SUPERNATURAL.

COLD FIRE

SUPERNATURAL™

COLD FIRE

JOHN PASSARELLA

SUPERNATURAL created by Eric Kripke

TITAN BOOKS

Supernatural: Cold Fire
Print edition ISBN: 9781781166758
E-book edition ISBN: 9781781166765

Published by Titan Books
A division of Titan Publishing Group Ltd
144 Southwark St, London SE1 0UP

First edition: March 2016
10 9 8 7 6 5 4 3 2 1

Visit our website: www.titanbooks.com

Did you enjoy this book? We love to hear from our readers. Please email
us at readerfeedback@titanemail.com or write to us at Reader Feedback
at the above address.

To receive advance information, news, competitions, and exclusive
offers online, please sign up for the Titan newsletter on our website:
www.titanbooks.com

A CIP catalogue record for this title is available from the British Library.

Printed and bound in the United States.

For Andrea, who takes care of the real world while I explore imaginary ones.

HISTORIAN'S NOTE
This novel takes place during season ten, between "About a Boy" and "Halt & Catch Fire."

ONE

With no complaints about the division of labor, Dave Holcomb lugged whole panels of six-foot stockade fencing from the dinged bed of his Ford F-150, which he'd backed into the driveway, through the propped-open gate into the backyard of his new home. He placed each section of pressure-treated spruce in a growing and orderly pile on the small cement patio that overlooked the wedge-shaped yard, opposite the utility shed that had been a selling point for him. A guy could never have enough storage.

As he ferried a dozen loose fence posts, pickets and rails from the truck to the patio and lined them up beside his red metal toolbox, he had no regrets about staying home, working up a healthy sweat outdoors while his wife Sally spent the afternoon shopping. She was eager to check out the Braden Heights mall, followed by a selection of specialist stores touting local artisanal wares their new neighbors insisted they simply *must* try. But shopping—specifically window shopping—made Dave fidgety. Before hitting the local home improvement store, he had inspected the deteriorating fence one last time and prepared a checklist of items he'd need to whip it into shape. Later, at the store, he'd grabbed one of the industrial-strength wheeled carts, the kind that never seemed to go where you steered them, and collected each item on his list, drawing a line through each one after he placed them on the cart. Each step placed him incrementally closer to completing the task at hand, and Dave was all about getting things done.

They'd been in Braden Heights, Indiana little more than a week and Dave had allotted himself a month, six weeks max, to spruce up their new home. He'd never classify it as a true fixer-upper, but he'd added enough tasks to his repair list—and yes he had a master list, one list to rule them all—to keep himself busy every weekend and more than a few weeknights within that timeframe. No real burden since Dave enjoyed working with his hands, and the list gave him a solid excuse to stay far from the jostling crowd of shoppers and the anxiety of aimless wandering past endless window displays. Besides, the repairs had given them negotiating leverage on the purchase price of the home, far from the familiar surroundings of San Bernardino, California they'd left behind.

Compared to the stingy plot of land that backed their old townhouse, the new yard seemed enormous, a luxury that would require a lot more upkeep unless they hired a crew of professionals for regular maintenance. Even with the generous salary of his new job, he'd probably opt for the DIY route. Time permitting, of course. Along with the fancy title and big salary, the new job would no doubt require a chunk of hours above and beyond the standard forty-hour work week.

Hefting a fence panel in two gloved hands, Dave side-stepped his way across the overgrown lawn. Landscaping filled half a page in his master list, along with the overgrown bushes surrounding the utility shed, but the patchwork fencing came first. He'd often heard good fences made good neighbors. Based on the leaning panels, rotted rails, and crumbling pickets, the Holcombs' reputation teetered equally in the balance. Dave figured the benefit-of-the-doubt grace period from their settlement date was fading fast.

Manufactured drama aside, Dave admitted to himself he cared what others thought about them, and first impressions were often visual ones. Before his job claimed the majority of his waking hours, he was determined to correct the exterior faults. If he fell behind his self-imposed timetable for addressing interior repairs and upgrades, only he and Sally would know. Well, at least until Sally's inevitable housewarming party.

Dave leaned the new fence panel against an old one, on the near side of the one he intended to replace. Based upon his inspection, the posts on either side would remain, but the panel had rotted so much it had pulled free of many nails that had once secured it. The wood at the top of the pointed pickets crumbled in his gloved hands, falling through his fingers like pieces of mulch.

"And so it begins…" Dave muttered as he walked back to the patio for his claw hammer. He debated returning to the garage for his old radio. As much as he enjoyed the solitude of working alone outside, listening to music always made the work go faster…

Dave stopped. Listened.

Coming from behind him, a faint sound… A baby crying?

Though faint, the crying seemed close. Too close. In-his-backyard close.

"What the hell…?"

He turned around, looking first toward the fence panel he'd set down less than ten feet away, canted his head. Turned slightly. The utility shed?

For a brief moment, he entertained the possibility that someone had abandoned a baby in the Holcomb utility shed. Then he imagined a more farfetched scenario. What if a homeless family had moved in there? The storage unit even looked like a tiny house, with a peaked and shingled roof, curtained windows on either side of the door—and no lock on the door handle.

Taking a step toward the shed, Dave tentatively called out, "Hello?"

He felt ridiculous for even considering the possibility but stranger things had happened, and if squatters had taken up residence in the shed, they might be armed. Even discounting the possibility of a gun or knife, the shed housed enough potentially deadly tools to warrant caution.

"Anybody in there?"

The faint cry of an infant continued, and Dave had now half convinced himself the baby, if not a whole family, occupied his shed. But when could they have… moved in? He'd been inside it that very morning, before he'd left to purchase the new fencing. There was no place to hide in there, a single room, approximately twelve-by-ten. From the center, you could see all four corners. Besides, the gate into the backyard had been padlocked while he was out.

He debated grabbing the claw hammer from his toolbox, so he'd have his own makeshift weapon to defend himself, but the idea made him feel ridiculous. Shaking off his paranoia, he strode to the front of the shed, turned the handle and pulled the door open. Even in early afternoon, the interior remained dim, lit only by sunlight filtered through dingy curtains on the two small windows.

His gaze swept across the assortment of tools and yard supplies, checking any potential blind spots, those large enough to conceal an infant. But judging from the assortment of cobwebs, the only living residents of the utility shed belonged to the arachnid family. Stepping inside, he moved a folded tarp, pushed aside a red wheelbarrow, and lifted a bunch of hanging lanterns. Nothing.

And yet the baby continued to cry.

Low but clear, a forlorn sobbing, as if the infant lacked the energy to produce the type of indignant wailing that would draw the attention and assistance of anyone within a three block radius who had an ounce of paternal or maternal instinct. To Dave, it seemed oddly personal, as if he were the baby's only hope.

Now that he was inside the shed, he could tell the sound came from outside. That's when he thought about the clutter of overgrown bushes obscuring the windows. He'd never really had a good look at the fencing in back, only a small section he'd glimpsed through a tangle of branches when they'd first inspected the house.

Leaving the shed, he turned the handle behind him, to secure the door as much as possible without a lock. Now convinced that somebody had abandoned a baby behind the shed, he looked for the widest gap between the bushes and wondered how someone could have gone back there without leaving a path of freshly snapped branches in their wake, coming and going. Then he had a worse thought. What if somebody had approached the yard from the other side, through the overgrown field of grass and weeds to drop the baby over the fence—from a height of six feet?

It made no sense.

Halfway through the tangle of branches and having already accumulated an impressive collection of scratches on his face, neck and forearms, Dave belatedly wished he'd gone back into the shed for trimming shears, if not a damned tree saw. *Too late to turn back now,* he thought. But how would he bring the baby out without causing more harm?

The baby's wailing softened into quiet sobs and snuffling sounds.

For some reason, this alarmed Dave more than sudden anguished cries would have. Abandoned and injured, the infant could be near death. Dave might literally be hearing the baby's last gasps. He forged ahead with renewed purpose, barely noticing when a thorny vine raked across his palm, drawing stipples of blood like beads of crimson sweat. "Hold on!" he said softly, then louder. "Hold on, I'm coming!"

The last branch whipped back behind him, rustling its

neighbors into a chorus of arboreal admonishments. The scent of pine trees washed over him, briefly reminding him of Christmas, happy childhood memories of giftwrapped surprises and lavish feasts. Which was odd, because there were no pine trees on their property and none that he'd noticed nearby. But that hardly mattered at the moment. He pushed the thought aside and turned the corner into the narrow space between the back of the shed and the fence.

Naturally, he scanned the small patch of ground where he expected to find a baby wrapped in swaddling clothes or a soiled diaper. What he saw instead was sparse grass and decaying plant matter, along with the desiccated carcass of what could have been a squirrel.

And then he was no longer alone…

He caught a brief glance of legs, standing before the rotted fence pickets where no one had been a moment before.

"How—?"

His gaze darted upward, more confused than afraid.

It happened so fast, he had no time to process what he saw. A vague, dark shape, tatters of cloth—but before his eyes could focus on the image before him, something flashed in front of his face; the movements were animalistic, and definitely inhuman in their speed and ferocity. Something sharp and painful struck his face, tugging and tearing—

He cried out at the sudden, unbelievable pain.

—then another impact, much lower, doubling him over in searing agony, ripping the breath from his lungs, and he dropped into numb darkness, welcoming it…

* * *

Sally Holcomb returned from her extended shopping trip a couple hours later than she had anticipated. *Almost time to get dinner started or call in a takeout order.* Dave had backed his pickup into the driveway, angled toward the backyard gate, so she assumed he continued to patch up the fence.

"I'm home!" she called as she passed the gate on the first of several trips from her Camry to the kitchen, emptying the trunk and backseat of numerous shopping bags; first the plastic grocery bags—stowing the perishables in the fridge or freezer—followed by the home decorations; everything from artisanal candles and storage cubbies, to window treatments and bed linens.

By the time she made her last trip, holding a ceramic planter wrapped in both arms, she paused to wonder why Dave hadn't offered to help her with the bags. Sometimes, in the midst of a complicated home improvement project, he'd enter a trancelike state of concentration and fail to register the details of a conversation she thought they'd been having. More than once, she'd had to remind herself that his mumbles of assent and understanding had no correlation to the actual subject matter at hand. Over the years, she'd learned to recognize the signs of his worker-bee single-mindedness and would postpone any casual discussions until he finished the job or came up for air on his own. When she really needed his attention, her go-to move was offering him a cold beer. But as she stood before the gate, she heard nothing to suggest he was absorbed in the repairs. No rap of a hammer. No clunking of wood.

"Dave?"

Again, no response. Not completely unexpected if he'd entered trance mode. As she walked through the gate into the backyard, she noticed the lack of progress. She scanned the fencing. Nothing new or patched. To her right, she saw the reason why. The cement patio held everything Dave must have bought for the job and unloaded from the pickup, with the sole exception of one new fence panel leaning against the rotten old one. She never considered herself any kind of handyman—handy*woman*? handy*person*?—but her immediate impression was that nothing had been done, that he'd carried the panel across the yard but nothing else.

"Dave!"

No answer.

Empty yard. Utility shed closed. Naturally, she assumed he'd gone into the house and gotten involved in some other project, abandoning the fence, even if that was so unlike her methodical husband, a man who made prioritized checklists for every project no matter how small. Unless an emergency had come up. A busted pipe, maybe, an overflowing toilet. She'd only breezed through the kitchen to unload her bags and the house was much bigger than their old townhouse, plenty of rooms she hadn't passed. She made a complete sweep of the place with no sign of Dave or the remnants of any household emergency, her anxiety building with each step.

"The shed," she mumbled. "He must be in the shed."

She imagined he'd hurt himself with a power tool, her mind miles ahead of rationality, concocting bizarre and gruesome scenarios. Perhaps he was unconscious, lying on the floor of the shed, bleeding…

Why close the door? She hurried out back, across the patio and overgrown lawn to the shed. She gripped the metal handle, pausing to take a deep, calming breath, preparing herself as much as possible for the worst case scenario. *So why did you leave your cell phone in your purse on the kitchen counter?*

She yanked the door open and peered inside, through dust-filled shafts of sunlight. Holding her breath now, she entered the shed, her gaze darting toward every corner until she convinced herself of Dave's absence. As she backed out of the shed, uncertainty filled her, the names of her neighbors bubbling to the surface of her thoughts. If he'd left home without the pickup, maybe he'd accepted a neighbor's offer to watch a ballgame or have a beer. But her reasoning crumbled before she could even build a case for either scenario. She'd been gone for hours and Dave hadn't even begun work on the fence. No distraction would have lasted so long.

As she stood there, seeking an answer that made sense, she noticed broken branches on the bushes pressed against the right side of the shed. The breaks looked fresh...

That was the only place she hadn't checked, as it was invisible to casual inspection. But it seemed like the only place he could have gone.

"Dave!" she called, rubbing her arm in anticipation of the awkward tangle of branches and prickly leaves that awaited her if he failed to come out on his own. "Dave, are you back there?" A deep breath. "Are you hurt?"

Silence.

She stepped forward, snapped a few branches to allow her as much unmolested passage through the bushes as possible without the benefit of garden shears. That's when she noticed bright red spots on some of the leaves… drying blood.

With a renewed sense of urgency, she flung herself forward, eyes closed, left forearm shielding her face as she broke through the last of the bushes and thorny vines. Stumbling free, she rounded the corner of the shed and saw more blood splattered across the old fencing, some patches so wet that long crimson drip lines had formed underneath them. Numb, she took a step forward and her foot struck something, throwing her off balance. A frantic windmilling of her arms helped her avoid a fall, but in the process of catching herself, her gaze had dropped to the obstruction at her feet and an involuntary gasp escaped her throat.

Dave. Sprawled face down before her, motionless, right arm tucked under his midsection, left arm above his head, fingers clutching loose weeds, his legs splayed inelegantly to the sides. For a few agonizing seconds, her heart seemed to pause as she strained to see if he was breathing, the slightest rise and fall of his chest.

"Oh, my God! Dave!"

She dropped to her knees beside him, shook him and called his name again and received no response, not even a moan or grunt of pain. If not for the blood all over the fence, she might have thought he'd had a heart attack and simply collapsed, unnoticed back here. She spared no time speculating on the reason why he'd gone behind the shed. Instead, she focused on what she could do now, alone, since she'd left her cell phone in the kitchen. Although she'd never taken a CPR class, she'd seen the procedure performed on television often enough to give it a try. Grabbing his right shoulder and hip, she flipped him over to—

"Oh! Oh—oh, oh, God, please no," she sputtered as she recoiled, flinging herself backward and slamming painfully into the back wall of the utility shed. "No, no, no, no!"

For a terrifying moment, it seemed as if Dave was staring accusingly at her, but that was impossible. He couldn't stare. Not without eyes. Only bloody gaping sockets where his ice-blue eyes had been. Dark voids in a blood-smeared face, shockingly pale. And less than an instant must have passed before she noticed another bloody void, a ragged hole in his midsection, extending from beneath his ribcage to his waistline, and framed in the dripping, shredded remains of intestines. Small twigs and bits of dried leaves clung to the gore. And insects were already—

Whipping her head to the side, Sally dropped to all fours and expelled the remains of her food court lunch, gagging interspersed with uncontrollable sobbing until only thin strings of bile remained. She pushed herself to her feet, shaking as she stumbled away from her husband's body, shrieking once as her foot slipped in blood-matted leaves. Irrational fear surged through her. She imagined some evil presence—a monster born of nightmares—had caught her ankle, determined to pull her back to finish its macabre task.

Screaming as conscious thought abandoned her, she flung herself around the corner of the shed, tearing several fingernails, and charged through the tangle of overlapping bushes as if her very survival depended on it.

TWO

Two minutes in, and Dean was gone.

Preferring a more cautious approach, Sam took in their surroundings. The setting sun leached all color from the graffiti decorating the drab and cracked walls of the abandoned three-story factory that dominated this particular city block of urban decay. A poured concrete foundation supported a ground floor of bleached cinderblock beneath two additional stories of faded and crumbling red brick. The hundreds of upper level windowpanes, perhaps intended to provide visual relief from the oppressive monotony of brick, had been transformed into endless daggers of glass, which caught the fading light in a golden glow and seemed to set the condemned structure ablaze. Whatever dark secrets the building held, they were hidden from the street view.

At some point after the factory closure, most likely after the majority of the graffiti artists tagged the then-fresh urban canvas, the building owners had erected a cyclone fence topped with loops of barbed wire around the perimeter, in

case the metal No Trespassing – Private Property sign—
now tagged as well—affixed to the padlocked gate provided
insufficient deterrent.

Rather than scale the fence and navigate the barbed wire,
Dean had removed a pair of bolt cutters from the trunk
of the Impala and made short work of the padlock. Then,
exchanging the bolt cutters for a long-handled ax, Dean
slipped through the gate, told Sam to take the front, and
sprinted toward the rear of the forgotten factory.

"Dean!" Sam whispered, too late for his brother to hear,
and shook his head in resignation. Not that they needed a big
discussion or an elaborate plan, but he doubted their quarry
had any intention of slipping out the back and fleeing. And
it might have been wise to stick together for this final assault.

After a week of brutal assaults perpetrated by what several
terrified eyewitnesses described as strange, mutated beasts, the
Winchesters had determined the abominations had somehow
been created by the mythological Chimera, a creature
described in lore as a lion with the head of a goat rising from
its back and a snake's head for a tail. While the Chimera itself
had remained in the shadows during the attacks, a couple
of witnesses caught glimpses of its telltale features, but they
also had the impression of a massive, lumbering presence,
indicating something larger and more fearsome than the
sum of the Chimera's supposed parts. Unfortunately, as the
frequency and ferocity of the assaults escalated, the Chimera
had become more elusive. The brothers speculated that it
had retreated to some kind of lair, a place secluded enough
to avoid chance discovery while orchestrating its expanding

reign of terror. In order to find it, the Winchesters needed to wait for one of its minions to "escape" a battle long enough to report back to the lair and secretly follow it to its master.

Sam assumed once Dean and he located the lair, they would plan and coordinate their attack together. But one of the consequences of Dean's bearing the Mark of Cain was a penchant for expediency, straight line thinking. In a way, Sam supposed Dean had made a concession by not barging in through the front door, figurative guns blazing. Sam suspected Dean merely wanted to wade into the battle without discussion or delay and the quickest way to accomplish that was to forge ahead on his own, whether Sam had his back or not.

While Dean insisted he remained in control of the Mark, and to all appearances he hadn't succumbed to the unreasoning bloodlust it induced in its owner, this particular hunt might prove too much for Dean to handle alone. Hell, if the creature was as massive as those early reports suggested, Sam worried both of them together didn't stand a chance. They'd witnessed firsthand the deadly nature of the Chimera's creations, which the Winchesters discovered were actually supernaturally fused combinations of one or more animals with a human victim in the mix. Not that the word "nature" applied to these bizarre hybrids. At best, they were short-term weapons, animate grenades.

The last one had practically ripped a police officer's spine out of her back before hurling her from an overpass into the path of an oncoming semi. The resulting twenty-three-car rush-hour pileup would occupy police and emergency services throughout the night. But the Winchesters had managed to track the Chimera's minion back to this gutted factory. Unless they ganked the source of the hybrids, the reign of terror would continue unabated.

Sam crept along the interior of the fence, taking note of the shadows gathered near the building's front entrance and along the walls, wondering what type of madness they might contain. In passing, he spotted a few sections where the chain-link fence had been snipped in a vertical line to allow furtive passage onto the factory grounds. Of course, the Chimera and its creations—at least those which couldn't fly—would need a way in and out of the building. With the padlocked gate undisturbed, the area would appear secure to the occasional patrol car sweep.

Finally, Sam stepped forward, toward the front door and the impermeable shadows, hefting the meat cleaver he'd taken from the Impala's trunk. Let Dean have the long-handled ax. Sam had a feeling the night would involve a lot of close combat. They'd already discovered guns and knives weren't up to the task of dispatching the strange creatures.

From the rear of the factory, Sam heard a clang of metal on metal. Dean? Knocking? *Doesn't get much more direct than that,* he thought, with another shake of his head.

Distracted, Sam almost missed the growing shadow—or rather something dark rising from within the shadows. With a loud, brutish snort, the creature lumbered toward him, gathering momentum. In the fading light, Sam glimpsed the black bear's head, and the fur pelt covering the shoulders in an uneven line above a man's torso, with human arms terminating in clawed bear paws. Eerily the eyes and ears appeared to be human, the right one milky, as if it hadn't adapted well to hybridization. The same creature that had tossed the police officer off the overpass, now on guard duty.

Assuming—and hoping—the bear–human hybrid was blind in its right eye, Sam darted to his left. While the hybrid was fast, it relied on one bear leg and one human leg for movement and its gait included a lot of dipping and swaying, especially on turns. Sam imagined he could hear the mismatched bones in its legs and spine grinding together with each ungainly step.

He moved beyond its blind spot to its rear and drove his right foot into the creature's lower back, shoving it toward the fence and letting its own momentum work against it. With a grunt, the hybrid reached up with both arms to catch itself against the fencing, bear claws scraping against metal, seeking purchase. Approaching from the creature's blind side, Sam raised the cleaver and brought it down in a two-handed grip. The blow jarred him momentarily before the blade severed the creature's forearm above the bear portion of the limb. The key was to attack the unnatural joins. The fresher the hybridization, the weaker the connections between one species and the other.

Briefly, the severed forearm dangled from the fence, claws snared in the gaps, before slipping free. The creature's stump dripped blood, much less than expected for such a grievous wound. Which helped explain why bullet and knife wounds were ineffective. Whatever preternatural energy allowed the hybrids to live in the first place, it kept them ticking even after they suffered what should have been mortal wounds. A dozen Detroit cops had learned that lesson the hard way. Their instincts and logic had failed them. And yet, the key to destroying the hybrids was logical after all. The trick to their undoing was to, literally, undo the hybridization itself. In layman's terms—or rather, hunter's terms—that meant strategic dismemberment.

Seemingly unperturbed by the loss of its right arm, the hybrid spun around and swiped at Sam's face with its remaining bear paw. Sam ducked beneath the formidable set of claws, but the bear limb passed so close to his head that ursine musk filled his nostrils.

Before the hybrid could recover its balance from the missed blow, Sam propped himself on his left palm and drove his right foot into the kneecap of the creature's human right leg. The joint buckled the wrong way and, with an animal roar, the man-bear fell on its left side, mangled right leg high and dangling unnaturally—even for a hybrid.

But the shattered right leg was not Sam's target. He planted his foot just below the human elbow of the left arm and hacked off the bear paw, the tip of the cleaver sparking as it struck the busted concrete below.

Undeterred, the man-bear curled its body upward, attempting to lash out with the claws on its one bear leg. With a backhand blow, Sam drove the butt of the cleaver's handle into the temple of the bear head, just above and in front of a human ear. The one functioning eye rolled upward. The deep-throated bear growl turned into a groggy grumble of pain and confusion. Long enough for Sam to remove the head of the creature. Although the body continued to twitch with preternatural life and the bear's jaws worked as if attempting human speech, Sam hacked the bear leg free of the human torso. Seconds later, the disparate pieces of flesh sagged and decayed eerily fast as the unnatural energy that had kept the hybrid alive dissipated.

Sam rushed the front door of the factory to join Dean inside.

The oversized hybrid guarding the rear door charged, determined to keep Dean out—for good. If Dean had to name the creature barreling toward him out of the shadows, he would have said *Minotaur*. Horned bull's head on a man's body: check. Murderous attitude: check. One slight problem with the Minotaur comparison—well, two actually: a pair of problems in the shape of oversized lobster claws for hands.

Dean stood his ground, swinging the long-handled ax behind his right shoulder then bringing it forward in a powerful two-handed grip a moment before the Minotaur's horns would have gored him. The wedge-shaped blade of the ax drove through the center of the bull's skull, three inches deep into bone and brain matter. Keeping his grip on the wooden handle kept the twin horns at a safe distance, but the jumbo lobster claws were another matter.

As the Minotaur's charge continued unabated, lifting Dean clear off the ground and carrying him backward, one claw snapped at Dean's face. Twisting away, Dean avoided that claw but left himself open to attack from the other. On a sudden impulse, Dean released the ax handle and switched his grip to the base of the horns, one in each hand, his face now close enough to the bull's head to feel the hot snort of moist air from its flared nostrils. *Grabbed the bull by the horns,* Dean thought. *Now what?*

He pulled downward, using the creature's own momentum against it and, as they both fell, Dean drove his feet into the human torso the same instant he released the horns. If the creature had the full body and mass of a bull, the throw wouldn't have worked and Dean would have been summarily trampled. Instead, the hybrid slammed into a nearby overflowing dumpster with an impressive thud and fell on its side, dislodging the ax from its skull.

Dean scrambled to his feet and retrieved the weapon.

Groggy, the Minotaur shook its head, seemingly oblivious to the ooze of blood ferrying dislodged bits of gray matter down its broad face. Lobster claws scraped against cracked concrete as the hybrid attempted to rise. Dean had no intention of giving it a second chance to make Winchester kabob with its horns.

He raised the ax overhead. "Party's over, Surf and Turf."

The hybrid raised one lobster-claw arm to shield itself from the blow.

Dean took it off at the elbow, the ax blade slicing through flesh and bone at the seam and rebounding off the side of the dumpster with a metallic clang loud enough to wake the dead—or rouse the recently vivisected. If the Winchesters had expected to benefit from the slightest element of surprise, that hope was dashed.

No time to waste.

The Minotaur reached for its severed appendage with the stump of its right arm and the bloody end of the lost claw twitched, like a piece of metal the instant before it surrenders to the pull of a nearby magnet. Once before, Dean had watched in amazement as a dismembered hybrid reassembled itself. As long as the head was attached…

Despite the gruesome head wound, the Minotaur remained a threat. Taking a moment to kick the dismembered claw away, Dean swung the ax overhead, again driving the blade into the split skull. This time the blade bit much deeper, sinking down the back of the skull and spine. Enough damage to subdue the creature, but Dean wouldn't be fooled again. Changing the angle of attack, he chopped through the thick neck until the head rolled away from the torso. Quick work to remove the other limbs.

With the Minotaur dismemberment complete, Dean loped toward the back door, which hung askew on rusted hinges, and kicked it in. The base of the door scraped the floor as it whipped inward before striking something partially human that emitted a startled squeal-growl. One of many similar creatures, waiting to pounce on Dean as he entered the gutted factory.

Before they circled him, he had a moment to assess the factory's interior: An expansive and gloomy rectangular space nearly three stories high, exposed girders, banks of window panes, many broken, floor space littered with wooden and metallic debris. A second-story walkway, its safety railing in disrepair, bisected the factory and housed several cramped offices in a single row. Currently dark, the glass-enclosed rooms would have given supervisors a clear view of the factory floor. Across the dark factory—moonlight filtering through the banks of windows and irregular gaps in the ceiling provided the only illumination—Dean caught a glimpse of Sam near the front door, facing a few mismatched problems of his own.

Once again, Dean's mind tried to make sense of the hybrids. This time, the task remained relatively simple as he faced five identical half-human creatures. All had wiry human torsos, replete with an assortment of tattoos, but grafted hyena heads, arms and legs. At one time, Dean imagined, they had been human teenagers, possibly gang members, captured and hybridized together to form an internal security force for the Chimera. And they operated as a pack, human individuality absent as their hyena heads circled him warily, each one seeking an opening, after which the others would move in a concerted attack to bring him down.

Rather than delay the inevitable, Dean feigned a vulnerability, stepping deeper into the factory and away from the doorway. As expected, one of the hyena-teens slipped behind him, no doubt intending to tear into an Achilles tendon to bring him down. At the first sound of scrabbling claws, Dean swiveled and drilled the butt of the ax handle into the head of the attacking hybrid. With a pained squeal, the hyena-teen stumbled, fell and scrambled away, shaking its head.

Bringing the weapon forward, Dean slapped the flat of the blade across the muzzle of a leaping hybrid, knocking it aside. An overhead swing lopped off the head of a third attacker.

He'd need to chop off the limbs to finish the disassembly, but he'd bought himself some time to deal with the others. The hybrids were slowest to recover if they lost their heads. Lop off an arm or a leg and they'd continue to fight, though less effectively. Remove the head, and all the preternatural energy in the hybrid turned to self-repair.

From across the factory, Dean heard simian screeches and howls, but he needed to dispatch the hyena-teen gang circling him before he could help his brother. Besides, Sam could take care of himself. And, unlike Dean, he didn't have to worry about giving in to the Mark of Cain and letting the unreasoning rage take over and consume him until it burned itself out in a river of blood.

No, Dean had to stay focused on killing monsters without becoming one in the process.

Sam barely had time to think before the creatures attacked. Swinging from exposed steel girders in the ruined shell of the factory, they moved with simian grace, though something was off about them. What initially seemed an illusion of motion resolved into a grotesque multiplicity of limbs.

Two hybrids dropped to the floor on either side of him while a third, larger than the others, sprouted oversized bat wings as it descended, touching down silently. The confusion of limbs became clear, though no less disconcerting. Each hybrid had a human torso and human arms, with a pair of large simian arms above those, for a total of four upper limbs. The hybrids flanking Sam had orangutan arms and legs, judging by the orange-reddish coloring, while the bat-winged leader had the arms and lower body of a gorilla. All three had incongruously smaller chimpanzee heads, filled with a mismatched assortment of crocodile teeth, which became apparent when they screeched in unison, a moment before attacking.

Sam swung the cleaver at the face of the gorilla hybrid, knocking the leader off balance, while jamming his elbow into the face of the orangutan hybrid on his left and narrowly avoiding the reaching hands of the one on his right. Human and simian hands pawed at him, scraping and clutching, determined to get a hold. Technically, he was outnumbered three to one, but the odds felt much steeper with twelve hands and fists pitted against his two. As the number and weight of his assailants threatened to overwhelm him, Dean chose that moment to kick in the rear door, which struck a hybrid on the far side of the factory judging by its yelp of pain.

Startled, the simian hybrids paused, looking toward the source of the disturbance. Sam allowed himself an almost involuntary glance Dean's way, long enough to see a pack of four-legged hybrids circling his brother, without relinquishing the advantage of the momentary distraction. A fierce swing of the cleaver hacked off the face and front of the skull of the orangutan hybrid on his right, then a second quick chop sunk deep into the neck of the gorilla hybrid. Both staggered and fell away, the first blinded, the second clamping both human hands to an apparently severed artery. For such a grievous injury, the blood seeped out in a steady flow, no spurting or gushing. With hands compressing the wound, the hybrid could probably heal itself in minutes without the threat of bleeding out.

From behind Sam, four arms wrapped around his chest and abdomen, squeezing with inhuman ferocity. A moment before he expected his ribs to crack, Sam slammed his head backward into the chimpanzee head, no doubt preempting an intended crocodile-teeth bite. The grip around his torso slackened and with his arms free, Sam took the cleaver in a two-handed grip and swung the blade wildly behind his head. He felt it bite into flesh and bone. Finally, he broke free of the four-armed hold, spun on his heel, and hoisted the cleaver at the neck join. Another chop beheaded the orangutan hybrid. Headless, it stood there, swaying slightly, as if confused how to proceed. The moment it fell, all four hands would reach for the missing head and begin the reassembly, so Sam left it standing there and went to work on the other two.

The faceless one cocked its head, orienting itself by sound. The gorilla hybrid crouched, its bat wings snapped outward and it was aloft, but Sam anticipated the move and jumped, timing his leap to catch the top of its right wing with his left hand, then swiping down with the cleaver in his right to sever the wing from the hybrid's back. The blow was beyond the join, not a true dismemberment at the seam, but effective nonetheless. With only one functioning wing, the gorilla hybrid spun out of control, turning in midair, exposing the back of his neck to Sam and his cleaver. A vicious blow to the right side of the neck from behind, combined with the early deep wound on the left front of its throat, was enough to complete the decapitation.

Sam sprang back as the gorilla hybrid crashed to the

ground and kicked the head clear of its frantically searching limbs, long enough for him to hack them off. And so his own battle continued, long and bloody work. At some point, he heard the repeated clang of an ax from across the factory: Dean completing a similar chore on the pack of four-legged hybrids that had ambushed him.

Down on one knee and drenched in sweat, head bowed as he completed his grisly task, Sam froze at the sound of serpentine hissing combined with light, almost delicate footfalls crunching on bits of debris strewn across the factory floor.

"Sam!"

As Sam rose to his feet, Dean pointed upward with the dripping blade of his ax, indicating the second floor offices. A long undulating shape—or series of shapes—darker than the darkness it inhabited roiled behind the glass, slouching and rolling, as if rousing itself from a dormant state. Sam had the impression of vast size, and somehow knew that whatever it was, it had destroyed the walls between offices to accommodate its girth.

The factory itself seemed to rumble.

Metal creaked, bolts popped and the entire walkway trembled, shedding dust and rust in equal measure. A billowing haze rolled outward and descended around them. A moment later a strained window cracked, followed by others; a short series of distinct breaks, then an overwhelming explosion of sound as the offices erupted, blasting a hailstorm of broken glass in all directions. Only the Winchesters' distance from the central walkway saved them from serious harm. Sam shielded his face with his right forearm and flinched as a piece of glass nicked his ear, a larger piece glanced off his thigh, and another pinged off the blade of the cleaver.

The large, misshapen mass of the Chimera, hidden until now within the dark offices, brushed aside the damaged safety railing and launched itself off the walkway, a confusion of multiple heads, limbs and tentacles swirling around the central mass. Until the wide dragon-wings snapped open, Sam couldn't even guess which way it had been facing. But that word lost meaning when something had multiple faces all over its sprawling body.

Movement directly in front of Sam commanded his attention.

In the confusion, he'd only registered the serpentine nature of the hybrid approaching him. Now he saw a scaled woman's face, seemingly emerging from the thick, tubular body of a python, as if she'd been consumed whole and was somehow able to push her human essence through snake flesh. Bipedal, she had scaled human legs and feet with a mostly serpentine torso and cobra-hooded neck supporting a mostly human but hairless head, with ear holes and a flattened nose. She had two snakes—complete with heads—in place of human arms and hands. When she spoke, he noted her long fangs and forked tongue.

"Please"—she said plaintively, with a slight lisp—"kill me!"

Before Sam could react or respond to her plea, her long snake-headed arms darted toward him and she attacked.

THREE

Having suffered a few scrapes and bruises but no serious injuries, Dean finished dismembering the hyena-teens to defuse the hybridization process. As he severed the remaining sutures, each hybrid seemed to deflate and rapidly decay. Dean started forward in case Sam needed help dispatching the last of the ape hybrids, but the situation was in hand. Many loose hands, judging by the tangle of hacked-off limbs at Sam's feet.

He stopped short when he noticed a pit in the floor. One more careless step and he would have pitched head-first into the recess, which had probably housed the base of some robotic assembly equipment years ago, but was now home to something much more disturbing. Glowing with eerie energy in the pale, filtered moonlight writhed a mass of white shapeless flesh in various states of viscosity. Intermittently, unattached limbs would emerge from the surface, twitching and twisting, hands reaching, fingers grasping at nothing, searching for something. Every few seconds, a face—human or ursine or reptilian—rose to the surface, eyes milky, dazed or darting left and right in fear or hunger, before submerging again. Other than a liquid churning as the surface roiled, the mass remained silent until one of the faces appeared and a mouth gaped open to sigh, moan or pant.

Instinctively, Dean kept his distance from the pit. Shaking his head in undisguised loathing, he muttered, "Nuke it from orbit."

Creaking and rumbling from above caught his attention, drawing his gaze to the observation deck and something large and menacing rising from the shadows of the dark offices. Their suspicions were confirmed. They'd found the lair of the Chimera and killing its hybrid henchmen—hench*fiends*?— had finally drawn its attention.

Raising the long-handled ax to point at the commotion above, he called, "Sam!"

Dean had time to notice the snake-woman blocking Sam before the office windows exploded and the massive Chimera clambered over the ruined safety railing and glided down to the factory floor with the aid of what seemed like expansive dragon wings. Whether the wings were the mutated-beyond-recognition contribution of some unfortunate gliding reptile or actual wings from a real dragon, Dean couldn't guess. Hell, maybe they were appropriated from an honest-to-god gargoyle. A hunter should know better than anyone that the lines between myth and reality were blurry, and sometimes invisible.

The Chimera's unnatural girth settled on a mass of giant squid tentacles ringed by at least a half-dozen lion legs.

Closer to the interior of its enormous body, Dean spotted a grizzled lion's head near a goat's head with one milky eye—facets of its original design, along with a tail that ended in a snake's head, though it had three of those now. Over the centuries, the Chimera had added other limbs and heads to its mass—animal and human—in an indiscriminate display of self-modification, or self-mutilation. No rhyme or reason to the assemblage of parts. Trying to make sense of where one species ended and the next began seemed like a short trip to crazy town. There was something profoundly disturbing about the construction of the creature, like the collective nightmares of humankind come to life in one monstrous being.

Most of the Chimera's heads focused on Dean, so he had to assume he faced the front of the creature, which was confirmed when it lurched toward him, lion paws scrabbling for purchase along the cracked concrete floor as the tentacles heaved and shoved its bulk from behind, aided by the pounding of its massive wings. The fetid smell of the creature wafted toward him: eau de zoo layered with more than a hint of overflowing septic tank.

"Hey, Jabba," Dean taunted. "Think maybe you got carried away with the spare parts?"

By way of answer, a tentacle lashed out and looped around his left arm as the serrated ring of one of the suckers tore through the sleeve of his jacket and dug into his flesh. Pulling against the hold of the tentacle, Dean shortened his right-handed grip on the ax and lopped off the end, freeing himself. The Chimera lumbered forward again and Dean backed away, narrowly avoiding the swipe of lion's claws.

When Dean cast a nervous glance backward to be sure he was in no danger of stumbling into an unformed flesh pit, another tentacle lashed out, wrapped around the ax handle and lifted him off the ground, hurling him toward the nearest cinderblock wall.

He struck the wall with enough force to knock the wind out of him, falling to all fours as he gasped for breath. More importantly, he'd lost his grip on the ax and, as he struggled to his feet before the approaching monstrosity, he spotted the weapon, ten feet away, its long wooden handle split in half.

As the Chimera bore down on him, one of the human heads—a Latino male with a teardrop tattoo—partially raised from the dark pelt like an impacted wisdom tooth, spoke to him. "You will... join me."

Literally. Dean pushed the image from his mind as he took an involuntary step back, only for his heel to hit the wall.

A woman's head, her left eye sunk below the flesh-line, spoke next.

"Join me now."

Sam leaned backward, away from the striking snake-headed arms of the woman–serpent hybrid. If the twin snake heads belonged to constrictors their bites wouldn't be deadly, but their grip could be. And while her earless human head couldn't strike like a snake thanks to her mostly human torso, he imagined the venom dripping from the impressive fangs in her too-wide mouth was definitely poisonous.

"Kill me," she begged.

Sam dipped out of range as the snake attached to her

right shoulder snapped at his face.

"Please!" she said, frantically, her plea at odds with her continued attack. "I'm losing—me."

Sam bobbed right and left, like a boxer ducking a flurry of jabs while waiting to land a devastating counterpunch. With each step backward, his boxing ring grew smaller. He needed to stop her before she cornered him.

"Can't live like—like this," she wailed, staggering forward as a battle raged inside her, the remnants of her former self struggling against the murderous will of her inhuman creator.

Taking advantage of her hesitation, Sam shrugged off his jacket and wrapped it around his left forearm to build a thick layer of padding, like a man in a bite suit training an attack dog. He thrust his arm out and let one of the snakes sink its fangs into the jacket. The moment it took hold, he brought the cleaver down at a point where a human elbow would have been. Not a species join, but one less obstacle to ending the hybrid for good.

The snake-woman took a startled moment to process the loss of her limb, long enough for Sam to swing his padded forearm to the right and avoid a bite on his unprotected side. The second snake arm bit the rolled jacket, right next to the dangling, severed snake head, and suffered the same fate.

The hybrid's arms swayed to and fro aimlessly, blood oozing from the twin stumps. She walked forward, flashing fangs, droplets of venom falling to her scaled chin. "Now, finish it," she said. Her neck thrust forward, jaws snapping. The snake heads still dangling from his forearm twitched as she neared him. Her arms suddenly had purpose, reaching toward their missing heads, seeking reconnection.

"Do it!" she screamed, once again snapping at Sam with her fangs.

He shoved her back with the butt of the cleaver, buying time, if nothing else.

So much simpler to kill the monsters when they had animal heads to go with human parts. They behaved more like rabid beasts, murderous and vicious. Killing them was the only rational choice. But when the hybrid had a human face and a human voice—even if that voice pleaded with you to kill it and end its misery—it wasn't so simple. She hadn't always been a monster. She'd had no choice in her re-creation.

But she had a choice now.

She was living a nightmare. She would never be anything close to human again. Sam could honor her last human choice.

He shook his head, tightened his grip on the cleaver. "I'm sorry..."

Whether she doubted his resolve or could no longer offer even token resistance to the unspoken imperative of the Chimera, she screamed and lunged toward Sam, mouth wide, fangs extended, forcing the issue. The internal debate ceased in an instant. One moment she'd been about to plunge her fangs into his throat, the next she staggered backward and toppled over, headless.

After detaching her snake-scale-covered limbs, it dawned on Sam he might have to skin her to completely reverse the hybridization. But that gruesome task could wait. Stepping around the snake-woman's remains, he sprinted toward the Chimera.

When he saw Dean, bloody and smiling, behind the bulk

of the attacking creature, he couldn't help but worry about his brother. What if he won the battle with the Chimera at the cost of losing the war to the Mark?

If there was a fate worse than becoming a hybrid, it had to be becoming part of the monster that created hybrids, nothing more than a fleshy ornament on a living, metric ton of nightmare fuel. *Not happening*, Dean thought.

A third head, probably belonging to one of the hyena-teens, echoed the Chimera's refrain, "Join me."

"Like hell."

The long-handled ax, now broken, lay out of reach. But Dean hadn't come without backup party favors. From inside his jacket, he took out a metal-handled hatchet and a long hunting knife.

"Way I see it, you're just one big plate of sushi."

The Chimera lurched forward—its weight buoyed by powerful dragon wing thrusts, undulating forward on giant squid tentacles and multiple lion legs—attempting to trap Dean against the factory's cinderblock wall. Diving to the side, Dean drove the point of the hunting knife through a meaty paw as he somersaulted out of range. Multiple arms reached out for him and he managed to hack a hand off at the wrist when it attempted to pin him to the floor. He sprang to his feet in a heartbeat, slashing at one arm, chopping another, stabbing a third. Severed fingers spun through the air, followed by the cheek and nose of an impacted face he caught with a backhanded blow of the hatchet. With every opening in the creature's defenses, he plunged the knife into the rolling flesh, but despite the flurry of wounds he inflicted, the damage was superficial, with minimal bleeding and no true dismemberments, at least not at species joins.

He caught a blur of motion in the periphery of his vision and narrowly avoided the darting snake heads that sprouted from the creature's long tail. But a tentacle slammed into his back and knocked him to the ground. When it tried to wrap around his leg, he slammed the hatchet into the slick flesh, only partially severing the appendage. Another tentacle struck his chest, hurled him into the wall again and he lost his grip on the weapon.

The Chimera's mass leaned forward, its center of gravity close to a tipping point if not for the wide base of the tentacles, and the lion's head stretched forward with a roar. Dean figured that this was the Chimera's command center, despite all the talking human heads that riddled its flesh like a scattering of warts. Leaning against the wall to catch his breath, he grabbed the hilt of a throwing knife hidden in his belt and fired it at the lion's head, grinning when the flat blade sank deep into its left eye.

The resultant roar, accompanied by the indignant screams of all the other Chimera faces, was deafening. Dean doubted the wound was life-threatening, but it struck at the core of the monster, blinding one of its primary eyes and inflicting a substantial amount of trauma to the lion's brain. The Chimera lurched forward so suddenly, Dean had no time to evade the body slam it delivered. The malleability of the Chimera's ever-expanding fleshy frame saved him from serious injury, but it smothered him in a suffocating embrace. Turning his head aside, he gasped for the slightest sip of air while the creature's unrelenting stench burned his eyes. If the military had been involved in the hunt, Dean imagined they'd spare the Chimera's life in hope of weaponizing its body odor.

Fortunately for Dean, the creature's rage was too pure to grant him death by suffocation. It backed away, looped Dean's leg in a tentacle and hoisted him into the air, spinning around on a procession of lion legs. As Dean dangled upside down in the tentacle's grip, wishing he'd packed more throwing knives or, hell, maybe a flamethrower, he glanced down and his eyes widened in alarm. In about two seconds, the Chimera would have him directly above the roiling flesh pit. He'd be dropped into that infernal soup of miscreation. Before he could be reassembled as part of a hybrid—or grafted onto the Chimera itself—he'd be disassembled: his head, limbs and organs dispersed but still somehow alive, awaiting whatever horrific reassignment the Chimera deemed appropriate.

Lion claws tap-tap-tapped across the broken concrete flooring, spinning the Chimera's body, the tentacle swooping in an arc like an airplane carnival ride. The pit was six feet away… four feet…

Sam yelled, swinging a section of twisted rebar overhead, striking the tentacle inches away from where it gripped Dean by the ankle. Instantly, the tentacle flinched, flinging Dean two feet from the hellish pit. Skidding forward, his legs flailed wildly over the edge before he could steady himself.

Below, the mass of flesh rolled like a wave. As it crested beneath him, a forlorn face rose to the surface, wide mouth moaning. Then an enlarged scorpion tail rolled toward him, its tip striking the near wall before sliding back into the mass, giving way to a pair of mismatched arms whose fingers strained to reach Dean's right leg as it hung over the pit.

"Hey!" Dean shouted, yanking his leg clear. "I'm not spare parts!"

"Uh, Dean," Sam said beside him. "Any suggestions?"

Dean scrambled to his feet. His hatchet was momentarily lost on the other side of the Chimera, but he'd somehow retained his hold on the hunting knife. Sam held the rusty section of rebar in his left hand, spear-like—though Dean doubted the warped metal would fly true—and a bloody cleaver in his right.

The Chimera surged toward them, a chaotic but effective pursuit aided by dragon wings, lion legs and seething tentacles.

"Separate—away from that damned pit!"

They spread out, Dean to the left, Sam to the right, far enough apart that the Chimera had to choose which Winchester to attack. Normally that would leave the attacker vulnerable on the opposite flank, but the Chimera had faces, arms and clawed legs scattered around its bulk.

"Now what?" Sam said. "Where do we start?"

"Anywhere," Dean said. "Keep whaling on it until it runs out of parts."

One of the Chimera's human arms yanked the throwing knife from the lion's eye and hurled it at Dean. But the arm protruded from the creature's flesh at an awkward angle and the throw was obviously unpracticed. Dean dodged the blade easily and heard it skitter across the concrete without taking his eyes off the monster, even for a moment.

Sam attacked the same instant the Chimera threw the knife, lunging forward to drive the tip of the rebar deep into the rolls of flesh, barely avoiding the powerful claws of a lion as he jumped backward, abandoning the makeshift weapon.

Dean doubted the attack inflicted much damage on the Chimera. Other than the reflexive swipe with its claws, it hardly reacted to the impalement. Nothing like the roar and screams of the beast when Dean punctured the lion's head eye with the throwing knife. Almost as if the—

Two tentacles whipped around in opposing arcs, attempting to loop around Dean's legs as the Chimera surged forward again. As both tentacles swept across the ground Dean leapt straight up, avoiding the trap, but a third struck the point of his shoulder, spinning him away to land awkwardly and stagger into a concrete pillar.

Sensing an advantage, the Chimera rumbled forward with frightening acceleration. Dean spun around to the back of the pillar a second before the Chimera struck the front with the full force of its weight. Wary of the long reach of the tentacles, Dean almost fell to his hands and knees as he stumbled away. Then the tip of a tentacle swatted the heel of his back foot and he went down. He rolled away awkwardly as the Chimera shambled around the obstructing column to continue its pursuit.

Damn thing's on a mission to destroy me.

"Sam," Dean called. "Spare parts!"

"What?" Sam asked, tracking the Chimera from behind, his cleaver poised to attack the nearest limb.

"Ignore the spare parts," Dean said, finally understanding.

"They're like—decoys! Distractions. Sever the original parts."

They'd both studied the illustrations from mythological texts. Sam would know what and where to attack. From behind the creature, Sam tossed his jacket over the multi-headed snake tail, blunting its attack long enough for his cleaver to slice through its base. One of those snake heads had been part of the original Chimera body and now it was gone. The Chimera reared back, multiple faces shrieking as the lion head roared. Before making a strategic retreat, Sam snatched the embedded rebar from the Chimera's body.

"That's more like it," Dean said, approaching carefully but with renewed purpose, hunting knife clutched at his side.

As the Chimera spun around on its lion legs and mass of tentacles, dragon wings beating furiously, to retaliate against its most recent attacker, Dean caught sight of his hatchet and, a bit farther away, the broken-handled ax. For the moment, Dean held no interest for Chimera-prime. But some of the tortured human and animal faces looking down on him raised quite a vocal protest, in the combined form of howls, screeches, and useless shouts: "No!" "Stop him!" "Kill him!"

Whoever had most recently attacked the original Chimera body became enemy number one. Though its spare parts became distracted, the Chimera's attack retained laser focus. As Dean retrieved his other weapons, Sam backed away from the creature, evading the vicious swipes of its original forelegs, his rusty rebar and cleaver poor but more lethal substitutes for a lion tamer's whip and chair.

Nevertheless, they'd stumbled upon an effective strategy of alternating tag-team attacks, ultimately targeting the

Chimera's original heads and limbs, whenever they sensed an opening, blinding and dismembering. Dean's ax and knife became natural extensions of his arms and he entered a zone where he anticipated the path and strike of each claw and tentacle, meeting them with sharp steel, chopping and slicing to devastating effect. Then Sam lopped off the blinded lion's head. A moment later Dean countered with the decapitation of the similarly incapacitated goat's head. And it was basically over.

Sam noticed the difference immediately.

Without the original Chimera heads to take charge, the monster lost any semblance of focus in its attacks. Any distraction set it on a new course, as if a dozen feuding minds vied for control of the massive body. Given time, one of the voices might establish itself as the new leader—at least until the Chimera could reattach or possibly regrow its original heads—but Sam and Dean were unwilling to give the abomination time to recover from internal anarchy. Taking turns, the Winchesters attacked one side, then the other, completing one dismemberment after another.

When only the legless, armless, headless and tailless husk of the body remained, a bloody mass of quivering flesh and fur, Dean made a quick trip to the Impala and returned with a few containers of lighter fluid. Sam checked on the snake-woman, whose head remained far from her scaled, armless body. She presented no immediate threat. After the Chimera's body and severed parts burned, her snake-skinned form would succumb to the rapid decaying process, ending any chance of an unnatural resurrection. Spared the gruesome chore of skinning her from head to toe to separate snake from woman, Sam's relief was palpable. After several intense days and nights of beheadings and dismemberments had turned the Winchesters and the Impala into a mobile slaughterhouse, that was a final mercy.

He couldn't recall a time he'd been more grateful at the end of a hunt. Which made him turn his attention to Dean, standing beside him as the Chimera's flesh sizzled and charred to ash. Twice during the final battle, Sam had noticed the intensity with which Dean had torn into the Chimera, first when he'd been backed against the wall and later, when he'd faced an onslaught of tentacles. Though Dean insisted he was in control of himself, Sam couldn't help but worry that the Mark seized any opportunity for violence to take over.

Dean noticed Sam staring at him. "What?"

"You okay, Dean?"

"Other than bruises," Dean said, spreading his arms, "I'm fine."

His tone seemed casual, rather than evasive.

"And the Mark never…?"

"Took control?" Dean finished. "No. Of course not."

Sam nodded, wanting that to be true. But took in the surfeit of blood smeared across his brother's face, the torn and bloody clothes, and yet more blood slowly dripping from his shirt cuffs and fingertips. As if he'd bathed in the stuff.

Again, Dean noticed the wordless appraisal, took note of his own appearance, smiled and shook his head.

"What?"

"You're worried about how *I* look?"

"Well," Sam began, cleared his throat. "Now that you mention it."

"Dude, look in the mirror."

Sam examined his own hands, streaked with tacky red fluid layered over dried, almost black blood, caked into his knuckles. His shredded jacket was sodden and speckled with gore, from finger-sized chunks to confetti-sized bits. Neither his pants nor his shoes had been spared the reeking mess of the slaughtered hybrids and their maker. If Sam and Dean had brought a spare set of clothes, their outfits would have certainly ended up in the Chimera bonfire without a second thought. Nothing worth trying to salvage in a basic spin cycle.

Without a mirror, Sam couldn't examine his own face, but he imagined it looked no better than his brother's frightening visage. They looked like a pair of serial killers after a murderous bender, the stuff of nightmares.

"Point taken," Sam said.

Feeling vindicated, Dean replied with an emphatic nod, "Damn right!"

Nevertheless, Sam couldn't forget the unbridled glee with which Dean had attacked the Chimera. Though not without satisfaction, hunting was grim work. Sam never considered it a source of entertainment. It was a job. Sometimes the killing felt like a necessary evil. They'd both had to cross some gray lines over the years, often with regrets and sometimes resentments that lingered.

They'd agreed to be honest with each other. No more secrets. Dean said he remained in control of himself, that he wore the Mark without it controlling him. But they both knew that couldn't last. The Mark would eventually have its way. And when the scales tilted, when the Mark claimed its inevitable hold over Dean, would his brother even know that moment had arrived? Or would his own will be swept away as he lost the battle for control? And if that fateful day arrived, would Dean still retain enough of himself to admit the truth to Sam?

FOUR

The newest Braden Heights housing development remained a work in progress.

Yet from Day One, the builder had made sure to have the decorative wooden sign erected at the eventual entrance, facing the busy highway, with COVENTRY CROSSING emblazoned in a flowing script font, painted green, very official, as if the houses had already been built and were home to many happy families. If not for the white vinyl banner below the wooden sign, stating FAMILY HOMES IN THE $200,000S – COMING SOON! A year later, the permanent sign and a new vinyl banner with an updated enticement remained, with twenty percent of the projected 110 homes unfinished. Traveling from one of the developments to the other, finished homes gave way to skeletal wooden frameworks of future homes, which gave way to several lots which had seen utility work completed but little else.

Since Sal Fanizzi operated his bulldozer on the edge of the development farthest from the finished homes and the families living in them, he had no qualms about blasting the volume on the old radio he'd duct-taped to the window of the cab. Listening and singing along to the classic rock station helped the day go by faster, especially when stuck in the noisy bulldozer, cut off from the rest of the construction team. All afternoon he'd worked his way along the packed earth roads between the lots, clearing the building sites of trees and brush.

Driving from one end of the development to the other seemed like traveling through time. It reminded him of fast-forwarding through a movie or watching time-lapse photography. Head toward the finished homes and you jumped to the future where the homes had already been built. Turn around and drive away from the completed section and you traveled into the past, watching roofs and walls vanish, lumber come down to reveal rectangular foundations, exposed earth and finally open land, nothing but trees and brush and the occasional patch of wildflowers. At the moment, Sal worked in the past while listening to a commercial-free block of music from what seemed an equally distant time.

He'd been tasked with clearing the far perimeter of the land the builder had purchased for the development. Sal couldn't believe this preliminary work hadn't been done already, but he'd heard some whispers about "bad mojo" and the "creeps" or the "willies" that others had experienced while working this portion of the property. Hardly mattered if it was the guys getting their hands dirty or the supervisors directing the operation, they all seemed to find something better to do a little farther away and the work never got done. Sal had laughed, called it a bunch of superstitious bullshit. Guys looking for any excuse to get out of some work. How long before one of them said he spotted Bigfoot roaming through the woods? Eventually, the task of clearing the final bit of land fell in Sal's lap. So he put on a brave face, tugged down his trucker hat and told his foreman, "No problem."

Naturally, within an hour or so, the other guys had wandered off and he worked the final lots alone. The bulldozer's blade rumbled through the dirt and ripped out the snarls of brush same as anywhere else. Yes, the air seemed unnaturally still, the breeze from earlier in the day gone, but on the "unusual" meter, that hardly budged the needle. True, he neither saw nor heard any signs of wildlife out here, but why would he? The powerful growl of the bulldozer's engine combined with the gouging destruction of the blade would have scared off any bird, mammal or reptile with the slightest instinct for self-preservation. As for the occasional chill Sal felt down his spine, he imagined he might be coming down with the flu bug going around.

He made a mental note to toss back some vitamin C and zinc tablets soon as he got home. In the meantime, he sang along to the radio, Mellencamp's "Rain on the Scarecrow" segueing into Zevon's "Werewolves of London."

Besides, he was almost done with that section of the property. All that was left was the removal of a stand of dead trees, not a bit of foliage on them. The trunks had shed most of their bark, their branches brittle, skeletal limbs. A bunch of dried timber too stubborn to fall down and crumble to mulch or turn into a massive buffet for termites. Enter Sal Fanizzi to help the process along.

If he was honest with himself and beyond earshot of any of the superstitious bozos on his crew, he would admit how odd it was for this one stand of trees to have died in the middle of lush growth. They were like a stain on the landscape. He wondered if the previous owner of the land had dumped something toxic on the back corner of his land. Out of sight, out of mind. Whatever it was, it happened long ago and the effect hadn't spread. Tucked away in the cab of the bulldozer, Sal had no worries about exposing himself to whatever might have killed those trees. He simply took a great deal of satisfaction in watching them tumble over, their withered roots tugging clumps of earth up with them, giving way almost too easily after all the superstitious mumblings had bestowed this block of the land with almost mystical powers.

As one tree after another toppled over, seemingly in slow motion, Sal accelerated into the muck and drove them back beyond the perimeter, backing up and circling around to repeat the process as many times as needed. Once the trees were well clear of the final lots, he dropped the blade into the tossed earth, plowing the excess back into the darkness of the surrounding woods and packing the earth left behind in the process.

Mangling the lyrics to Springsteen's "The Rising," Sal smiled as the last of the dead trees fell.

Focused on the removal of the trees and the bragging rights he now possessed for finishing what the others had been too scared to attempt, he never noticed the long shapes scooped up within the mounds of earth. Partially obscured from view by the bulldozer's massive blade, the shapes offered no more resistance than the withered trees. Rootless and silent, they made no protest to this latest mistreatment, beyond the fluttering of ragged cloth that continued to cling to them after so many years.

When the bulldozer backed up and turned away, they settled into the loose earth, once again hidden from view. Once again ignored and forgotten...

FIVE

Pharmaceutical sales rep Elijah Green often referred to his silver Audi S3 as his mobile office. Considering the long hours spent and the many miles logged in the sedan, traveling between pharmacies, doctors' offices, hospitals and outpatient clinics, his nickname had a certain inescapable logic. Unless he was taking a client out for a business lunch, the passenger seat of the Audi functioned as a mini desk, holding his samples trunk, laptop computer and an old-fashioned clipboard and legal pad. But he had a dashboard mount for his smartphone, which allowed him to see notifications of incoming calls and texts without fumbling in his pockets while navigating the highways and side streets of Evansville, Indiana.

If he received an important call, he'd pull over and answer rather than dividing his attention between the caller and the road. Some days he drove well over a hundred miles before heading home to Braden Heights. He'd seen more than his share of distracted drivers and refused to become one. They came in all shapes, sizes: chatting or texting on phones, eating fast food lunches out of paper wrappers cradled in their lap, applying makeup with the aid of a sun visor mirror, yelling at kids in the backseat to behave, even a few who'd spent too many hours on the road and dozed off at the wheel.

After a brief, hopeful flirtation with a Bluetooth earpiece—a gift from Brianna—in an effort to communicate hands free, Elijah finally concluded that phone conversations, no matter how they were conducted, remained too much of a distraction for him. During his one-week trial with the earpiece, he'd caught himself drifting into the next lane twice; on a third occasion, he'd been scolded by a passing motorist who laid on his horn for three indignant seconds. Elijah might as well have been dozing. Another time, he hadn't noticed traffic slowing ahead in a construction zone and a tailgating situation quickly escalated to a near-miss fender bender. To avoid the collision, he'd stomped on the brake pedal and watched helplessly as his trunk, laptop and clipboard slammed into the dashboard. After that incident, he took the hint and tossed the earpiece into the dinged glove compartment.

Sometimes days on the road seemed like a war of attrition, or at least an erosion of concentration. And while he might joke about the car being his mobile office, anyone who carried a smartphone knew that possessing one of the miraculous devices, with constant access to email, text chat and voice calls, meant that the owner never left the office. Being on-call 24/7 was not always a blessing, but Elijah was particularly grateful for the freedom it allowed him these past few days. He'd made Brianna promise to text him whenever she had news. Sure his schedule in the field remained busy and hectic, but almost anything on that schedule could be rearranged. All it took was a few calls. Problem solved.

Naturally, her first text came during rush hour, while traffic maddeningly alternated between too slow through the bottlenecks and much too fast when the lanes opened. While slogging through the former, he'd turned on the radio to take his mind off of how slow so many cars could move in unison. The Stones' "Mother's Little Helper" was playing when his dashboard-mounted phone's screen lit up to display the text notification. Considering his situation, he vacillated between recognizing the appropriateness of the song and believing it was far too cynical for a pharma rep to ever include on a playlist.

His gaze darted between the uncomfortably close rear bumper of the PT Cruiser in front of his Audi and the short text message on his phone's screen.

"Gotta go!"

At the moment, he was stuck between lanes of slow-moving traffic, no opportunity to pull over and too risky to attempt a fumbled reply. He'd narrowly avoided one fender bender. Best not to push his luck. Instead he wondered why she'd waited so long to text him. He'd asked her more than once to text him right away. And she had promised, playfully offering to pinky-swear if he doubted her.

The phone chimed again. *"Can't wait!"*

Frowning, Elijah jabbed his finger at the radio to switch stations.

Another text chime: *"Sorry!"*

Strangely, the new station was also playing "Mother's Little Helper." Hell of a coincidence. He was used to hopping between stations and hearing the same irritating commercial, those things were impossible to avoid, but what were the odds of both stations playing this old song?

He was mentally rambling, a familiar habit when his anxiety climbed, which happened when he felt himself losing control of a situation. Nothing he peddled in his samples case would treat that condition.

Chime: *"Malik's here."*

Fortunately, Elijah was nearing the end of the bottleneck. Ahead, he saw cars accelerating, the mass of metal expanding and flowing away from him at unsafe speeds, many drivers determined to make up for lost time. Today of all days, he could sympathize. As the PT Cruiser sped away from him, he pressed down on the gas.

Supposedly, Brianna's brother was the backup plan, in case she couldn't reach Elijah. She hadn't wasted any time, though. She must have called Malik first, before bothering to text her husband. Maybe she thought Elijah would find his way home in time, but planned all along to have Malik take her. To keep her own anxiety under control. To be fair, her needs came first and his being there for the main event was more important than being the chauffeur.

Feeling control coming back into his grasp, he punched in a third radio station.

"Seriously…?"

Once again "Mother's Little Helper" played on his car

speakers. An earlier part of the song, enough of a change to assure him the programmed radio buttons still worked. But the same song on three stations at once? He shook his head.

Chime: *"Meet us at LMC! If you can!?!"*

Elijah decided to let the damn song play and risked a very quick text reply, a mere three letters, *"OMW,"* which automatically expanded to *"On my way!"*

After allowing himself this small infraction of his self-imposed rules, he leaned back in the driver's seat and took a deep breath. Not that he'd been too worried about risking an accident for three letters' worth of distraction, but simply to calm his own nerves. He still had quite a drive left, plenty of time to consider their life going forward. Normally, he'd pull over, review his schedule and make the few calls necessary to juggle the last few appointments of the day, but that could wait. And Brianna couldn't.

His nostrils flared at the strong scent of cinnamon. Like some kind of weird, reverse memory association. He'd want to remember this moment, and now he would associate it with one of his favorite scents. Was his brain playing some weird trick on him? The symptom of a stroke?

Sudden movement reflected in the rearview mirror. His gaze darted there, expecting to see the approaching bumper of a car or truck whose driver had overestimated Elijah's speed. Instead, he saw something dark and wretched rise into view, eyes black as coal under a foul mat of straggly hair. For a brief moment, he believed a homeless person had stowed away in the backseat of his car and had somehow gone undetected while he made his rounds.

Unspoken outrage on the tip of his tongue, he whipped his head around to face the intruder and before the grotesque face could come into focus, clawed hands flashed in front of his face, first blocking his vision then destroying it. Searing pain ripped through the flesh around his eyes—then utter darkness.

Instinctively, his hands flew from the steering wheel to his savaged face, and he felt the Audi swerve out of control, heard the protracted warning blare of a tractor-trailer's horn and felt, for the briefest moment, a jarring, thunderous impact immediately followed by explosive white-hot pain throughout his body—

SIX

Hunched over a table covered with leather-bound tomes and a few vellum scrolls in the library of the Men of Letters bunker—which he had at one time affectionately referred to as the Batcave—Dean searched for any mention of the Mark of Cain. Any information he discovered about the Mark could lead him a step closer to learning how to remove the damn thing. The scar—brand—whatever the hell it was, came with an unknown remove-by date. At some point in the not-too-distant future, the Mark would turn its current bearer into a mindless, murdering rage machine. A mystical ticking time bomb, but without the ticking. Unless you counted the occasional trembling in Dean's hands. And without a convenient set of red LED numbers counting down the seconds to the final explosion. It could happen in a week or two, maybe in a few months, but Dean doubted he had a year or even six months of control left.

Cain himself had reached an accommodation of sorts with the Mark, but only after centuries of killing. Not really an option as far as Dean was concerned. He wanted it gone as soon as possible. Hell, he'd have it surgically removed from his flesh if he thought the mystical mumbo-jumbo that attached the Mark to him would part ways that easily. Consenting to a partial flaying of his right forearm would no doubt lead to the Mark reappearing on his body as quickly as it had transferred from Cain to him. Even if he paid the ultimate price and killed himself with the First Blade—because nothing else could kill him while he bore the Mark—he'd be resurrected as a demon and a Knight of Hell. That wasn't a guess on Dean's part, Cain had done exactly that—and continued to bear the Mark.

Dean tapped his fingers impatiently on one of the few areas of the tabletop not covered with musty old books. His gaze flitted from one text to another, flipping pages, skimming entries. Now and then, a profound sense of déjà vu filled him and for fleeting moments he believed he had the answer in sight, but squeezed his eyes shut in disgust when he realized he'd simply read the same passage before, sometimes more than once. Was there such a thing as reading in circles?

The one book that might have the information they needed was the *Book of the Damned*, which, unfortunately, was not part of the Men of Letters collection, at least not in the Lebanon, Kansas bunker where the Winchesters had taken up residence. Now that she had returned from Oz, Charlie Bradbury had volunteered to track down the *Book of the Damned* but so far they hadn't heard a peep from her. Dean wondered if they'd sent her on a fool's errand. Maybe the damn *Book of the Damned* was a myth or, if it had existed at one time, had been destroyed years ago.

Tugging back the plaid sleeve of his shirt, Dean stared at the symbol representing the First Blade, which Crowley had agreed—not without a bit of self-preservation—to hide from Dean to slow the transformative effects of the Mark. Clenching his fist in frustration, he swept his arm across the table, sending half a dozen books and his empty coffee mug flying across the room.

Exhaling forcefully, Dean held out both arms, palms down, fingers spread. A quick test. No trembling. "Okay," he said softly. *Still in control.*

He pushed back his chair and walked away from the table, twisting his head and rolling his shoulders to relieve his tension, determined not to let the fruitless search get under his skin.

He recalled Sam's words about the Mark. *"We'll figure it out. We always do."*

One part of Dean believed that sentiment. They'd been to hell and back and parts in between. They'd overcome considerable odds on multiple occasions. But that track record led them to take greater risks, and they'd lost plenty of people they cared about along the way. And, really, how long could you keep beating the odds before the house won a round? With the Mark bound to his flesh, a continuous visual reminder of a murderous fate, Dean couldn't help but wonder if this, finally, was the losing hand.

Sensing movement, he looked up, saw Sam standing at the entrance to the library, watching him.

"How long?"

Sam inadvertently glanced at the books and the shattered mug scattered across the floor. "Long enough."

Dean tried to shake off his concern. "What? You never get frustrated with this stuff?"

"That's all it is?"

"Absolutely."

"And the Chimera?"

"We've been over that," Dean said. "That was me. Not the Mark. I was in total control."

Looking doubtful, Sam said, "Really?"

"Yes, that was me. In a zone. Firing on all cylinders. Eye of the tiger. Pick one." He took a deep breath. "Look, Sam, you saw that thing. Anything less than one hundred percent focus, and I would have ended up in that spare parts flesh pit—or worse."

Sam nodded. "You're right."

"Of course I'm right," Dean said jovially, displaying more confidence than he felt. "I'm in total control."

"For now," Sam said solemnly.

Dean wanted to argue the point, insist that he could fight the effects of the Mark indefinitely, but they'd both know he was lying.

They turned at the sound of footfalls on the stairs leading down from the abandoned power plant that loomed over the bunker. Warded against any evil that ever existed, the bunker had become their headquarters and their home base, if not truly a home, though it featured bedrooms and a kitchen in addition to the vast library, war room, laboratory, shooting range, observatory, and even a dungeon of sorts, hidden behind a storage area. The bunker had become the one place they could relax, even if the time spent there was sometimes infuriating.

"Cass," Sam informed Dean, a moment before the angel walked through the doorway into the library, wearing the somewhat rumpled trench coat over two-piece suit and loosened necktie that had become his uniform.

While surviving on a diminished and fading Grace, Castiel lacked the full powers of an angel of the Lord. No longer able to teleport, he traveled by conventional means. More often than not, that meant his old Lincoln or shoe leather. Restoring Castiel's Grace was a problem for another day. Something else they would, they hoped, figure out. In the meantime, the world-weary angel seemed resigned to a fate that meant gradually fading away.

"Sam. Dean." Castiel glanced at each of them in turn, then took in the mess on the floor. "I assume Charlie has not returned with the *Book of the Damned*."

Sam gave a slight shake of his head, downplaying the lack of results on their end.

"No word," Dean said. "I, on the other hand, found a whole lot of nothing."

"I see," Castiel said, glancing at Sam, an unspoken question passing between them. Sam shook his head.

"Guys," Dean said, arms spread. "I'm right here. You got a question, ask. But stop passing notes."

Castiel cleared his throat. "So… you're well? In control?"

"I'm good," Dean said, smiling. "Complete control. Living a life of reluctant moderation. No coloring outside the lines."

"Good," Castiel said, either missing the sarcasm or taking Dean's statement at face value. Sometimes it was hard to tell with Cass.

"Any word on Cain?" Sam asked the angel.

Castiel frowned. "Nothing yet, unfortunately," he said. "But maybe something else. A possible lead on someone who may have information about a cure."

Dean took a step forward but caught himself. "That sounds like a whole lot of maybes."

"There's an answer out there somewhere," Sam said. "In the *Book of the Damned*. Or here, in some book or scroll we haven't checked—"

"I've checked everything here, Sam," Dean said. "Five or six times. Hell, I've got some of these books damn near memorized."

"—or it's out there," Sam said, pointing up and away. "All I know is, we keep looking for the answer. That's what we do."

"The lead's worth checking," Castiel said. "Until I find Cain, it's the… best option."

Dean guessed that he'd been about to say "only option" but that would've sounded too fatalistic. Last lead. End of the line. "Fine," Dean said. "Nothing to lose, right?"

Castiel nodded, unable to hide his concern. "Either way, this won't take long."

"You know where to find us," Dean said, pacing along the length of the table. At some point he'd pick up the scattered books and coffee mug shrapnel, but right then he had some pent-up anxiety to expend and pacing was definitely the better option. *Some justifiable frustration,* he assured himself, *no oncoming rage-a-thon, no trembling hands.* "I'll be reading these same books again, working on my teetotaling ways."

"Or not," Sam said, navigating around the books on the floor to the neighboring library table, where he'd left his laptop to fix something to eat in the kitchen.

"What?"

"Let's do something else," Sam said, looking to Castiel for support. "Don't get me wrong, the bunker's great. But we're underground here, no windows, staring at books or screens all day. Recipe for cabin fever, right?"

"Cabin fever," Castiel said, supportive but waiting to see where Sam was going with his line of reasoning.

"So we stop looking for a cure," Dean said. "And we go… out?"

"On a hunt," Sam said, waking his laptop from sleep mode. "But, no, we don't stop looking. Ever. We… take time to recharge."

"On a hunt?"

"Yes," Sam said. Then, acknowledging Dean's skepticism, he continued, "Look, Dean, we can bang our heads against a locked door until we knock ourselves out. Or we take a step back, and notice a window open around the corner." Sam paused, working the keyboard until he brought up the information he sought. "Let's take time for a hunt. Then maybe we find a way to come at this from a new direction."

"A valid suggestion," Castiel chimed in.

"Sure," Dean said. "Why not? We've done it before."

Sam was right in one aspect. A hunt kept Dean's mind off the impending doom the Mark represented. Work on a smaller, fixable problem, while the big problem simmered on a back burner. The time between hunts was what got to him. Sitting around with nothing to occupy his time or thoughts brought the big problem to the fore. The bunker may have been their safe zone, but it couldn't protect them from themselves. With no outside threats to worry about, the only thing Dean thought about was the internal threat waiting to overwhelm him. Better to leave the sanctuary and face something that could be defeated than to sit underground in a quiet corner and wonder how much time he had left before Mr. Hyde kicked Jekyll to the curb and signed the long-term lease on his body and soul.

"What have you got?"

Sam spun the laptop around to Dean.

"Disembowelment murder," Sam said. "Dave Holcomb, Braden Heights, Indiana. Wife comes back from a shopping trip, finds her husband gutted behind their toolshed."

"Angry lawn gnome?" Dean said as he sat down in front of the laptop to read the news report.

Castiel came forward, looked over Dean's shoulder.

"I know it's not much," Sam said. "Just the one incident. And other than the brutality of the—"

"Animal attack," Dean said, pointing. "According to police."

"Maybe, but—"

"Gouged out eyeballs," Dean continued, not really ignoring Sam, just his hard-sell masquerading as a soft-sell. "That a message? Or a delicacy?"

Sam shrugged. "Let's find out. You in?"

"I'm in."

"I'll join you," Castiel said. "After I follow up on my lead."

"Great," Dean said as he picked up the scattered books. "Lot of irons in the cure-the-Mark fire. Unfortunately, these"—he dumped the stack of books back on the table—"aren't one of them."

SEVEN

After lying to his parents that he'd finished his homework, Aidan Dufford ducked out for the evening to spend some time with his friends, which basically meant wandering around Braden Heights with no clear destination in mind. Technically, he hadn't lied. He'd told them he was finished *with* his homework. Which was true. He'd had more than enough of term papers, essays, reading assignments and math problems for one day. Really, teachers should get together and declare a mercy rule, especially for seniors. Even prisoners were granted early release for good behavior. But to his mind, his teachers did put their heads together, like a gathering of psychological torturers, to decide the best way to drive their students crazy before they escaped the drab walls and crowded halls of Braden Heights High. Sadistic bastards, the whole bunch of them. And, really, how much of the crap they tried to stuff into his head would matter one week after graduation? The whole system was designed to keep teens busy during as many waking hours as humanly possible. Idle hands and all that bullshit…

Well, whatever. Just because they played a tune, it didn't make him a dancing idiot. But dropping out wasn't an option. Not this close to the finish line. He'd play along just enough to get by. Get the diploma and get the hell out.

Problem was, he'd skipped too many classes and missed too many assignments to give himself any wiggle room. Every day remaining in the school year meant another tightrope walk to avoid expulsion, summer school or failure. Another day of nodding his head as one person after another told him what to do and where to go and how to be, starting and ending with his parents, with his teachers and the vice principal in between, and even Chloe when everyone else was too busy to nag him.

So, really, who could blame him for wanting to blow off some steam? It was so much easier to hang out with Wally and Jay. They got it. They got him. And so what if they got into a little mischief now and then. Wasn't anything major, really, just kids clowning around. A little loitering, a little smoking, with an occasional side of vandalism, but mostly decompressing. Wasn't as if anybody their age could find jobs these days. And even if something turned up, some minimum-wage slave job, they had their whole freaking lives to work from dawn to dusk or vice versa. What was the goddamn rush?

Lately, between the home and girlfriend situations, he'd much rather stay out and tune out, walk the streets with his friends, vent about the indignities of his daily life and ignore the uncertain future. If he tried to take it more than one day at a time, he really would go crazy.

"Everybody keeps telling me I'm an adult now," Aidan said as he walked down the street three abreast with Wally and Jay. He could see the wrought-iron fence ahead at the corner of Second and Hawthorne. That's where they'd split up, Aidan heading east and the others north. In other words, his freedom walk was nearly over. "As if turning eighteen flipped some magical damn switch in my DNA and changed me somehow. Know what I mean?"

Jay nodded.

Wally said, "Yeah, like, 'Welcome to the club.' And you're like, 'What club? That's it? That's all there is?'"

"And nothing they teach us in school makes any difference," Aidan continued. "None of it really matters."

"I have no clue," Jay said.

"It's like they want to confuse us," Aidan said. "Pretend like they're preparing us for something, but the stuff in the books is all crap."

"It's a conspiracy," Wally said. "Joke's on us, man."

"You know what?" Jay said. "I bet they don't have a clue either."

"You're onto something," Aidan said, laughing. "Making it up as they go along."

They paused by the wrought-iron fence that marked the perimeter of Halloran's Life Celebration Studio. Which, once you turned off the bullshit force field, was better known as a funeral home. For a while, their running joke had been to refer to every location as a "celebration studio" of some kind. Braden Heights High became the Education

Celebration Studio, Madonado's Deli was rebranded the Sandwich Celebration Studio, and Grand National Bank's new moniker was the Fat Stacks Celebration Studio. Not that they had any stacks, fat or otherwise, with which to celebrate. But upcoming graduation gifts kept the hope alive.

Aidan nodded toward the funeral home. "How many dead people are celebrating in there right now?"

"How should I know?" Jay said, taking the question literally.

"Just wondering," Aidan said. "People are always dying, right?"

"Half dozen, maybe," Wally said. "Just the ones ready to get burned or buried, right? And it's not the only stiff shop in town, right?"

"Stiff shop?" Aidan asked, smiling.

"Whatever," Wally said, shrugging. "Corpse club? Zombie hatchery? Listen, man, we gotta go."

"Right," Aidan said. "See you guys tomorrow."

Once they were a block away, their chatter fading into the night, Aidan crossed the street heading west a couple blocks before circling behind Kirkwood Plaza. He was already late and figured a few more minutes wouldn't hurt. If his parents held true to form, his mother would already be sound asleep and his father, if he hadn't passed out from putting a major dent in a case of beer, would be warming a bar stool until closing or until they cut him off. Either way, Aidan's lateness would go unnoticed.

By ducking behind Kirkwood Plaza, a strip mall with a dozen stores facing Second Avenue, his presence would also go unnoticed by any patrolling cop cars. At the rear of the first store in the strip mall conga line, he reached into his left inner jacket pocket and pulled out a wrist rocket. Basically a slingshot on steroids. In the right inner pocket, he had a hundred-count bag of steel ball ammo, each one about the size of a marble.

Behind the stores after business hours, on the private access driveway with barely enough room for a trash truck to trundle through and empty the row of fetid dumpsters, he risked little chance of discovery. A cop car might pass by every few hours, but Aidan would be long gone in five or ten minutes. At the first glare of headlights, he could duck into the line of bushes on the far side of the driveway, stay low and avoid detection. Until then, he planned to engage in a bit of what he called "sanity preservation."

At some point, venting to his friends fell short of the mark. On these occasions, some target practice usually improved his mood. He'd practiced on bottles and empty pop cans until he got good enough not to waste too much ammo. This late at night most stores were closed and dark, except for security lights and—in the case of the strip mall—the steel-caged lights over the rear doors. He preferred the caged lights to exposed bulbs. The metal grid protecting them provided a higher degree of difficulty and the extra challenge of a direct hit provided more satisfaction. Hit one of the cage bars instead, and his shot ricocheted into the night—or, worse, right back at him. He'd had the welts and bruises to show for it. But knocking out a caged light required precision, like zipping a puck through a goalie's five hole.

For each light, he imagined the head of some teacher or administrator or store clerk who had pissed him off recently. But he kept his "hit list" internal, completely memorized, no written record that could ever lead to suspension or expulsion. Besides, he had no actual plans to go after anyone with fists, ball bearings or real bullets. He was blowing off steam, nothing more. So what if he broke a bunch of fifty-cent light bulbs? It was—what did they call it?—the cost of doing business. The shop owners should be grateful he didn't smash their big display windows or break into their shops and steal stuff.

Taking position behind Flanagan's Pub, he took careful aim. "This one's for Mrs. Garrity and the never-ending term paper," he said with a wicked grin, imagining the mole on the corner of her forehead, and launched a metal ball at the first caged light. Direct hit! The bulb burst with a deep *pop* sound and a slight sizzle of electricity before bits of glass clinked all over the ground, like a miniature orchestra warming up.

His steel ball rattled around the cage for a moment before striking the wall and rolling toward his feet. Plucking it off the ground, he moved to the rear of the next shop, Sal's Pizza Palace, if he recalled the order of the stores correctly. Again, he took aim. "Ah, for Mr. Uphoff and that D+ on my last exam. Writing 'Try Harder' followed by three exclamation marks really helps. How about you try harder to be a better teacher, jackass!"

He released the shot—missed. Though he flinched at the steel-on-steel ping, the ricochet sailed wide, harmless. "Figures," he muttered. "Guess I need to try harder!"

His next shot scored. Definite sizzle this time.

Moving sideways down the line, he positioned himself behind the rear entrance of the third shop, a dry cleaner or temp agency, he couldn't remember. He fished a shot out of his plastic bag, deciding whose face would make a perfect target, when his cell phone buzzed. Heaving a sigh, he said, "What now?"

He tugged the phone from his back pocket, checked the caller ID: Chloe.

"C'mon," he said. "Give it a break already."

He tapped the ignore button and shoved the phone back in his pocket before proceeding to knock out the third light. Unfortunately, he'd been so upset by yet another call from Chloe that he'd forgotten to pick a target for the light. *Wasted a bulb for nothing!* Not like he could retroactively assign a face to the bulb.

With a sigh he moved on to light number four, but was interrupted by another call. Chloe again. "She can*not* take a hint," he mumbled. "Save it for tomorrow, Chloe. I'm fried over this crap."

Maybe she can be the face of light number four, he thought. She wouldn't give him a moment's peace. Worse than his damn parents. Powering off the phone, he put it away and tried to shake off the interruption.

He took aim—

And smelled freshly popped popcorn. Made him think of settling into the darkness of a movie theater to see the latest summer action blockbuster; overhyped more often than not, but a happy diversion for a few hours, away from people making demands of his time, an island of serenity during the projected chaos and one-liners. He pulled back on the rubber tubing and took aim at the fourth light again—

—and the light blew out.

But he hadn't released the steel ball. It sat in the rubber pad, full of potential energy, as his physics teacher might say. Then, one by one, each caged light in the row of stores popped out. Some merely winked out. Others shattered. But he hadn't moved.

"What the hell—?"

Something scraped the ground behind him.

For a moment he worried the shopping center had hired a security guard to patrol the place at night. A security guard with a popcorn cart. But as he spun around, an apology or some lame excuse trying to take form in his mind, he caught a whiff of something foul, like an animal carcass left on the side of the road too long. But what he saw was not an animal.

He had the fleeting impression of utter darkness mixed with corpse-pale flesh, straggly hair and strangely elongated fingers, somebody in a horror costume maybe, but he sensed she—yes a *she*—was not entirely human. Something that emerged from the nightmares of a fevered mind after gorging on tainted food in a serial killer's house, something that couldn't exist but terrified at the level of instinct.

The wrist rocket and ammo slipped from his numb hands.

"What—?"

His gaze tracked toward her partially obscured face, trying to focus despite his revulsion. In that moment, she switched from inhuman stillness to surging forward, inhumanly fast, reaching for his face—his eyes!—with those disturbingly long fingers. Fire ripped through his face, and then lower, the intense pain scorching him until he welcomed—

EIGHT

After a ten-hour overnight drive from Lebanon, Kansas, the Winchesters rented a room at a local motel, switched into their Fed suits and made their way to the Public Safety Center in Braden Heights, Indiana. Of recent construction, the sprawling complex had a modern aesthetic with a curved driveway leading to the landscaped, tree-lined front entrance with access to rooms designed to accommodate town and school board meetings. An exterior directory pointed them to the rear of the building for police-related matters. The rear parking lot was smaller than the front and side lots and the occupied spaces held police cruisers, a K-9 SUV, and a police van. Dean parked the Impala in a corner spot, nearest the side parking lot, possibly to look less conspicuous among all the law enforcement vehicles.

The receptionist, behind her bulletproof glass barrier, buzzed them through into the police office area. If they were to maintain their FBI covers and receive cooperation from local authorities, the first order of business called for checking in with local law enforcement. They made it past a mere half-dozen low-walled cubicles, and only a couple of those occupied by uniformed police officers working at computers, when Assistant Chief of Police Francisco Cordero intercepted them. Since Sam had suggested the hunt to help take Dean's mind off the ongoing futility of searching for a cure to the Mark, he let Dean take the lead.

"Agents Banks and Rutherford, FBI," Dean said with the aplomb of a seasoned con man, flashing the fake FBI laminate and exchanging a quick handshake. Sam already had his ID out, and displayed it simultaneously with a curt nod.

"Assistant Chief Francisco Cordero," the man said, introducing himself with a quick, amiable smile as he moved from shaking Dean's hand to Sam's. Medium height, approaching fifty while maintaining a trim, muscular build, Cordero sported a thin black mustache trimmed with a laser's precision. "But you can call me Frank. What brings you to Braden Heights, gentlemen?"

"We're looking into the Holcomb murder," Dean said, "and hope you can answer a few questions before we visit the scene."

"Ah, that's a bizarre one," Cordero said, nodding. "And gruesome, besides. But we're not ready to call it a murder just yet. Preliminary opinion of our medical examiner is animal attack."

"Animal attack?" Dean said, arching an eyebrow.

"There's the matter of the murder weapon," Cordero said.

"What about it?" Sam asked, recalling no mention of a recovered murder weapon in the report he'd read online.

"Technically, there isn't one," Cordero said. "Whatever killed Mr. Holcomb did so with claws and teeth."

"Teeth?" Dean asked. "He was bitten?"

Cordero frowned and waved them back toward his office, as if reluctant to speak about the case in the open, even though the only potential eavesdroppers were fellow officers. On their way, the Assistant Chief was interrupted by a uniformed woman in her mid-thirties, blond hair pulled back in a bun, with the two bars of a captain's rank pinned to her shirt collar.

She gave Sam and Dean a quick appraising glance before turning her attention to Cordero. "The Green file you requested, sir," she said, handing him a manila folder.

He thanked her, introduced her as Captain Jaime Sands and informed her that they were investigating the Holcomb case. Cordero lowered his voice. "Captain Sands and I basically run the place while Chief Townshend attends conferences with other chiefs. Homeland terrorism or emergency crisis management or—what is it this week, Captain?"

"Effective Budgeting with Limited Resources, sir," she said, exchanging a conspiratorial grin with Cordero. "I think."

"I'm sure that's it," Cordero said. "Anyway, I'm usually stuck here with meetings, reports and analysis. Captain Sands is most likely to be in the field, so you may need to liaise with her if you need anything." From his wistful tone of voice, if not for the change in pay grade, Cordero would have preferred to have their roles reversed.

Before she left, Captain Sands removed two business cards from her shirt pocket and passed them to Dean and Sam. Cordero ushered them into his spartan office. His desk held a computer workstation, two stacks of folders, a tray of business cards and a family photo in a silver frame. The wall behind his desk had one row of framed photos—Cordero with the absentee Chief Townshend, Cordero in an official department group shot, Cordero wearing a racing bib and medal at a childhood brain cancer charity 5K event, Cordero shaking hands with the mayor—and a plaque denoting a commendation for bravery.

Cordero didn't invite them to sit in the two wooden chairs facing his desk, so Sam guessed whatever he had to say wouldn't take long. The Assistant Chief stood with his hands on his hips, thumbs tucked under his police belt. "Where were we?" he asked.

"Teeth," Dean provided.

"Oh, yes, teeth," Cordero said. "This was left out of the information released to the public, but some of the victim's organs were missing. At first the medical examiner suspected these organs had been… harvested. But teeth marks seemed to indicate something else."

"The organs were consumed," Dean guessed.

"Exactly," Cordero said. "Along with the evidence that the victim had been viciously clawed, the consumption of human organs… well, you can see how he came to the conclusion that Dave Holcomb was the victim of an animal attack."

"But the case remains open," Sam said.

"Yes," Cordero replied, glancing away for a telltale moment, curled hand to his mouth as he cleared his throat, uncomfortable. "There are a few… inconsistencies with the animal attack theory."

"No animal tracks in the yard," Sam said.

"None consistent with the size of an animal capable of such an attack."

Dean nodded. "Guessing none of the neighbors noticed any wild animals roaming the area."

"No reports," Cordero said. "My officers canvassed the whole block. Nobody noticed anything unusual."

"So what's the explanation?" Sam asked.

"The property faces an unoccupied lot," Cordero said. "Something could have come over the six-foot fence, but again…"

"No claw marks on the fence," Dean said.

"No," Cordero admitted. "And the fence has rotted. The weight of a large animal scaling it would have caused additional damage."

"What's left?" Dean asked. "Large bird of prey?"

Cordero shrugged, at a loss. "Turkey vulture could have fed on the body after the initial attack," he said, "but they're carrion eaters. Dine on roadkill, mostly."

"And something—someone—else killed Holcomb," Sam said. *Something with claws and fangs, possibly, that left no tracks.*

"If, as you believe, some*one*—and not some animal—killed Holcomb," Cordero said, "that person is one true sicko."

"What can you tell us about Dave Holcomb and his wife?" Dean asked.

"Recent transplants from the west coast," Cordero said. "Job opportunity for the vic—husband. Haven't been in town long enough to make many friends—or any enemies. Of course, it's always possible an enemy followed them here."

Easier for the Assistant Chief to suspect an outsider with a specific motive, Sam imagined, rather than a homegrown menace that might stick around and continue to terrorize Braden Heights.

Cordero had the department secretary print out a copy of the official report, which included contact information for the widow, Sally Holcomb, along with her street address.

"Listen," Cordero told them as they stepped out of his office, "I have a good department here. Not likely we missed anything relevant to the case."

"No doubt very thorough," Dean said agreeably. "Consider us two pairs of fresh eyes. That's all."

"Make that three," said a familiar voice, approaching from the reception area.

"Our colleague," Sam said quickly, as Castiel joined them. "Special Agent Collins. Agent, this is Assistant Chief Cordero. He's been filling us in on the Holcomb case."

Castiel's usual attire—open trench coat and loosened necktie—and default demeanor—a carrying-the-weight-of-the-world-on-his-shoulders seriousness—was more than appropriate for the grim nature of the Holcomb case. In other words, he fit right in. "I came as soon as I could."

"Wrapping up that other case," Dean said.

"Yes."

"Looks like we have the makings of a full-blown task force here," Cordero said in a mixture of amusement and genuine curiosity.

"We're nothing if not thorough," Dean said. "That's the Bureau for you."

"Well, good to meet you, Agent Collins," Cordero said. The Assistant Chief gave them copies of his own business card, which Sam and Dean added to their growing Braden Heights Police Department collection. Castiel looked at the card for a moment as if he were expected to memorize it, then shoved it absently into the pocket of his overcoat.

"Thanks for your time, Chief," Dean said. "We'll bring our colleague up to speed at the crime scene. And get back to you with any developments."

"I'll do the same," Cordero said, thumbs tucked in his belt again.

Sam couldn't help but wonder if the man's suspicions had been raised by the arrival of three FBI agents to investigate an apparent animal attack. They'd stay out of his way and hope he did the same.

Cordero returned to his office while the Winchesters and Castiel headed toward the reception area. Dean cast a sidelong glance at Castiel that spoke volumes without his uttering a word. He seemed about to say something out of FBI character, thought better of it considering the presence of police officers within earshot, and gave a slight, disbelieving head shake instead.

Once they were in the rear parking lot, where Castiel had parked his gold 1978 Lincoln Continental Mark V next to the Impala, Dean stopped and looked around before addressing the angel. "Look, Cass, I'm in control," Dean said. "Got it? I don't need a freakin' babysitter."

"Dean, I'm not here to... babysit," Castiel said. "We all want the same thing."

"Fine," Dean said. "One for all and all for one. I get it. Just stop staring, okay?"

Without waiting for an answer, Dean continued to the Impala.

Castiel turned to Sam. "I wasn't staring."

"Yeah," Sam said. "He's a little on edge. Think you remind him we're no closer to removing the Mark."

"That's unfortunate," Castiel said, as if the unwanted association physically pained him.

"Got to say, Cass, wasn't expecting to see you so soon," Sam said.

Castiel frowned. "My contact dug a little deeper. And the lead was worthless after all."

"What happened?"

"Let's just say it involved a series of vellum forgeries hoarded by a cave-dwelling hermit who apparently lost touch with reality several decades ago."

Sam glanced at his brother, sitting in the Impala's driver's seat, staring through the windshield, apparently lost in thought. *Dark thoughts,* Sam suspected. "Dean doesn't need to know about this."

Again, Castiel frowned. "You want me to keep it from him?"

"No," Sam amended, "but let's not rub his face in more failure. If he asks, downplay it. We've still got the search for Cain and the *Book of the Damned*. We'll figure something out, find another way. We always do. Right?"

But Sam could tell by the way Castiel avoided his gaze that the angel had begun to have his own doubts, that maybe the

Mark of Cain was an unsolvable riddle. They weren't buying time for Dean, they were simply ignoring the meaning of its passage, filling their days with wishful thinking and fruitless searches instead of preparing themselves for the inevitable day when Dean finally succumbed to the Mark.

Sam refused to believe that. Not while they had options and avenues to explore. As far as he was concerned, they only failed if they quit looking for an answer before time ran out.

He climbed into the passenger seat of the Impala, clutching the police report in his hands. "You got the address?"

"Read it to me," Dean said.

Sam opened the folder, read the street address aloud, along with some scribbled driving directions courtesy of Cordero.

After Sam tossed the folder on the dashboard, Dean backed out of the parking spot and drove out of the lot, Castiel following behind him. He gave a slight nod toward the rearview mirror. "So?"

"What?"

"Cass's lead," Dean said. "A bust, right?"

Sam stared ahead, feigning more interest in the road than the conversation. "It was a long shot."

After a long moment, "Yeah."

NINE

From the outside, nothing distinguished the suburban Holcomb residence from the other homes on the block. No visible indication that tragedy had befallen this house in particular. The lot boasted the same well-manicured lawn and neatly trimmed bushes as the others. So often personal tragedies remain hidden to the casual viewer, only to be experienced in painful solitude.

But Dave Holcomb's widow was not home alone.

When Sam rang the doorbell, an elderly woman opened the door, her twinkling gaze taking each of them in turn, attempting to make a careful appraisal before addressing them. "Yes? How may I help you?"

"Hello, ma'am," Sam said, showing his FBI credentials. "Special Agent Rutherford. With Agents Banks and Collins. We're looking into the death of David Holcomb. Is Mrs. Holcomb home?"

"I'm her grandmother."

"Could we have a few minutes of her time?"

"The poor dear is in a state," the woman said. "She's already talked to the police. Can this wait?"

"Grandma Mary, who is it?" called a masculine voice.

The old woman looked over her shoulder. "Three FBI agents," she said, adding, "And I asked you not to call me that, Ramon."

From her tone of voice, Sam had the impression she'd made the request on repeated occasions but had no illusion that compliance was forthcoming. Turning her attention back to Sam, she said, "I'm sorry, it's a bad t—"

"The police believe Mr. Holcomb was the victim of an animal attack," Sam continued, hoping he wouldn't have to wedge his foot in the door to stop her from slamming it in his face. "We have reason to believe that's not the case."

Frown lines joined the assemblage of wrinkles on her brow, whether from curiosity or suspicion, Sam couldn't tell. "What reason?"

"We've... seen this kind of thing before," Sam explained. *Maybe not the exact M.O. but enough inconsistencies to point to a supernatural menace at work.*

"It's okay, Grandma Mary," a younger woman said as she approached the door, a wad of damp tissues clutched in one hand. "I'll talk to them."

The grandmother backed away, but not without a pointed finger and a chiding tone as she said, "You set a bad example for your little brother, Dalisay."

"He started it," Sally Holcomb said, allowing herself a blink-and-you-miss-it smile as the old woman surrendered the doorway to her.

Couched within the old woman's admonition, Sam sensed true affection and warmth in the term of endearment. No wonder they ignored her request. Sam guessed the teasing and easy familiarity was a small comfort during this time of shock and grief.

In her early thirties, Sally Holcomb had shoulder-length black hair currently in a slight bit of disarray, and a natural caramel skin tone. Devoid of makeup, her face showed signs of stress and sleeplessness, her lips pressed tight but at times trembling with repressed emotion as she struggled to maintain her composure.

"I'm sorry for your loss, Mrs. Holcomb," Sam said, again making introductions and flashing his fake ID. "As I mentioned to your grandmother, we don't believe your husband was the victim of an animal attack."

"What else could it have been?" she asked. "The way he was…" She sniffled a bit, pressing the crumpled tissues to her nose.

"That's what we want to find out," Dean said, behind and to Sam's right. Castiel stood another step back, on Sam's left.

"If you could spare a few minutes for some questions," Sam said. "And allow us to review the crime scene. Won't take long. Promise."

"You really think you'll find something the police missed?"

"We won't know for sure," Dean said, "until we check."

"Okay," she said. "Come in."

Little brother Ramon joined his sister at the door as the Winchesters and Castiel entered the home. Ramon stood an inch or two shorter than his sister, with matching hair color and complexion, and had the solid build of a welterweight boxer. He placed his hand protectively on his sister's shoulder as he examined the three ostensible FBI agents with a slow nod.

"Police okay with you guys second guessing them?"

"Assistant Chief Cordero knows we're here," Sam said, avoiding a direct answer. Some police departments resented outside interference. Some welcomed the assistance. Sam couldn't guess if the man fell into the former or latter group. "He's given us a copy of the case file."

"We have more experience with… unusual cases," Dean added.

"Some very unusual cases," Castiel said absently as he took in the new surroundings.

"Can I—we get you anything," Sally asked, glancing at her grandmother for potential assistance. "Water? Brownies? Some neighbors brought casseroles, but…"

"No, thank you," Sam said. "We won't take up much of your time."

"Okay," Sally said. "Please have a seat. This is all—you can't prepare yourself for something like this. I don't know how to act… how to be… Inside, I'm falling apart and it feels like the walls are crumbling around me but…" Her voice caught in her throat. She dabbed at her eyes as tears welled, catching them before they could roll down her cheeks. "I'm lost without Dave."

Sally sat in the middle of the sofa in the living room, Sam and Dean on either side of her. Castiel sat in a wingchair angled toward the sofa on the other side of a glass coffee table. Ramon stood behind the sofa, maintaining physical contact with his sister, leaving the matching wingchair unoccupied, obviously expecting his grandmother to take that seat. But the old woman wandered into the kitchen on some unspoken errand. Maybe she needed to keep herself busy. Everyone handled grief differently.

"Do Ramon and your grandmother live here with you?" Sam asked.

"No," Sally said, pausing each time her emotions threatened to overwhelm her. "They came to help me out. Dave's parents are on a Caribbean cruise. They'll be here as soon as they can. Right now, everything's in a holding pattern. I'm not sure what to do about... about Dave's body."

The grandmother returned, bearing a tray with a water pitcher and glasses, in case anyone changed their mind about refreshments. "I told her to put the house back on the market," the old woman said. "This is no place for her now."

"It's our home..." Sally began halfheartedly, even failing to convince herself.

"This is a house," Mary said, shaking her head. "Not a home. Just because you sign some papers doesn't make it a home. There wasn't time for that."

Sam looked around, noticed some unpacked boxes here and there against the walls. They really hadn't been in Braden Heights long enough to settle in. And now that was hardly possible given the circumstances.

Ramon said, "They moved here because David had a job offer. That don't matter no more."

Sally nodded. "That's true. Dave's old friend from high

school, Stanley Vargus, offered him a job as night manager at
a factory he owns in Evansville. Dave met everyone, toured
the place, but he hadn't even started yet. He wanted to fix
up… fix things before…" Another long pause while she
tried to compose herself. "There really is nothing for me here
anymore. Those neighbors? The ones who baked the brownies,
brought the casseroles… I don't even remember their names.
And the idea of staying in this house, where Dave…"

Ramon leaned down, wrapped his arms around her
shoulders and gave her a fierce hug. "No reason you gotta
stay, sis. We're here for you until you're ready to go."

Sally nodded, pressing the flat of her hand to her mouth.

"Is it possible," Sam began, "in the short time you've been
in Braden Heights, that your husband made any enemies?
Someone who might have wished him harm?"

"No," Sally said. "How could he? Dave's been a homebody
since we got here, checking off repairs on his long to-do list.
Other than the factory tour and the times he drove to the
home improvement center for supplies—he was probably
their best customer lately—he hardly left the house. Besides,
everyone liked Dave. He was easygoing. I doubt he's ever had
any real enemies…"

She alternated between present and past tense when
discussing her husband; it was obvious Sally hadn't adjusted
to his loss. Sam wondered if she could really look at the
situation objectively. Clearly, she was still in shock, her
coping mechanisms not yet in place.

Dean leaned forward, turning to address her. "You
found your husband and reported the attack." She nodded.

"Anything strike you as odd about the surroundings? The house? The backyard?"

"His pickup was backed into the driveway," she said. "To unload supplies. I thought he would have been finished by then and parked on the street so I could bring the groceries in through the garage. But when I checked on him in the backyard, I saw he hadn't done any work. Everything was stacked on the patio except one section of fence. I thought he left on foot, for some reason."

"He must have been... attacked soon after you left," Castiel said.

"Soon after he returned from the home improvement center," Sally said. "I'm not sure when that..."

"How did you find him?" Sam asked.

"I searched through the house when I didn't see him in the backyard," Sally said. "Then I thought maybe he went in the utility shed, maybe had an accident with a power tool or... a heart attack or something. I didn't know what to think."

"What made you check behind the shed?" Dean asked.

"The broken branches," Sally said. "Looked like he pushed his way through. And then I saw... blood on the leaves. Then..." Her voice hitched. "It was horrible. What happened to him... How could something like that...? In our own backyard?"

"We want to find out," Sam said sympathetically. "Do you mind if we have a look now?"

"No, but I can't..." Sally said. "The police are done collecting evidence, so you can—but..."

"She stays here," Mary said. "Once was enough."

"That's fine," Dean said.

The old woman led the three of them to the back door, which opened onto a cement patio that overlooked the wide yard and the utility shed. She followed them out but stayed on the patio—which remained encumbered with fence panels, posts and pickets—as if the artificial surface protected her from whatever evil had descended upon Dave Holcomb. She shook her head and clucked her tongue. "To come all this way, make such a big commitment, only to pack up and go before you even finish unpacking in the first place… Maybe this place is cursed for her, after all." She shrugged. "Sometimes life makes no sense."

"Man's mistake is assuming he has complete control over his life," Castiel said absently as his gaze wandered across the yard. "Free will exists, but some choices are forced upon him. And sometimes he has no choice."

"That's a debate for the philosophers, *diba*?" she said with a fatalistic air. "Right now, I have a traumatized granddaughter to comfort."

After she returned to the house, Sam, Dean and Castiel approached the utility shed, centered on the far side of the yard. Dean turned the handle and the three of them crowded into the twelve-by-ten structure. Dean and Castiel made a casual inspection of the assorted rakes, shovels, hoes and power tools while Sam took readings with an EMF meter.

"No hex bags," Dean said.

Castiel scanned the walls and ceiling. "No mystical symbols or sigils."

"Whole lot of cobwebs," Dean added, brushing his hands off.

In short order they concluded their search, finding no evidence of a struggle, no bloodstains, and no unusual paranormal readings.

Next they made their way through the overgrown bushes to examine the crime scene. Sam noticed that although some branches had been snapped, others had been snipped clean off. "Bagged for evidence," Sam said as he held one truncated branch up for visual inspection. The crime scene unit had removed any branches or leaves with blood evidence. In addition, it appeared as if they had cut away enough of the overgrown brush to allow for single file passage between the side of the shed and the bushes. Per the official report, the blood recovered from the bushes belonged to Dave Holcomb and his wife, both of whom had suffered scrapes and cuts pushing their way through the overgrowth. And, despite the medical examiner's working theory, no animal fur or blood had been recovered from the area.

The cramped space between the rear of the utility shed and the fence showed signs of a hasty departure. Sam noticed two torn bits of yellow crime scene tape in the dirt, with a third torn piece attached to the back wall of the shed. Dark stains from blood splatter remained on the fence panel opposite the rear of the shed. Where Holcomb's body had been found— face down per the police report—the ground dipped, as if the tragedy had left a scar on the land. The more likely explanation was crime scene excavation of topsoil to collect blood and loose viscera.

Again, Sam took readings with the EMF meter, walking the perimeter of the crime scene and finally bringing the meter down close to where Dave Holcomb had taken his last breath. And once again, no telltale spikes. As he returned the meter to his jacket pocket, he glanced over the rotting stockade fence, beyond a thin screening of trees and an open, weed-covered lot to a dilapidated rancher.

"What?" Dean asked.

"Abandoned house," Sam said. "Far side of the lot."

"Worth a look."

"Definitely," Sam said.

After Dean picked the padlock bolted to the front door, the rundown rancher yielded no unusual EMF readings or definitive clues. Any furniture had been removed long ago and the walls were bare. A lumpy, stained mattress had been tossed on the floor of a bedroom in the rear of the house, along with a scattering of crushed beer cans, an empty bottle of peach schnapps, and several candy wrappers.

At some point, someone had made an effort to clean the place, based upon the presence of two filled plastic trash bags placed against the front wall. Since then, a side window had been jimmied to bypass the padlocked front door. From what Sam could gather, somebody watched over the place, but not as vigilantly as necessary considering the determination of area teens eager for a private place to light up or down a few.

Breaking the eerie silence of the abandoned house, Dean's cell phone rang.

He grabbed it and checked the caller ID. "BHPD." He

cleared his throat and answered before the third ring. "Special Agent Banks." A pause. "Hi, Chief. What—?"

A longer pause. Dean nodded, eyebrows raised.

"Thank you," he said. "We'll be right there."

"What is it?" Sam asked.

"Another victim."

"Same M.O.?"

"Exactly," Dean said. "Disemboweled. Plucked peepers."

TEN

Dean parked the Impala outside the entrance to the alley that serviced the Kirkwood Plaza strip mall at the intersection of Hawthorne Street and Second Avenue. Castiel's gold Lincoln pulled in behind him and, based on Dean's frown directed at the rearview mirror, a bit too close to Baby's rear bumper.

"If angels were meant to drive," Dean grumbled, "they wouldn't have wings."

"In fairness," Sam said, "his wings have been clipped."

Police cruisers with light bars flashing blocked either entrance to the alley. Further in, more police cars, a medical examiner's SUV and a Crime Scene Unit van blocked their view of the victim. Several employees stood by the rear entrances of their respective places of employment, ostensibly on smoking breaks but more likely to gawk and gossip about the gruesome discovery. When a few strayed too far from the open doorways, a stone-faced cop shooed them back with perfunctory warnings about obstruction of justice and interfering with a crime scene.

On the far side of the alley, the driver of a local TV news van angled for a position close to the scene but clear of any overhanging tree branches that might block his ability to raise the satellite mast for a live remote broadcast.

With Sam and Castiel flanking him, Dean flashed his FBI ID to two uniforms standing together near the driver's side door of the patrol car blocking the near entrance. One of them decided to check Dean's credentials up close, and strode around the cruiser to intercept him.

"He's cleared, O'Malley!" Assistant Chief Cordero called from within the makeshift corral of crime scene tape, waving them through. "Over here."

Cordero stood next to an elderly man with a shock of white hair wearing a rumpled gray suit and a laminate ID dangling from his neck that identified him as Dr. Hugh Trumble, Chief Medical Examiner. The old doctor looked as if he'd been yanked out of bed and pressed back into service a decade after retirement. Nearby, crime scene photographers maneuvered around the confines of the yellow police tape and snapped photos of items on the ground, tagged with evidence markers, including a wrist rocket, a bag of steel balls and a cell phone. But the body of the second victim had already been zipped into a body bag beside a lowered gurney.

Dean and Sam ducked under the tape while Castiel drifted toward the rear of the stores, looking up at shattered light bulbs in wire cages over the doors. After a quick round of introductions, Cordero informed them that the body of Aidan Dufford—eighteen-year-old white male—had been found in the dumpster behind the dollar store.

"Killer making a statement about the value of human life?" Dean wondered.

Trumble gave a small snort of amusement—or derision. "Based upon the claw marks and depredation of the remains, this was an animal attack, plain and simple."

"Depredation?" Sam inquired.

"Clear evidence of consumption of the human remains," Doc Trumble said. "Although preliminary evidence would indicate that the victim was very much alive when said consumption began."

"Eaten alive?" Castiel said as he joined them, his revulsion evident.

"Initially," Doc Trumble said. "Blood loss and organ failure would have taken their toll rather quickly. There's also the matter of collateral brain damage from the forcible excision of the eyeballs. Let me rephrase: The ocular trauma, as evidenced by significant quantities of expelled vitreous humor, is more in line with destruction rather than removal."

"Meaning the eyes were gouged," Dean said. "Not plucked out."

"Precisely," Trumble said. "No planning, no forethought, no trophy collecting. Simply a matter of brute force and hunger. Nothing to indicate a human perpetrator."

"But other than the attack itself," Cordero said, "nothing to indicate an animal's involvement."

"Other than the attack?" Trumble asked incredulously.

"Maybe a paw print in the blood or a tuft of fur."

A nearby patrol officer stepped forward. "A rodent was nibbling on the corpse in the dumpster when we arrived, sir."

"A rodent, Coogan?"

"Yes, sir," the officer said. "A rat."

Dean looked at the medical examiner. "You're pinning these murders on a rat?"

"Of course not," Trumble said. "A larger animal, species undetermined."

Sam pointed to the body bag. "May I?"

Cordero glanced down the far end of the alley, checking on the news van. The satellite mast was up, but the reporter, a sharply dressed blond woman holding a mic, had her back to the crime scene, involved in an animated discussion with her cameraman. "Make it quick."

When Sam unzipped the body bag, all the way down to the victim's groin, Dean squatted beside the corpse for a closer look. The medical examiner dropped awkwardly to one knee, caught his balance by placing his palm on the blacktop, then pointed with his other index finger at the flesh surrounding the eye sockets and then lower, along the perimeter of the shredded abdomen. "There—at the edges of all these wounds—those cuts were not made by a knife or any type of edged weapon. Definitely claw marks." He tugged on a pair of latex gloves and reached into the abdominal cavity. "If you look closely at the remains of the liver, those smaller, ragged incisions are the result of teeth tearing into the organ."

Cordero stood over them, helping to obstruct the view of the corpse as he spoke. "From what we can determine, Aidan came back here for a little after-hours vandalism with that wrist rocket. Shot out the lights over the rear doors. The darkness made it easier for whoever—or whatever—attacked him."

"Any witnesses?" Sam asked. "Store employees?"

"None of the shops were open that time of night."

"According to the good doctor," Dean said, "what we have here is a considerate animal."

"Considerate?" Trumble asked. "In what way, may I ask?"

Dean indicated the dumpster. "After attacking and feeding on Aidan, this animal takes time to clean up after itself and throws its leftovers in the trash."

"Well, I'm sure stranger things have happened," Trumble said, a bit flustered. "I never claimed to be a detective." He turned to Cordero. "You'll have EMS take the body to the morgue for a more complete examination?" Cordero nodded and Trumble said, "Then I'm done here. Good day."

After Trumble stalked off, climbed into his SUV and slammed the door, Dean looked up at Cordero. "He always so cheerful?"

"Man's got an ulcer, and insomnia," Cordero said. "He really wants to chalk this up to an animal attack and be done with it. But I'm not convinced. We've still had no wild animal sightings and whatever attacked Holcomb and young Dufford here would have been noticed by someone."

"Were you hoping he'd convince you this time?" Dean asked. "Since you managed to get out of your office?"

"Had to see this for myself," Cordero said grimly. "Got a bad feeling."

"Bad feeling," Dean commented. "But good instincts."

Castiel pointed to the broken exterior lights. "Aidan shot out some of these bulbs before he was killed, but somebody else blew out or extinguished the rest. Some bulbs are broken. Others have burnt-out filaments. The killer didn't want to be seen."

"How can you tell the unbroken lights have burnt-out filaments?" Cordero said.

"I looked at them," Castiel said.

"You looked—?"

"Any security camera footage available?" Dean interrupted. He'd been scanning the exterior of the shops while Castiel brought up the broken lights. Sam saw no cameras in evidence.

"No such luck," Cordero said. "Some of the shops have interior cameras, some face the front entrance, but nothing back here."

Sam noticed Aidan's cell phone nearby, pulled on a pair of latex gloves and picked it up. "Several unanswered calls from the same number," he said. "Chloe Sikes."

"She's one of my daughter's classmates," Cordero said. "Chloe obviously knows the victim. They both attend Braden Heights High School. Seniors. Possibly dating."

"Let's find out," Sam said, and pressed the button to dial Chloe's number. He switched the phone to speaker mode. She picked up on the third ring.

"Aidan, what the hell—?" a young woman's voice yelled over the crackling connection. "I can't believe—do you have any idea how long I've been calling you? What I've been going through?"

"Chlo—?" Sam managed a single syllable before she cut him off.

"No more excuses! You said I could count on you! Or was

that another lie? Well, good thing this was a false alarm or I'd really be pissed at—Aidan? You there?"

"Chloe Sikes?"

"Yes—wait, who is this? Why do you have Aidan's phone? Is this some kind of joke? Jay, is that you? Did Aidan put you up to this? I swear, I'll—!"

"Chloe, this is Special Agent Rutherford, with the FBI," Sam said. "Where are you? We need to talk about Aidan."

"What? FBI? Oh, God! What the hell has Aidan gotten himself into this time?"

"Just tell me where you are," Sam said. "I'll explain everything."

"Okay," Chloe said. Over the phone speaker, they heard her take a deep calming breath. "I'm at Lovering Maternity Center."

ELEVEN

The entrance to Lovering Maternity Center passed through the ongoing construction around the adjacent and much smaller Stanton Fertility Clinic. Bulldozers and excavators transformed the open space bordering the clinic into an expanded parking lot. They drove past a schizophrenic medley of signs, some apologizing for the inconvenience, while others touted the benefits of the project. Every PARDON OUR DUST and UNDER CONSTRUCTION: PLEASE EXCUSE THE INCONVENIENCE alternated with a WATCH US GROW or WORKING TODAY FOR A BETTER TOMORROW.

With Cordero leaving the crime scene to notify Aidan's parents about his death in person, the Winchesters, along with Castiel, had the task of breaking the bad news to his apparent—and apparently expecting—girlfriend without a police presence.

An unprepossessing red-brick building with discreet signage nearly obscured by a framework of shrubs, the Stanton Fertility Clinic could have been mistaken for a generic office complex. In stark contrast, Lovering Maternity Center displayed a modern aesthetic, with a central circular tower encased in dark reflective glass flanked by shorter twin rectangular outbuildings of red brick. A circular driveway passed through a porte cochère bearing the large cursive letters LMC, where expectant mothers could be safely dropped off.

Dean bypassed the driveway entrance and parked the Impala in the visitor lot. Castiel parked in the nearest available slot. Sam twisted around to look out the back window.

"At some point we should carpool."

"If Cass is finished snipe hunting."

"Cain will turn up, Dean."

"Not in Braden Heights."

Sam couldn't argue with that and saw no sense poking holes in Dean's arguments with a logic stick. Castiel cared about what happened to them. And the feeling was mutual. They all had history together. Nobody was giving up on Dean. But repeated failures had a way of undermining confidence. Meanwhile, Sam worried about Dean, and Cass worried about Dean, and Dean… well, maybe Dean was beginning to see himself as a lost cause and worried that's what he would see in their eyes: The moment when they accepted there was nothing more to do. He knew Dean didn't want his pity and Sam was determined to never show his brother that emotion. Sam would fight Dean's fate until the last second… and even that wasn't quite right. That implied giving up at some point in time and he wouldn't do that. Not while he lived.

Silently, they entered the maternity center. Forming

a central island, a horseshoe-shaped reception desk was currently unoccupied. Marble walls to the left and right of the desk were mirror images of each other; both had glass-enclosed directories above sixty-gallon aquariums, each of which contained about a dozen exotic fish drifting aimlessly in languid silence. Branching off from both walls were identical banks of elevators, with a third set directly behind reception leading to the circular tower's birthing facilities. Along the far wall, someone had parked two wheelchairs on either side of the aquarium. Indistinct background music, set at an almost subliminally low volume and piped in through hidden speakers, provided a calming white noise.

Chloe had given them the address to the maternity center along with the office number of her OB/GYN, Dr. Vanessa Hartwell. Dean confirmed the office number via the directory—designated as "North"—mounted on the near wall.

"321," Dean said, referring to Hartwell's office number. "Like a countdown to delivery."

"Human childbirth traditionally takes much longer," Castiel said as they waited for the elevator.

"Wishful thinking," Dean said.

The elevator door opened and a distracted middle-aged woman in a jade-green smock emerged, almost running into them before stopping, startled. In lieu of a name badge, the letters LMC were stitched across the breast pocket in the same cursive style as those featured on the building's exterior. "Oh my! Can I help you, gentlemen?"

She glanced quickly to either side of them, as if looking

for the expectant mother who warranted a three-man guard detail. Finding none, she seemed perplexed.

"FBI," Dean said, flashing the ID. "Here to see a patient of Dr. Hartwell."

"This is a bit unusual," the receptionist said. "Is she expecting you?"

"The patient or the doctor?"

"Well, either."

"Yes."

"Okay, then," she said, still flustered. "But, um, you may need to wait until the end of the appointment. You know the way?"

"North 321," Sam said, nodding, as he caught the closing elevator door to hold it open. "Thank you."

"Okay, then," she repeated, forcing a smile as she nodded and nervously swiped her palms against the base of her smock. Backing away, she smiled again as she returned to the horseshoe reception desk and placed her hand on the telephone receiver. Sam guessed Dr. Hartwell would know they were on their way up.

After they boarded the elevator and Sam pressed the button for the third floor, Dean switched topics. "Not seeing a connection between our victims. Recent west coast transplant husband and a townie teen vandal."

"They're both male," Castiel offered, stating the obvious.

"Narrows down the pool of potential victims to fifty percent of the population."

"Place of employment," Castiel suggested.

Sam shook his head. "Holcomb hadn't started his new job."

"He frequented the home improvement center."

"Right," Dean said, catching on. "Maybe Aidan worked there."

"Based upon their relationship," Castiel said, "Chloe would know."

"Probably a long shot," Sam said.

"Hunters don't get many layups," Dean said as the elevator stopped with a chime a moment before the doors opened. Sam wondered if Dean was referring to his own predicament, but decided he was reading too much into his brother's words. He had to stop walking on eggshells around Dean.

They exited the elevator, where a sign at eye level directed them to the left down a wide corridor. As they neared the door to suite 321, it swung open and a man in his late forties with a few streaks of gray in his hair and a slight paunch above his belt emerged, back to them as he held the door open. Dressed casually in a yellow polo shirt and jeans, he was followed out of the office by the doctor. Around ten years younger, her brunette hair in a pixie cut, she tucked her hands into the pockets of a white lab coat and smiled at him reassuringly, confirming that everything was fine, right on schedule.

Dean, Sam and Castiel stopped beside them a moment before a very pregnant blond woman in her late teens came through the open doorway, one hand pressed supportively against her lower back. "Told you, Dad," she said. "It's all cool. It was only Braxton Hicks contractions last night, like Doctor Hartwell said."

"You weren't so calm last night, Chloe," her father said.

"Don't listen to him, Dr. Hartwell," Chloe said, smiling. "I was a cucumber. But he and my mom were totally—" Out of the corner of her eye, she noticed the Winchesters and Castiel and her head whipped around. "Jeez! You guys scared the freakin' crap out of me!"

"Sorry," Sam said, worried for a moment they might've scared her into actual labor.

Staring at her in apparent confusion, Castiel muttered, "Claire?"

Now that Castiel had mentioned it, Sam could see the similarities between Chloe and Claire Novak, the daughter of the angel's former host, Jimmy. Same approximate height, hair color and length, prominent eyebrows. Chloe could have easily been mistaken for Claire's long lost sister, if not her twin. Of course, there was one glaring difference between the two young women, which was the reason for her visit to an OB/GYN.

After the momentary confusion, Castiel seemed to shake off the false impression. Sam wasn't surprised by his reaction. Even though Castiel and Claire had reached a good place in their relationship, Sam imagined the angel still felt responsible for the girl and would always be concerned about her safety, now that she was out on her own. In that way at least, he was like a father to her.

"Oh—you're the FBI," Chloe said. "Wasn't expecting three of you. And, you—" she poked a finger against the right lapel of Castiel's trench coat "—explain yourself. Who the heck is this Claire person?"

"Nothing. It's—she's... the daughter of a close friend," Castiel began, a bit flustered. "You bear a striking resemblance."

"Yeah, right. Prove it, mister."

"What?"

"Chloe!" her father scolded, a half-formed apology on his lips.

"FBI?" Dr. Hartwell murmured, a frown of consternation creasing her brow as she glanced from father to pregnant daughter.

"Pictures," Chloe demanded of Castiel, ignoring her father's reaction and her doctor's concern. "You can't use a line like that on a girl without some proof."

"Sorry. I don't have any," Castiel began. Then he reached into his jacket pocket and removed his cell phone. "Correction. I have… Sa—Special Agent Rutherford—we put her photo in here."

Sam had snapped a photo of Claire with Castiel's phone, cropped it and put it in his phone's address book under her name. They couldn't be sure she'd keep the same phone or number, but it was a start in their nascent father-figure and daughter relationship, a bit of normalcy in a situation that was anything but normal.

"Give it here," Chloe said playfully as she snatched the phone from Castiel's grip. "You olds and your oh-so-limited grasp of technology. Way past charming, dude."

Sam shook his head in amusement. If she only knew Castiel's real age, her composure would be gone in an instant.

"So, yeah, wow," she said, pursed her lips and nodded. "Girl's got my look, for sure." She turned to her father. "I'm not adopted, am I?"

"What?" her father looked as off-balance as Castiel had a moment ago. "Of course not."

"Congrats," she said to Castiel, grinning as she slapped the phone in his hand. "You passed the test. You're not a creeper."

"No," Castiel said and looked at Dean and Sam for assistance. "I'm not."

"Agent Collins is many things," Dean said. "But a creeper's not one of them."

"I'm sorry," Dr. Hartwell said. "You gentlemen are with the FBI?"

"Yes," Dean said, flashing the credentials again.

"I have other patients coming in," she said, "but my immediate concern is the welfare of *this* patient and her unborn child. What are your—?"

"It's okay, Doc," Chloe said. "They're not here to lock me up and throw away the key. They're here about my bonehead boyfriend. I don't know what trouble he's gotten into this time, but he's working on my last nerve."

Chloe's father reached out and grabbed Dean's shoulder, then seemed to think better about physical contact with a federal officer and dropped his hand. "Chloe knows I'm not Aidan's biggest fan—" Chloe snorted and rolled her eyes "—but if he's gotten my daughter involved in something illegal, I will break every bone in that young man's body."

"Dad!" Chloe exclaimed.

Sam exchanged a knowing look with Dean. Papa Sikes had just become their number one suspect. He may not have been capable of committing the actual attack himself, but that didn't mean he hadn't painted a bull's-eye on Aidan's chest for whatever supernatural menace dined on human eyeballs and entrails.

"Aidan's not a serial killer or a bank robber," Chloe continued, "he's a rebel—correction, he likes to *think* he's a rebel, but he's just scared about—about the future, you know? You gotta admit, our future has gotten a whole lot scarier."

"And whose fault is that?" her father snapped, his parental exasperation surging to the fore in a stressful moment, one that was about to become exponentially more stressful for all of them.

"God, Dad, not this again," Chloe said. "We made a mistake. We're trying to make the best of this."

"One of you is."

"You'll never let this go, will you?"

"Chloe, you need to remain calm," Dr. Hartwell interjected. "And, Mr. Sikes, I must caution—"

Sikes raised his hands, palms out. "I'm sorry, Chloe. This isn't what your mother and I wanted for you. We're trying to—we promised we'd be supportive and—"

Dean had had enough of the pop-up therapy session. "Sorry to interrupt, but you need to know something," he said to father and daughter, frowning impatiently. "It's bad news."

"Yeah, I figured," Chloe said. "Aidan's latest screw-up."

"Really bad news," Dean amended. "Chloe, you tried to call Aidan last night."

"A bunch of times, during my Braxton Hicks contractions, when I thought—and he was supposed to bring me here today! But the jerk ignored my calls!"

"There's a good reason for that," Sam said sympathetically. He wasn't sure Dean, with his recent straight-line mentality, was the best one to break shocking news to a teen who looked about three or four days away from delivering a baby into the world.

"He's in jail," Chloe guessed, but her eyes had gone wide at Sam's grim tone and he suspected the awful truth might have begun to sink in before he even confirmed it. "And… and the police took his phone away."

"I'm sorry, Chloe. It's worse than that," Sam said. "Last night, Aidan was attacked."

"Attacked," she repeated, her voice faint, all signs of her earlier self-assurance gone. "What do you mean 'attacked'?"

"Viciously attacked," Sam said, skipping the gruesome details. "I'm afraid Aidan didn't survive."

"No—what? What are you saying? You can't be—Aidan? Aidan's dead…?"

With the last two words, the volume fled from her voice. Her knees buckled and she collapsed.

Castiel, standing beside her, reacted immediately, catching her in his arms and supporting her weight. Her father moved to her other side, each of them wrapping an arm around her back.

"Bring her inside," Dr. Hartwell said. "We have chairs in the waiting room."

Castiel and Chloe's father settled her into the nearest comfortable chair and stood nearby as her doctor checked her vitals. But Chloe hadn't lost consciousness and insisted she was fine, even as tears streamed down her cheeks and she fought back sobs. Once she appeared to have her emotions in check, Dean sat in the chair facing her and leaned forward.

"Can you think of any reason someone would want to harm Aidan?"

Before Chloe could answer the question, her father said, "I'm sorry, but can't this wait until a better time?"

"We need to stop whoever did this," Dean said. "Aidan is the second victim. Chloe could be the key to saving a potential third victim."

"It's okay, Dad," Chloe said, waving a crumpled tissue at him. "I want to help them catch whoever did this." She looked at Dean. "I can't think of anyone who would want to… to hurt Aidan. He's been in trouble before, but nothing that would make someone want to…"

"Have you seen any unusual objects around?" Sam asked. "Something that Aidan found. Or something somebody at school showed off?"

"No, nothing like—wait, Wally bought a Pokémon bong online and brought it to school. Does that count?"

"Probably not," Sam said. "Nothing else?"

"No," Chloe said, blowing her nose with a honking sound before grabbing a few more tissues from the box Dr. Hartwell's receptionist had placed beside her. "What am I going to do…?"

Her father put his arm around her. "Your mother and I are here for you, sweetheart."

Chloe started to reply but her voice caught so she simply nodded and dabbed at fresh tears. "Who was the first?" she asked Dean.

"First?"

"Victim," Chloe said. "You said Aidan was the second."

"Somebody new to Braden Heights," Dean said. "David Holcomb. Does that name mean anything to you?" She shook her head. "Aidan never mentioned anyone by that name?"

"No," Chloe said. "Was he a teacher or something?"

"He worked—was scheduled to work in a factory," Castiel said. "Was Aidan employed?"

Chloe shrugged her shoulders. "Off and on," she said. "He worked at the Hadley's Market for a while, couple fast-food places, and Cosmic Donuts. He always found something to hate about every job. The hours or his supervisor or the smell. But he never worked in a factory."

Dean looked at Chloe's father, who'd been frowning in obvious disapproval the entire time Chloe spoke about Aidan's job hopping. "Mr. Sikes, were you with your daughter last night?"

"Yes," he said. "Her mother and I were with her all night— thinking less than charitable thoughts about the boy, I'll admit, but we had no way of knowing that he was…" He took a deep breath. "Let's just say it wasn't the first time he's let her down."

"Aidan had a good heart, Dad," Chloe said, losing her composure again. "You never saw that. You never gave him a chance…"

Sam took down the names, addresses and phone numbers of Aidan's parents and two close friends, Jay and Wally. Beyond that, Chloe couldn't provide any information that might lead them to whoever or whatever had murdered Aidan or Dave Holcomb.

As Chloe's father walked her out of the office, followed by

the Winchesters and Castiel, a nurse in a green smock pushed a very pregnant woman in her late thirties or early forties in a wheelchair from the opposite direction. Walking beside the pregnant woman, a nervous man held her outstretched hand. Both expectant mother and father-to-be had a few wisps of gray in their hair. He stepped behind the wheelchair momentarily so that the others could pass on their way back to the elevators.

"Denise, Gary, good to see you," Dr. Hartwell said. "Everyone well?" They both nodded tentatively. "Ready to become parents to little Baby Atherton?"

"Yes. No. Is anyone? Ever?" Gary sputtered.

Denise reached over and patted his hand. "Better late than never."

Before leaving the LMC lobby, Chloe and her father— who finally introduced himself by his full name, Edward Sikes—made Dean promise to tell them when they found Aidan's killer. As Dean, Sam and Castiel watched them cross the parking lot, Edward's arm held protectively around his daughter's shoulders, Chloe's soft sobs faded away, swallowed by the rumble of traffic.

TWELVE

For several blocks and two or three traffic lights, Castiel followed the black '67 Chevy Impala four-door through the streets of Braden Heights. Dean intended to stop at the motel where they'd checked in shortly before Castiel arrived in town. As much as the brothers needed to take a break after the long road trip, followed by witness interviews and crime scene visits, Castiel suspected Dean, if not both Winchesters, wanted out of the Fed suits before continuing with the investigation.

So far they had discovered little in the way of clues to point them toward the culprit in the cannibalistic murders. But the term "cannibalistic" assumed the killer was human, and that was far from a given, especially in their line of work. The murderer might be something that was once human or something that had passed for human or something entirely inhuman. But what had become obvious during the course of the day was that the solution would not be a—what did humans call it?—a slam dunk. Perhaps the better metaphor was not a piece of cake… although Dean preferred pie. Not a piece of pie? Castiel did not believe that expression was part of the common parlance, but he thought that maybe they should be interchangeable. They were both baked desserts.

Human metaphors aside, the case was beginning to look like a longer term project than Sam or Dean had probably anticipated when they'd left the relative comforts of the bunker. So they probably wanted to review their progress at their motel room and make themselves comfortable before resuming the hunt.

At some point during the drive back to the motel, Dean turned left and Castiel reached for his turn signal to follow but hesitated. A moment later he had driven straight through the intersection. He recalled the names, addresses and phone numbers that Chloe Sikes had rattled off from her cell phone for Sam to write down. While that exchange of information occurred, Castiel had noticed again the young woman's resemblance to Claire, Jimmy Novak's daughter. But this time, that's all he saw. A resemblance. Gone was the uncanny mirror image of Claire that had momentarily haunted him when Chloe first turned toward him.

He believed it had been a human response, like a form of déjà vu. And he had trouble shaking it off. In his devout faith, Jimmy Novak had offered his body to Castiel's possession and because of that faith, Jimmy Novak had died. Unlike Hannah, his fellow angel, Castiel could never return the body to the man he had borrowed it from. That weighted the initial offering with greater importance, because a gift had become an ultimate sacrifice. And that sacrifice forced

Castiel to recognize what had been lost: a father's relationship with his daughter. And triggered by Hannah's selfless action, Castiel decided to embrace that responsibility; knowing that he could never replace him, he tried to fill the void that had been left after Jimmy's passing.

What if his acceptance of that emotional bond had changed something in his mind as well? He'd often heard it said that parents never stopped worrying about their children, no matter how old they were. Bringing a life into the world became a lifelong commitment for the parent. Castiel inhabited a human body with the DNA of Claire's father. And Castiel had chosen to take on the role of father figure to the young woman. Would it be so strange to consider the possibility that a mental connection had been forged between them, that Castiel had activated a dormant father–daughter link simply by his acceptance of the role?

Rationally, he knew she could think of him in a time of need and he would know she was in trouble. But he had an idea that the parent–child bond did not always result in rational responses. After all, Claire could only contact him if she was aware of any danger she faced and remained conscious long enough to make the "call." Any number of perils could befall her without her knowing until it was too late. A car accident, a gunshot, a stalker, a medical condition…

He was not omniscient. He wasn't even a proper angel at the moment, his Grace fading by the day. What would happen to Claire after he faded away for good? No, there was no certainty involved when it came to her safety. That had been her choice, to go her own way, but the change had been in him. He couldn't worry about her when it was convenient, when it fit his schedule. That meant that the job was a permanent, all-day responsibility. And most of the time, he had to take it on faith that she was okay. The irony was not lost on him. Someone once said the worst lies are the lies we tell ourselves.

So had Castiel suffered a moment of parental panic, seeing Claire in Chloe's condition, the pregnant woman's similarity triggering an anxiety that might always lie beneath the surface of his consciousness? *Where is Claire now, right this moment? And is she safe?*

A question that would quite possibly, on one level or another, haunt him for the rest of his life.

And because he could do nothing at the moment for Claire, he pushed himself onward, to do something now, for the young woman who had become, in some strange way, her stand-in.

He arrived at the Duffords' home just as Cordero was leaving, having already given the boy's parents the devastating news. The Assistant Chief of Police gave brief introductions to Donald and Paige Dufford, explaining that Castiel—Special Agent Collins—was also working the case for the FBI.

"I'm sorry for your loss," Castiel said on the Duffords' doorstep as Cordero drove away from the house. Fearing the bereaved couple would be loath to repeat whatever information they had given Cordero, Castiel preemptively added, "I apologize for not coming sooner."

"Please come in," Paige Dufford said, her red-rimmed eyes making only fleeting contact with Castiel's before she ducked her head and backed into the room.

A grim-faced Donald Dufford, his jaw set, seemed to stare into the middle distance. With a curt nod he stepped back and held the door open for Castiel, closing it softly behind him. Paige led the way past a dim living room into the kitchen, where afternoon sunlight streamed through gauzy curtains in dust-filled shafts. She removed a used mug from the table and placed it in the sink before offering him coffee. Castiel sensed that she needed to keep herself occupied with small tasks, to keep her focus limited to immediate mundane concerns rather than direct her attention to the vast gulf of dark emotion that threatened to consume her.

"Yes," Castiel said to her offer of coffee. "Thank you."

"Please, have a seat," she said, indicating the chair he supposed Cordero had occupied. Castiel sat, hands folded on the table.

She filled a black mug with white lettering and placed it before him. The text on the mug read "John Dillinger Museum." Castiel wondered if the mug selection, considering his guise as an FBI agent, was intentional or mere coincidence. Dillinger had been born in Indiana and the museum was local, so he was inclined to believe the latter. After all, the mug that had apparently served Cordero featured a pair of well-known cartoon mouse ears.

"Milk? Sugar?" she asked. "Sorry, we don't have any cream."

"Milk and sugar is fine," Castiel said, giving her a few more simple tasks to complete. She retrieved a carton of milk from the refrigerator and set a container of sugar before him, along with a teaspoon.

Donald Dufford stood to Castiel's right, his hands clutched on the top of a ladder-back chair, knuckles white. Only after Paige sat across from Castiel did Aidan's father pull back the chair and sink into it.

As silence began to fill the room, Castiel heard soft crying from above.

Paige sniffed. "That's Amy," she said. "Aidan's little sister." She pressed her palm to her mouth, her shoulders shuddering for a moment as she fought for control.

"I want to find the person responsible," Castiel said, adding a spoonful of sugar and a splash of milk to the coffee. "Can you think of anyone who harbored ill will against your son?"

"As we told the police," Donald said, "Aidan had no real enemies. He only had a few friends at school, but he never mentioned anyone like that."

"Why would anyone want to hurt an eighteen-year-old boy?" Paige asked. "He spent his days at school, doing homework and hanging out with his friends. How could any of that be the cause…?"

"Aidan didn't return home last night," Castiel said. "Was that unusual?"

"Yes," Paige said. "We—we didn't know. He often pushes his curfew, that wasn't unusual, but he's never been out all night. I fell asleep and Donald… Donald was out late."

Donald's gaze dropped to the tabletop. "I came home very late. I was… I was tired. Didn't think to check on him."

Castiel recognized the father's guilt over this lapse, but in all likelihood—Castiel couldn't be sure because he didn't have the coroner's estimated time of death—Aidan had already been murdered before his father came home. The police may have searched for and found the body several hours earlier, but the killer would have been long gone.

"We've had a bit of a rough time," Paige said. "Donald was laid off recently and is still looking for a new job. Getting out of the house was probably an escape for Aidan. I thought he needed…"

"Assistant Chief Cordero may have mentioned another attack in Braden Heights," Castiel said.

"The man attacked in his backyard," Paige said, nodding.

"Because of the similarities between the two attacks," Castiel continued, "we are looking for a connection between the victims. We're considering the possibility that both victims knew their assailant."

"I don't see how," Paige said. "Chief Cordero said that man was new in town. Unemployed. I can't imagine how or why their paths would have crossed."

"David Holcomb was new in town," Castiel said. "But not unemployed. He moved to Braden Heights because of a job offer in Evansville." Castiel checked his notebook. "A night manager position at Vargus Fabricators."

"Vargus?" Paige said, her surprise evident, her gaze shifting to her husband. "Don…?"

Castiel looked at Donald as well. "What am I missing?"

"Stanley Vargus, the owner," Donald said, "is my former employer."

"You worked at Vargus?"

"Yeah," Donald said bitterly. "For a year and a half."

"Was Dave Holcomb your replacement?"

"I don't know any Dave Holcomb," Donald said. "Never met the man. Besides, I was a grunt. Not management, by any stretch. Guys like me, we're a dime a dozen to somebody like Stanley Vargus."

Turning to Castiel, Paige said, "You can't think Donald is involved in this. Even if he is upset with Stanley Vargus, David Holcomb is—was a complete stranger to us."

"You're right," Castiel said. "This doesn't make sense."

And yet, he wondered if that job connection somehow tied Holcomb and Aidan together in the killer's mind. The line of animosity stretched between Donald and Vargus, but it may not have been mutual. Donald's resentment stemmed from his dismissal, but Vargus may have felt justified in terminating Dufford. He may have regarded it as a business decision, not a personal affront. Even allowing for mutual dislike between the two men, why target Dufford's son and Vargus' future hire?

"May I ask why you were dismissed?"

"I don't want to talk about it," Donald said with a brusque wave of his hand as he shoved his chair back and left the kitchen. "But it had nothing to do with my son!"

Confused, Castiel turned to Paige.

Lips pressed tight, she shook her head. After a few moments, she spoke softly, quiet enough that her voice wouldn't carry beyond the kitchen. "Attendance issues," she said. "Donald… he struggles with, you know… personal demons. He goes to meetings, but sometimes… sometimes that's not enough."

Castiel thanked her for her time, again expressing sympathy

for the loss of her son, and quietly left the gloom of the Dufford household and climbed into his Lincoln. For a few moments, he sat in the car, hands on the steering wheel, lost in thought. Finally, he took out his cell phone and clutched it in the palm of his hand. Before making a call, he scrolled through his contacts and settled on the picture of Claire, a wistful smile on her face, and wondered how different her life would have been if Castiel had never interfered with Jimmy Novak's life.

True faith would have him trust in God's plan.

Yet even a positive outcome never meant everyone involved received the best result. Some people were simply destined to suffer in this life. History had proved that time and time again. How many of those unfortunates saw the wisdom in the grand plan? Maybe only the martyrs.

He dialed a number.

"Hello," came the familiar voice of Sally Holcomb's grandmother, Mary.

"This is Agent Collins," Castiel said. "I have—"

"Have you found him?"

"Who?"

She lowered her voice before continuing. "The monster who killed David."

"No, not yet," Castiel said. "I have some follow-up questions for Mrs. Holcomb if I—"

"I'm sorry, Agent Collins," the old woman said. "The poor girl wasn't feeling well and turned in early. Can this wait until tomorrow?"

"Yes," Castiel said. "Yes, of course it can wait. Thank you."

Next he called Dean, to update the Winchesters about Dufford's connection to Vargus Fabricators. For a moment, he thought about calling Sam with the information, but Dean had been defensive lately, convinced Sam and Castiel were talking about him behind his back. Rather than feed the incipient paranoia, Castiel decided to keep the lines of communication open between them.

On the second ring, Dean picked up.

THIRTEEN

"You know what happened to Cass?" Dean asked Sam.

"No," Sam said, opening his laptop on the small table by the window in their shabby budget motel room, its only redeeming feature—well two if you counted the free Wi-Fi—being the framed photos of classic muscle cars on the wall facing the twin beds. A cherry red '67 Pontiac GTO and cobalt blue '70 Plymouth Hemi 'Cuda.

"Another wild goose chase?"

"Dean, I don't know."

"One minute he's right behind me. The next he's off into the wild blue yonder."

"You could call him."

"I'm good," Dean said, settling back on his bed, doubling his pillow to stare comfortably at the far wall. Those cars were sweet, but no competition for Baby. Still, better than gazing at another vase of impressionistic flowers or landscapes of apocalyptically vacant beaches.

Once they'd returned to their motel room, their first order

of business was ditching the Fed suits for more comfortable attire. Dean had picked the nearest bed and plopped down on it, hands interlaced behind his head, lamenting the poor quality of the mattress and the strange odor permeating their room. "Dude, I miss my bunker bedroom."

"Maybe get that on a tattoo," Sam had suggested sarcastically.

They had lived on the road for most of their lives, interrupted by brief periods of what passed for normalcy. All the crappy motel rooms had become anonymous pit stops along the way, with one fading into the next. When that's all you know, that's all you expect. But the bunker had changed their expectations, giving them a home of sorts. It represented downtime, but it also represented a standard of living no grimy motel clinging to an interstate highway exit could match. But maybe that was the point. The road kept them from becoming soft and complacent. For hunters, the road meant war and battle. So maybe it was best they find no comfort there.

"Could be a ghoul," Dean speculated while Sam poked around the Web on his laptop. "Or a rakshasa or a rugaru. Hell, maybe a wendigo. All flesh eaters."

"I don't know," Sam said absently.

"Victims still had their hearts and brains, so we can rule out werewolves and wraiths. And rawheads go for kids."

"Interesting," Sam said from across the room from behind his laptop.

"Aidan was eighteen," Dean replied, pushing himself up on his elbows. "Not technically a kid anymore. And Holcomb? Definitely not a kid."

"No, this local news article," Sam said, pointing at the screen, though it was directed away from Dean. "Traffic accident."

"Traffic accident?" Dean asked, perplexed. "Unless it involves a hook hanging from a door handle, how does that concern us?"

"Elijah Green," Sam said, skimming the article again to read the salient facts aloud. "Pharmaceutical sales rep, returning home to Braden Heights from Evansville, crossed into oncoming traffic, head on collision with a semi."

"Let me guess," Dean said. "Didn't end well for Big Pharma."

"Not at all," Sam said, shaking his head. "Killed on impact. Apparently he was rushing home to witness the birth of his daughter."

"Tragic on two or three levels," Dean said. "But unless this is some sort of *Maximum Overdrive* situation, what's the angle?"

"Green suffered head trauma," Sam said. "The details are a bit vague here, but from a comment the trucker made to the press, it sounds like both of Green's eyes were destroyed."

Dean sat up. "Faulty airbags?"

Sam shook his head.

"What about the rest of him? Insides still inside?"

"Doesn't say. But guess who was at the scene?"

"Cordero?"

"Sands," Sam said. "Captain Jaime Sands."

"The Green file!" Dean said, remembering their brief introduction. "Thought she was referring to color coding or a recycling report."

He sat up and flipped between the two business cards he'd

set on the bedside table in front of the digital clock radio, settling on the Sands card. He took out his phone to dial her number but the phone rang before he entered the first digit. He checked the caller ID.

"Cass," he told Sam before answering the call. Instead of a greeting, he said, "What happened?"

"Dean," Castiel said. "I interviewed Aidan's parents." After a moment, he added, "Were you expecting something else?"

Like another magical mystery tour that led nowhere? Dean thought. *No, not at all.* "No," he lied. "Another dead end, right?"

"Something," Castiel said. "Maybe only a coincidence."

"Tell me."

Castiel explained how Donald Dufford had recently been terminated by Vargus just as Holcomb was scheduled to start.

"So Vargus links one victim to the father of the other victim," Dean said. "I don't know."

"It's a stretch," Castiel admitted.

"It's something, anyway," Dean said. As leads went, it wasn't much, but it was more than they had an hour ago. "Sam also found something. Possible third victim." He told Castiel about the Green accident. "I'll talk to Sands. BHPD may have withheld some details from the press."

"Where are you?"

"Oh, that's right," Dean said, remembering Castiel hadn't been with them when they checked into the latest fleabag special. "Look for the Blue Castle Lodge on Front Street."

"That name is indecisive," Castiel said.

"Nobody will mistake this place for a castle," Dean said, "but there's a picture of one on the sign out front."

After ending the call, Dean dialed the cell phone number on the business card he still held and waited three rings for her to pick up.

"Captain Sands."

"Captain, this is Special Agent Banks."

"What can I do for you?"

"What can you tell me about the fatal accident involving Elijah Green?"

"Green? But that's—never mind," she said. "His wife had gone into labor with their first child. He was speeding to get home in time for the birth. He drifted into oncoming traffic. Hit a semi head on. Killed instantly. Car totaled. Driver of the truck was treated at the scene and released after declining hospitalization."

"What about Green's body?" Dean asked. "From the witness account, he lost his eyes. Was he disemboweled?"

"Disemboweled? No, of course not," Sands said. "But the eyes... yeah, that was odd."

"How so?"

"Some of these highway fatalities are gruesome, to say the least, especially on interstate; at those speeds decapitation is not uncommon. But with Green's eyes, whatever caused that damage, well, we were unable to tie it to anything specific in the wreckage. And he was the lone occupant of the vehicle. But I remember thinking at the time..."

"What?"

"Keep in mind," she said, "this is not something I put in the official report. Too 'out there,' if you know what I mean."

"Unofficially, then," Dean encouraged.

She sighed in resignation, obviously concerned she might be putting her professional reputation on the line by engaging in this type of speculation. "Unofficially—judging by some of the lacerations on his face—I had the impression that something gouged out his eyes before the crash."

FOURTEEN

Before they began, Jesse Vetter had been meticulous about covering every inch of the nursery's hardwood floor and baseboards with drop cloths, secured with two rolls' worth of masking tape. He'd bordered the windows and the doorframe with more tape and tossed another drop cloth over the door itself. Forbidding Olivia to lift a finger, he'd moved all the furniture to the center of the room, with a third translucent drop cloth tossed over the crib and fish mobile, dresser, changing table, standing lamp, and wooden rocking chair, commenting that the whole mass looked like the world's most ungainly ghost. Only then had they begun to paint the room in aquatic, gender neutral colors, banishing from existence its humdrum off-white walls.

"Really, Olivia," he'd said before they began, "where's the mental stimulation for an infant staring into a white void all day?"

Olivia had shrugged, smiling as she played along. With the palm of one hand on the eight-month swell of her abdomen, she'd said, "Maybe the baby will achieve a Zen state."

"No!" Jesse said. "Who wants a blank slate Zen baby? That's creepy. There's a reason chalkboards come with chalk."

"They use Smart Boards these days."

"As long as she—*or he*—finishes school before they decide to implant telepathic gizmos in students' brains, I'm fine with any kind of board."

For the messy occasion, she'd tied a scarf over her shoulder-length black hair and dressed in distressed denim maternity bib overalls over a roomy white cotton shirt, both of which she'd picked up for a song at a local thrift shop.

Rather than putting on some clothing well past its prime, Jesse had purchased a white cap and painter coveralls from the hardware store. Olivia had ribbed him mercilessly, calling him the Good Humor man and every so often asking for her Chocolate Eclair or King Cone.

"Is this too blue?" Jesse asked. Two days ago they had painted the base layer the lightest color, Pale Water, from floor to ceiling. The day before they had painted the next darkest color, Pale Adam Jade, in a wave pattern halfway up the wall. But now, for the deepest, and lowest wave, the green verged on blue.

"It's fine, Jesse," Olivia said.

"Hard to call it gender neutral if you do blue."

"I see green," Olivia assured him.

"If you do blue," he said, "you have to do pink to cancel it out or be inclusive or something. What do you think about a rainbow on the far wall? Too much?"

"Don't know if it's too much," Olivia said, "but believe me, you don't want me trying to paint seven side-by-side arcs."

"Seven?"

"Roy G. Biv," Olivia said, referring to the mnemonic device. Then in a sing-song voice, "Red, orange, yellow—"

"I know what it stands for," Jesse interrupted. "We don't need to be all literal and scientific about it. Three or four colors should be enough."

"Ah, so you would stimulate this infant's mind with misinformation, Mr. Vetter."

"Don't make me splatter you, Ms. Krum," Jesse said, waving a loaded paintbrush in front of her face.

"Don't splat," she said, hands raised, laughing. "I surrender!"

Smiling, Jesse lowered the paintbrush to the edge of the paint can and, after a moment, his face took on a serious cast. "Other than your paint-speckled nose," he said, "any regrets?"

With a thumb, she rubbed the edge of her nose and examined the green smear before wiping it on the sheets of newspaper under the paint can. She patted her large abdomen. "Not much I can do about it now."

Frowning, he asked, "Seriously?"

"I'm kidding," she said. "Seriously. No regrets."

They heard footfalls on the stairs outside the nursery.

"You're both great guys," she said as Brandon Perreault ducked in through the doorway, tucking in his elbows to avoid getting paint on his pinstriped business suit. "I've known you my whole life. You'll make wonderful fathers."

Brandon examined the nearly complete paint job, nodding to indicate his appreciation. "Looking good. Sorry I'm late."

"No, you're not," Jesse replied, threatening to flick the still loaded wet paintbrush at his husband's expensive suit. "You hate painting."

"That's not entirely false," Brandon admitted. "But I have other talents. I can cook dinner." He looked specifically at Olivia. "Or pick something up, if you'd rather...?"

"Yes!" she said. "Been craving Chinese all day."

"Liv!" Jesse said. "You should have said something."

"There was work to do," she said. "I'm not a shirker."

"Unlike Brandon here."

"Hey, it's not like I was feeding pigeons in the park all day."

"Why are you still standing there, B?" Jesse asked. "Get back in your car and get the food!"

"Right," Brandon said, turning to Olivia again. "The usual?"

"No," she said. "I waited too long." She pursed her lips. "Maybe a little bit of everything? I'm starving!"

"Yes, ma'am," Brandon said, executing a playful salute. "Anything surrogate mother wants, surrogate mother shall have."

Brandon refused to admit to Jesse or Olivia that he had hung around the office later than strictly necessary to finish his work. He'd worked up a to-do list for the next day and completed a few other low-priority tasks, checked on some preliminary vendor bids even though the deadline was two weeks away, because he never joked about disliking painting. He hated getting paint in his hair, under his fingernails or on his clothes, even if they were old or ripped and he intended to toss them in the trash immediately after painting. He hated the anxiety of having wet paint on his person, to be smeared on anything and everything he might bump into or squeeze past.

That was the one area of baby-prep where he fell short of full participation. He'd helped buy and assemble the nursery furniture and he'd gone through endless paint swatches and samples to help pick the final colors with Jesse, but the actual painting, no thanks! He'd rather pay a handyman to do that dirty work. But if Olivia and Jesse for some reason wanted to take on that job, they were more than welcome to it.

He'd play errand boy and pick up the food and clean up afterward. He'd even help clean the nursery, as long as it could wait until after the paint splashed on the tarps and masking tape had completely dried. The idea of peeling off paint-wet tape and rolling up drop cloths with glistening gobs of the stuff ready to soil anything in the vicinity was almost worse than the idea of painting itself.

The nagging guilt gnawing at him, he hurried down the stairs and exited through the kitchen into the garage, jumping into his silver Prius. He pressed the button on the garage door opener clipped to the sun visor, tapping his fingers impatiently on the steering wheel as the wide door trundled open. He turned on the ignition and waited.

The garage door stopped halfway up, maybe high enough for the Prius to squeeze through but just as likely to scrape a layer of paint off the roof, assuming the main spring didn't snap and drop the door on the car like a guillotine blade as he tried to shoot through the gap.

He recalled the safety sensor on the door, which stopped it from closing if something blocked the infrared beam traveling from one side of the door to the other. That stopped the door from closing on a person or an object left in the door's path. But in this instance, the door was on the way up, not down. Nevertheless, he jumped out of the car and checked the sensor on both sides to make sure nothing obstructed the invisible beam. Everything seemed fine, so he climbed back into the Prius and pressed the button a second time, which brought the door down without a hitch.

"Okay, let's try this again," he said aloud as he pressed the button a third time. Once again the door rumbled its way up and… stopped again, lower than before. This time, if he hoped to escape the confines of the garage while inside his car, he'd have to crash through the door like a Hollywood stuntman. Another button press to close the door.

"Fine," he said. "You don't want to work, don't work."

Once again he exited the car, but this time he pulled the overhead release cable to switch the chain from motor operation to manual. If he could just get the door open tonight he'd call a repair service in the morning.

Bending at the knees, he gripped the door handle and tugged upward, nearly stumbling when the door remained closed. It hadn't budged an inch. He glanced up at the main spring, checking for a break but finding none. All the cables were intact. Nothing seemed wrong. He tugged again, grunting with the effort. The door creaked, but wouldn't budge.

Immediately, he thought of backup plans. He'd need to take a cab to work the next morning and as for picking up dinner tonight, he had three options. Have the food delivered, which would add another delay, borrow Olivia's red Honda Civic, parked out front, or take Jesse's Prius, parked across the street.

He leaned into his car through the open driver's side window and snatched his keys out of the ignition—and caught a strong scent of gingerbread. He inhaled deeply. Always loved the smell. Took him back to his childhood, eating gingerbread cookies fresh out of the oven. But the last thing he expected to smell in his garage, or any garage for that matter, was gingerbread. He'd passed through the kitchen two times since he came home and hadn't smelled anything baking and, as far as he could recall, the oven hadn't been turned on. So how—?

He'd already started toward the door, to call up to Jesse to ask for his car keys, when he noticed movement in the corner of the garage.

Turning, he saw her standing there, in dirt-smeared tatters, and immediately assumed a homeless person had somehow snuck into their garage and had been hiding among the shelves, ladders, bikes and lawn care supplies. His reflexive fear and sudden sense of violation left no room for sympathy. Whatever he glimpsed in that moment was not a homeless person—its otherness defied classification.

Head bowed slightly within a matted tangle of long, straggly hair, her claws—yes, claws—twitched in anticipation. In that moment, his prior fear at the sight of an intruder was distilled into the primal variety, a deep-seated revulsion to this inhuman entity wearing a human mask.

With a strange jerk of lateral motion, she blocked his access to the kitchen door.

Backing away, toward the closed garage door, his intent to place the Prius between him and whatever the clawed thing was, Brandon's gaze traveled from her strangely hunched torso to her lowered face, a need to identify what stalked him in his own home.

As her head rose ever so slightly, Brandon caught a glimpse of dark, sunken eyes that seemed to boil with hatred beneath the surface, the tension of a coiled spring in her taut features.

Briefly, he considered calling out for help, but what if that brought Jesse or Olivia running to the garage? He could yell to them to call the police, but they might still come to investigate. He had the undeniable sense that any exclamation on his part would trigger an attack. With the garage door stuck, his only option was to put the car between them and then, when she circled to pursue him, escape through the kitchen door.

Again her claws twitched.

His throat utterly dry, he implored, "Don't... don't do this."

Not a flicker of reaction to his words. Nor had he really expected any. The creature seemed beyond reasoning.

As he reached into his jacket pocket, considering the idea of blind-dialing 911 on his cell phone, he took a cautious step back. And another. A third brought him to the corner of the Prius. One more and he could—

With a raspy roar, she leapt into the air and dashed across the roof of the car, her dirty bare feet with claw-like toenails thumping lightly across the silver metal with the sound of a distant drum.

Startled, he had a split second to notice her strange, malformed abdomen before she shoved him forcefully against the garage door, which groaned under the stunning impact, its hinges creaking.

Woozy, he tried to run and wondered why his legs refused to cooperate. Another moment passed before an intense burning sensation registered, prompting him to look down. She hadn't simply shoved him against the garage door, she'd sunk her claws into him, ripping him open from the bottom of his ribs to his groin, slicing through his clothes, skin and muscle in that first attack.

One clawed hand pinned him upright against the garage door. Otherwise, his legs would not have supported his own weight. He watched in mute horror as her other clawed hand tore into his abdomen, slashing through his organs, slicing and tugging out his intestines. She brought slimy handfuls of organs and flesh to her mouth, gulping greedily. Lower, her swollen abdomen undulated each time she swallowed.

He stared down at the ruin of his body. It looked as if a bomb had exploded in his stomach. The pain was excruciating, a flare of white fire at the center of his consciousness, with rapidly encroaching darkness crumbling the corners of his vision, reducing his whole world to agony and the promise of nothingness.

Slowly, her face rose into his rapidly diminishing field of vision.

He saw his own blood dripping from her cracked lips and pointy teeth.

Then her sunken eyes met his through the veil of her

matted hair, but before he could make sense of her half-rotted visage, she shrieked and her blood-drenched claws shot toward his face, digging into his eyes, gouging deep and slamming his head repeatedly against the garage door as she ravaged both sockets.

This new pain was a mere echo of what he'd experienced moments ago, like a memory of recent pain and then an impression of how pain might feel and then only numbness, the sounds of her devouring his flesh fading to wet murmurs and finally silence in his new dark world. Just as, one by one, his senses had abandoned him, his consciousness scattered into bits of disconnected thought, like fireworks fading in the night sky, until the last pinpoint of hope winked out...

FIFTEEN

One moment tears of grief rolled down Brianna Green's cheeks; the next she flashed a smile of pure, unadulterated joy. Back and forth, from one extreme to the other. To Dean it was an unfathomable rollercoaster of emotions, how one person could sustain devastation and elation in such close proximity. But even when she smiled at Kiara, her infant daughter, the tears continued to flow.

She held the swaddled baby in her lap on the sofa, while seated next to her brother, Malik, who had taken her to LMC in her husband's absence. To hear Brianna tell it, Malik hadn't left her side since Elijah's fatal accident.

Back in their Fed suits, Dean and Sam sat facing the sofa from across a coffee table in matching chairs. Despite taking time to change, they had left the Blue Castle Lodge before Castiel returned from his own interview. But they could compare notes later.

"I blame myself," Brianna said, pressing her thumbs into the baby's tiny hands. "I shouldn't have texted Elijah. I knew there was nothing he could do in Evansville. But... I was so excited. I wanted to let him know and for him to meet us at LMC."

"You can't put this on yourself," Sam said. "Elijah chose to respond. And from the police report, he only texted a three-letter reply."

"He was so good about not using the cell phone while driving," Brianna said. "But I must have seemed frantic instead of excited. He probably worried about me... about us."

Sympathetic, Sam said, "We don't know if that one brief text caused the accident."

Dean kept silent. As far as he was concerned, Elijah had been distracted by the news of the impending birth and by texting a response. Either that was the direct cause of the collision or the attack itself resulted in his losing control of the car and driving into the oncoming lane. The problem was that they couldn't offer the latter as a cause because it would sound like crazy talk. Something attacked Elijah in his car and subsequently vanished, leaving no trace. Yeah, there was no way that would sound rational, even to a grief-stricken widow and her overprotective brother.

"The worst part was I didn't even know... that he was gone," Brianna said. "The last message from him was that 'on my way' and I kept expecting him to show up at LMC. My labor was relatively fast for a first child, only a few hours. I planned for an epidural but it was too late by the time we got to the hospital. Before too long, I had blocked everything out to get through the pain. In the back of my mind, I expected him to be there, eventually. Then, after Kiara came into the world, I was so relieved it was over and she was healthy… I called and got no answer."

Malik shook his head slowly. "I had a bad feeling something was wrong, but I didn't say anything to Brianna."

"Why not?" Sam asked.

"You kidding, man? She already had too much on her plate," he said. "Way I see it, bad news can wait. Like, it's not real until you acknowledge it. After that, no going back to the way things were." He ran the palm of one hand lightly over the baby's head. "No way Elijah would have missed the birth of his baby girl. When he didn't show… But I kept quiet. By the time Brianna found out for sure, she had Kiki in her world."

Kiara had begun to cry, a thready, quivering sound, so Brianna lifted her up and, after a quick smell test, held the baby against her chest. "I sure did, didn't I, baby girl?"

"She alright?" Malik asked.

"I fed her right before the FBI agents came," Brianna said. She laid a white cloth over her shoulder and patted the baby, trying to coax a burp out of her. "And she doesn't need to be changed. Maybe she just wants to be close."

Malik nodded, and looked back at the Winchesters to finish his thought. "Life takes stuff from you, year after year. But sometimes it gives back. That's what you hold onto."

Without a noticeable burp, the infant fell quiet in her mother's arms and drifted into a peaceful sleep. After exchanging a look with Malik, Brianna passed the baby to him. Malik cradled the baby in his arms, rose gracefully from the sofa and crept upstairs to keep the jostling to a minimum.

Brianna took a deep, shuddering breath and clenched her hands together as if she no longer knew how to occupy them. "She's a blessing," Brianna said. "I don't know how I'd get through this without her. And Malik... he's so strong, especially when I slip." She pressed her lips together and shook her head. "But you're not here to see how I'm getting along. You have questions for me?"

Dean glanced at Sam, who nodded ever so slightly, so Dean took the lead. First he wanted to rule out another possible connection between victims. "You had your baby at Lovering Maternity Center," he said. "Are you a patient of Dr. Hartwell?"

"I've heard good things about her, but no, she's not my doctor."

"So you've had no interactions with her?"

"No," Brianna said, confused. "Why?"

"Something else we're looking into," Dean said. "Probably unrelated."

"Okay," she said, glancing briefly at Sam, who gave an encouraging nod.

Dean continued on a different tack, into delicate territory. "Did you notice any changes in Elijah's behavior lately?"

"No, not really," she said and allowed herself a fleeting smile. "Except for the father-to-be nerves, checking that everything was ready, making lists, jumping every time I had an ache or a pain."

"Any trouble at work?" Sam asked.

She thought for a moment and shook her head. "Other than a cancelled or postponed appointment here or there, everything was the same old same old. He had his routines, doctor office and pharmacy visits, meetings, presentations. Nothing I would call unusual."

"No competition at work? Promotions on the line?"

"He had his territory," she said. "But I wouldn't say he was in competition with anyone. Maybe another pharmaceutical company's competing product. He never mentioned anything like that. And if he was up for a promotion, he kept it secret."

"Any unusual objects he may have found? Or saw in somebody else's possession?"

She frowned. "No." She twisted her engagement and wedding rings on her finger. Either a nervous habit, or something to help her focus on her husband. "Did the police find something in his car they haven't told me about?"

"No," Sam said. "Not at all."

"I'm confused," she said. "These questions make it seem like you suspect Elijah's crash wasn't an accident."

"We're considering the possibility of... interference," Sam said.

Dean raised his eyebrows, shorthand for asking his brother, *Are we going there?*

Sam fidgeted slightly, brow furrowed, a sure sign he was hesitant about how to begin the next line of questioning. "How much did the police tell you about the condition of your husband... after the crash?"

Brianna visibly recoiled, her back arching, as she pressed her hands to her mouth and inhaled deeply through her nose. She shook her head several times as if trying to rid herself of the thought or at least the mental image. "Oh,

God, it's so horrible… like some cruel punishment, Elijah not seeing his daughter in life or in death. His eyes… the police have no idea how that happened." She swiped at a tear before it streaked down her cheek. "Head trauma, they said, from the wreckage."

Malik, having settled the baby in her crib, had quietly descended the stairs, almost on tiptoe to avoid the slightest creak of wood. He settled in beside his sister as she spoke about the loss of Elijah's eyes, shaking his head. "Terrible thing," he said softly.

"Kiara?" Brianna asked.

"Still sleeping, Bree," he said, patting her knee. "Don't worry about her." He turned his attention to the Winchesters. "You think the police got it wrong? About Elijah's eyes?"

"We're investigating some recent assaults," Dean said. "In reviewing Elijah's accident, we noticed some similarities."

"Elijah was alone in his car," Brianna said. "How could he have been attacked?"

"Right now, we don't know," Sam said truthfully. "Just due diligence. Following up any leads. If someone else was involved, we want to stop them."

Stop meaning gank, Dean thought. "Thank you for your time in this difficult situation," he said, rising from his chair. Sam followed suit and Malik walked them to the door.

With the brothers on the doorstep outside, Malik leaned forward through the open storm door. "You find out somebody did this to Elijah, you let me know, all right?"

"We'll keep you informed," Sam said.

"When you get the bastard," Malik said, "you give me five

minutes alone with him. That's all I ask."

"When we find him," Sam said, "we'll bring him to justice."

Of course, that was the party line, had they been genuine FBI agents instead of hunters. In all likelihood, finding whoever or whatever was responsible was synonymous with discovering its weakness and killing it. No exchange of information with the families of the victims would be forthcoming. The Winchesters would end the killing and leave town. Malik's desire for personal vengeance would go unfulfilled, but the scales would be adjusted in his favor.

SIXTEEN

Back behind the wheel of the Impala, Dean tried to reconcile Elijah Green's apparent accidental death with the murders of Dave Holcomb and Aidan Dufford. "Three victims," Dean said. "What are the odds that the husband and boyfriend of women in late-term pregnancies are two of the victims of the same killer?" He shook his head. "It's not much. But is it enough?"

"Based on eye gouging alone?" Sam said. "Considering it occurred immediately before a head on collision—yeah. But you're forgetting the other connection."

"What?"

"LMC," Sam said. "Lovering Maternity Center."

"Not much of a connection there either," Dean said. "Brianna and Chloe have different doctors. The simple explanation? Pregnant women don't go to a general hospital when there's a maternity center in town."

"Makes sense."

"And unless I need my eyes checked," Dean said, "Sally Holcomb wasn't pregnant."

Dean's cell phone rang.

"Hey, Cass," Dean said, after spot-checking caller ID. "Missed you again. On our way back now."

"Dean, I'm not at the motel."

"What?"

"There's been another… incident."

As Dean pulled in behind Castiel's gold Lincoln, Sam looked across the street, where a row of police and emergency vehicles lined the curb of a craftsman-style home now bathed in flashing light, which revealed intricate and impeccable landscaping. From the outside, Sam saw no clue that something horrible had happened there a short time ago. As the Winchesters approached the house, walking up the long driveway, Sam spotted Castiel on the covered front porch, situated perpendicular to the paneled door of a two-car garage.

"Captain Sands is inside with the crime scene team," Castiel said when they reached the two steps leading up to the porch. "Medical examiner is reviewing the body. The attack happened in the garage."

"Lead the way," Dean said.

Castiel took them through the front door, across a small foyer and into the kitchen where an open door led out to the garage. Through the door Sam heard several overlapping conversations, while the occasional burst of flashbulbs cast stark shadows along the back of the garage.

Castiel waved to Captain Sands, who stood on the far side of a silver Prius by the garage door, Dr. Hugh Trumble beside her, bent at the waist as he studied the corpse. From their vantage point Sam couldn't see the body, only blood splatter on the second and third horizontal garage door panels.

"Victim was Brandon Perreault, mid-thirties, purchasing manager at a financial services corporation in Evansville."

"Coming or going?" Dean asked. Sam looked at him. "Attacked in the garage."

"He'd returned home from work minutes before the attack," Castiel said. "According to his husband, he was leaving to pick up dinner. Chinese takeout, apparently. But he never made it out of the garage."

"His husband?" Dean asked.

"Yes," Castiel said. "Jesse Vetter."

"Okay, then," Dean said, glancing at Sam again.

Sam was having the same thought: The pregnancy connection was mere coincidence. Unlike Elijah Green and Aidan Dufford, Dave Holcomb and now Brandon Perreault were not married to or dating pregnant women.

"Any chance Jesse works at Vargus Fabricators?"

"Currently between jobs," Castiel said. "Last position was in the admissions office of a community college."

Sam frowned. Another possible connection dismissed.

They edged forward, circling around the busy crime scene techs as much as the garage allowed, hoping for a look at the victim. By the time they reached the front of the Prius and glimpsed the body, the medical examiner stood upright and leaned back, massaging his lower back with both hands.

"Another animal attack, Doc?" Dean asked, unable to conceal a hint of sarcasm.

"Very likely," Trumble said, glancing over his shoulder. "Unless you have a better explanation?"

We will, Sam thought, *but not yet.*

Dean glanced at Captain Sands, "Any indication how this mystery animal got into and out of the garage?"

She shook her head and spoke softly. "No."

Trumble refused to give up his animal theory. "Entry is simple enough," he said. "Victim opens garage door from inside his car with an automatic opener. Obviously the animal darts inside. Victim fails to notice its presence. Victim enters house, comes out a few minutes later, and the cornered animal attacks."

"Judging by the blood spatter on the garage door," Dean said, "looks like your animal cornered the victim, not the other way around."

"Obviously the animal turned the tables on the victim," Trumble said. "Then slipped out through the kitchen door."

"So this *cornered* animal had the run of the place."

"Easy to criticize a theory when you have none of your own," Trumble said. "Look at these wounds! The only rational explanation is an animal attack."

While Dean goaded the medical examiner, Sam had inched forward for an unobstructed view of the body. To Sam, it appeared as if Perreault had been held against the garage door and, when released, had slipped down into a seated position, slumped to one side, hands palm up on the concrete garage floor, his head hanging at an angle. Whatever attacked him had impressively sharp claws, capable of slashing through several layers of clothing—

including the tailored jacket of a business suit—to eviscerate him. From sternum to mid-thigh, he was covered in dripping blood, ravaged ropes of glistening intestines and chunks of unidentifiable flesh. And as with the other victims, both eyes had been viciously gouged out of their sockets. The skin around the empty eye sockets showed the clearest evidence of claw marks, narrow but deep jagged lacerations inconsistent with a sharp-edged weapon.

Trumble didn't know any better; his experience only attributed the possession of claws to animals. But Sam did.

"What should animal control look for?" Captain Sands spoke to Trumble in such a measured tone Sam couldn't tell if she'd bought into his weak theory or if she was subtly mocking him. "Brown bear? Coyote? Mountain lion?"

"I don't know," Trumble admitted, heaving a frustrated shrug. "Most likely a brown bear."

Sam was certain somebody near one of the crime scenes would have noticed and reported a bear roaming the suburban streets. Then again, Trumble's theoretical brown bear entered and exited homes and the backseats of cars without leaving any noticeable damage or disruption other than the eviscerated corpses. But, to be fair, any theory Sam came up with to counter Trumble's would be met with equal derision by Braden Heights' law enforcement officers, so he kept his mouth shut.

"But I am certain of one fact," Trumble added, casting a significant look at the three professed FBI agents, while jabbing an index finger in the direction of the body. "No human committed this crime."

Castiel caught Sam's eye and motioned him over. When he stood nearby, Castiel spoke softly, "Look at the roof of the car."

Sam looked. "What about it?"

"Closely," Castiel advised.

Sam took a step closer and another, his gaze sweeping across the gleaming silver paint. Something was off. He tilted his head down to change the angle of light and then he noticed three faint indentations alternating along the roof. The impacts had dented the metal but the coat of paint hadn't been scratched. Moving forward, he examined the hood of the car and saw two more of the dings. If Sam imagined the path of the dents, they originated by a freestanding shelf near the kitchen door and arrowed directly at the body, had it once been standing where it now lay.

He looked at Castiel. "Footprints?"

"Whatever attacked him leapt onto the car," Castiel began, "and ran across the roof and the hood before pinning him to the garage door."

"Bear's light on his feet," Dean said.

Sam debated bringing the new evidence to the attention of the medical examiner, if only to see how he'd spin the information as further confirmation of an animal attack. Might be amusing to watch the pompous old man squirm, but ultimately pointless. Besides, if the police bought into his man-eating animal theory, the Winchesters and Castiel would have more latitude to continue their own parallel investigation.

Before Sam could change his mind about not mentioning the footprints, he heard a disturbance in the kitchen.

"Just, please, cover him," a distressed male voice pleaded. "It's not right to leave him exposed like that."

Castiel returned to the kitchen with Dean following him. Sam took one last look at the car roof footprints, then hurried to join them. Jesse Vetter, the husband, might have heard or seen something. The other three victims had been isolated when attacked: Holcomb in his backyard; Aidan behind a closed shopping center; and Green alone in his car.

A patrol officer blocked Jesse Vetter—also in his mid-thirties but wearing green-speckled white coveralls instead of a business suit—from entering the garage. Jesse clutched a pale blue blanket against his chest while the cop held him in place with a hand on each of Vetter's shoulders. "Please wait here, Mr. Vetter," the cop said. "Once the medical examiner is finished, I promise we'll cover the—Mr. Perreault."

"It's not dignified," Jesse Vetter said, his face raw with emotion. "All those people just staring…"

"They're professionals, Mr. Vetter," Sam said. "Just doing their job."

"We'll catch whatever did this," Dean said. "I promise."

Jesse turned his back to the open garage door, as if he needed to remove it from his field of vision in order to cope with what was out there. He wiped at his swollen eyes with the back of his hand. When he spoke again, he had regained some control of his voice, suppressing his grief long enough to help with the investigation. "I don't understand how this could happen," he said. "I was in the house all day. How could something get in here—hide in here—and I never knew?"

"Did you hear the attack?" Castiel asked.

"No," Jesse said. "I was upstairs, painting, when he left. I heard the door slam when he went into the garage and… I thought I heard it slam again, but—I don't know—I thought he came back in because he forgot his keys or a coupon or something. But I had a feeling something was wrong and couldn't understand why. Then I realized I never heard the garage door open or close when he left." He took a deep breath. "The house was quiet and I don't think the garage door is properly balanced. You can always hear it bang shut. But I never did."

"Is that when you called 911?" Castiel asked.

"No," Jesse said grimly. "I came down to check, to see if he had car trouble or a problem with the door. I didn't know… how could I ever imagine? This is a good neighborhood. Something like this…"

"You found the body?" Dean asked.

"Yes," Jesse said. "But not at first. I saw the car, parked and empty. But then I saw the stains… the blood stains on the door and I walked around to the front of his car and he was… he was… like he was sitting there but… I must have gone into shock. I thought I would scream, but I was gagging, choking on bile, burning my throat…"

"Through all of this, you never heard or saw the attacker?" Dean asked.

"Nothing," Jesse said. "Just that second slam… and the garage door hasn't opened since then. He… whoever did this must have crept through the house after… left through the front door or a window. The first police officers checked the entire house. No sign of forced entry, they said. But someone came into our home. Someone did this." He shuddered. "Seeing him—seeing Brandon... after was horrible enough. Thank God I came down alone."

"Who would've come down with you?" Sam asked.

"Olivia, of course," Jesse said, as if his answer should have been obvious. "But in her condition, she only takes the stairs when absolutely necessary. That's why I was alone."

Confused as Sam, Dean looked at Castiel and asked, "Olivia?"

As if on cue, a woman's strained voice called down the stairs, "Jesse, I'm all packed. We can go now."

Jesse looked at them. "She can't possibly stay here tonight," he said. "I couldn't do that to her." He pressed the folded blanket to his chest. "Don't think I can stay here tonight either. Every time I close my eyes, I see him out there. One minute we were joking around and the next he's just... gone. I have no idea what to do now. All our plans... Without Brandon, nothing makes sense anymore. The baby will be here any day. I'll be a single parent. And a widower. He'll never see... God, what do I do now...?"

Sam had a sense the question was more than rhetorical. The man seemed at a loss, buffeted by a whirlwind of consuming and dark emotions. "It's overwhelming now," Sam acknowledged. "Stay focused on short-term decisions. Call a friend where you can crash for the night or pick a hotel. Get through tonight. And then find a way to get through tomorrow morning."

A uniformed policewoman came down the stairs carrying

a soft suitcase with an extendable handle and wheels a few steps ahead of a very pregnant woman wearing threadbare denim overalls with black hair tucked under a scarf. Her face was red, her eyes puffy from crying.

Castiel nodded toward her. "Olivia Krum," he said. "The surrogate mother."

SEVENTEEN

Less than ten minutes had passed since Gary Atherton dimmed the lights in spacious birthing room 3C of Lovering Maternity Center and settled into the padded, reclining lounger reserved for new fathers. In the bed next to him, his exhausted wife slept, propped up at a thirty-degree angle with their newborn son asleep on her chest. The only other source of illumination came from the hallway through the doorway, open a few inches to give the new family some quiet privacy to regroup after a tiring day. Deeper in the room, by the bed and lounger, warm shadows ruled, and the ambient sounds of the round-the-clock hospital staff transformed into a soothing white noise.

Head turned toward his wife and son in a state of pleasant exhaustion, Gary had smiled in the moments before he too fell asleep. As new parents, he and his wife had already been given advice about catching sleep whenever the opportunity presented itself, that the demands of a hungry, soiled or lonely baby would preclude the previously taken for granted restful nights filled with extended hours of uninterrupted sleep. In a few hours at best, young Gabriel Atherton would rouse his mother and father with a tremulous cry, a parental call of duty, but for now all three slept soundly.

Beyond the intermediate shadows of the mother's bed and the father's chair, in the farthest corner of the room, by the closet where Gary had stashed an emergency duffel bag filled with clothing and reading material and other supplies, a dark figure waited, inhumanly still.

Straggly black hair obscured her pale face as she stood in the corner, head slightly bowed, clawed hands resting atop her protruding midsection. When the father's breathing deepened, she moved forward in a silent gliding motion and slipped between the large padded chair and the hospital bed. But her urge to savage the man remained suppressed, overruled by a deeper need. Instead of sinking her claws into his abdomen, she leaned over the hospital bed, letting her matted hair fall away from the back of her neck to reveal a pulsing, slimy hole at the nape.

The strange orifice puckered and swelled, extruding a slender, quivering tentacle. Unerringly, it snaked its way across the bed covers and over the mother's chest. Nearing its target, the tip of the thin tentacle flexed outward to reveal a ring of tiny lamprey-like teeth coated in a clear viscous fluid. A moment later, they clamped onto the infant's neck, establishing a gentle seal. After the clear fluid numbed the delicate skin, the narrow teeth sunk further into the newborn's flesh. Then the tentacle pulsed, contracting to suck, feeding...

Knuckles rapped on the heavy wooden door.

Lulled by the feeding cycle, the dark figure took a moment to react to the interruption. Then her head swiveled toward the door as the shaft of light from the hallway widened, banishing shadows across the room.

"Excuse me, folks," the young nurse said as she took a step into the room. "Wondered if I could get you—?"

The question forgotten, the nurse stared back at her, also momentarily frozen as her mind attempted to make sense out of something from a waking nightmare. Failing, the nurse screamed, her hand sweeping against the wall as she frantically tried to flip the light switch.

In that confused moment, the dark figure stopped feeding. The tentacle retracted into the neck orifice much quicker than it had appeared. If the intruder had glided forward before the feeding, she now rushed backward, faster than human legs and feet would allow, instinctively returning to the darkest corner of the room.

When the nurse found the switch and flicked on the overhead lights, the intruder was gone, the far corner no longer dark, but empty.

Nurse Maggie O'Brien stood in the doorway with her hand clamped over her mouth. She barely trusted herself not to scream again. If anything had stood in the corner, revealed by the light, she would have screamed. Of that she was certain.

The sound, however, had been more than sufficient to wake the entire Atherton family, mother, father and child.

Gary had startled awake, as if he'd been jolted by a powerful electrical charge, back arched, feet instinctively dropping to the floor to prepare himself for an emergency. But Denise had merely flinched, her entire body tensing as her arms wrapped protectively around her child. Following the nurse's example, Baby Gabriel had decided screaming was a splendid idea and wailed with all the power in his newborn lungs.

Mothering instincts kicking in, Denise attempted to soothe Gabriel, hugging and rocking him while whispering soothing words into his ear.

"What the hell happened?" Gary asked, eyes wide as he shook his head to shake off the last traces of lethargy.

Maggie imagined the incident from his point of view: He'd heard their nurse scream at the top of her lungs and yet nothing seemed amiss. But she had yet to recover from the effects of the nighttime shock and couldn't begin to explain what she saw. With one hand pressed to her chest and the rapid pounding of her heart, Maggie tried to slow and deepen her shallow breathing. She pointed to the back of the room with her other, trembling, hand. "Did you—? I saw—I don't know what—! It was—was horrible."

Gary looked over his shoulder, but obviously nothing was there for him to see anymore, and returned his questioning gaze to her with a confused shrug. "What are you talking about?"

"It's gone now," she said. "But there was something by the bed, standing over Denise and the baby." She spoke slowly in an attempt to frame her overwrought words in a way that might preserve her reputation as a sane and rational maternity ward nurse while explaining the reason for her frightened outburst. But how could she explain the strange shape that looked like a woman but wasn't a woman—or human for that matter—or the snakelike appendage sticking out of her neck?

Having heard the commotion, Nancy Dougherty and Janice Aquino, the two other nurses from her station, arrived and posed the same questions the Athertons were asking. Questions that had no easy answers. "Somebody was in the room," Maggie explained over and over again. "When I looked in, I saw… someone standing there."

"It's past visiting hours," Nancy Dougherty reminded her. "If it wasn't one of us, who could it have been?"

"I don't know," Maggie said, afraid to cross the threshold of the room. What if she—it—came back for her, the only witness. "She was standing by the bed. But she heard me call out and before I could turn on the lights, she… retreated to the corner."

She remembered the freaky way the intruder had moved backward, not as if she took the required number of steps to walk from bed to corner, but almost as if she had willed her body to glide across the floor.

"A woman?" Gary asked.

"Think so," Maggie said. "But I'm not—I can't be sure. It was dark…"

Because she wouldn't commit to the truth, she realized how lame her explanation sounded. She wanted to tell them she couldn't be sure what she saw was human. In fact, she was almost certain whatever had been in the room was not human. But how could she admit that aloud to patients and colleagues?

With all the uncertainty hanging over them, Nancy Dougherty decided to search the room. She opened the door to a small supply closet—obviously much too small and confined to conceal a full grown woman—before crossing the room to look in the patient closet, where she revealed Gary's coat and duffel bag but nothing sinister. She faced Maggie, spread her arms and shrugged. A birthing room offered precious few hiding places for an intruder.

Finally, Nancy dropped to one knee and peered under the adjustable bed, which made Maggie feel like a small child frightened of her dark bedroom. Oblivious to the damage she continued to wreak on Maggie's self-esteem, Nancy said cheerily, "All clear!"

Maggie had to acknowledge this wasn't about her or her bruised ego. The lighthearted search was meant to calm and reassure the agitated patients, something Maggie herself was incapable of accomplishing in her present state. For that at least, she was grateful for Nancy's presence.

Janice took Maggie's hands. "You said the lights were out," she reminded Maggie. "I'm sure it was just a trick of light and shadows."

"Sure—you're right. You must be right," Maggie said, unconvinced but unwilling to jeopardize her reputation any further by insisting on an impossible explanation.

She fully expected the Athertons to lodge a complaint about her behavior as it was, without compounding the damage. But Nancy and Janice had certainly helped to smooth things over. Gabriel was quiet, his breathing punctuated by faint, hitching sobs as he drifted off to sleep again.

After the other nurses left the room, Maggie addressed the Athertons. "I'm so sorry. For startling you, for waking the baby. I'm near the end of a double shift and I must be more tired than I knew. I'm sure Nurse Aquino was right. Trick of the shadows."

Gary and Denise nodded as she backed out of the room, seemingly more concerned with getting Gabriel back to sleep than dwelling on what had awoken him in the first place. That was the best outcome she could hope for at the moment, a return to normalcy. Come morning, she might face consequences for her involuntary reaction. But she couldn't help what she saw—or thought she saw.

Mortified, she stood outside birthing room 3C and leaned against the wall for support. Her legs felt like limp noodles and her hands still trembled when she held them out. Though she had begun to doubt her own eyes, the fear she'd experienced in those brief, horrifying moments still coursed through her veins.

She had barely managed to calm herself when Dr. Hartwell showed up outside the Athertons' room, a look of professional concern on her face.

"Hi, Maggie," Dr. Hartwell said. "How are you?"

"Okay," she said unconvincingly. She attempted a smile and wondered if it looked as ghastly as it felt. "Hard to tell around here sometimes, right?"

Dr. Hartwell nodded. "I've been hearing some… odd stories about you and the Athertons from the other nurses."

"Not the Athertons," Maggie admitted. "All me."

"Everything under control?"

"Now?" Maggie asked. "I think so. Hope so, anyway."

"What happened—exactly?"

"I, um, startled the Athertons."

"Screamed, is what I heard."

"I would say that's accurate," Maggie said, mortified all over again. "The Athertons were sleeping. Baby too. So I managed to wake them up—suddenly."

"Want to talk about it?"

"Oh, that's probably not a good idea. All things considered."

"Let me rephrase," Dr. Hartwell said. "Tell me about it."

Forcing another weak smile, Maggie said, "You'll refer me to the psych ward."

"Let me be the judge of that."

"So, I went in to check on them," Maggie said. "Totally routine. See if they needed anything. Lights were dimmed, but I could see well enough. At least, I thought I could. Gary was in the chair, Denise in the bed, naturally, baby at her chest, all asleep."

"Go on."

"But, for a moment, I thought I saw something else in the room with them…"

"Someone else, you mean?"

"Right. Someone," Maggie said. Though her original description was more truthful, it would also be more damning to her reputation. "A woman, dressed in rags, with long stringy hair." She took a deep breath. "There's more…"

Dr. Hartwell held a patient chart on a clipboard in her hands. As Maggie described the intruder, the doctor clutched the clipboard against her chest. Maggie knew enough about body language cues to assume Dr. Hartwell rejected her account of the intruder, blocking her entire story, unconvinced or unswayed by Maggie's calm description.

Disheartened and knowing she had yet to reveal the most farfetched part of her account, Maggie continued. "Something stuck out of the back of her neck. Like a tube or something. And it seemed to... stretch from her to the baby."

"A tube?" Dr. Hartwell frowned. "Medical equipment?"

"Something odd," Maggie said. "I only saw it for an instant."

"Is that all?"

"It was so strange and... unnatural—" *I sensed it was evil, but how do I tell her that?* "—it startled me. That's when I sort of screamed."

"Sort of?"

"Actually screamed," Maggie said, chagrined. "But it was totally reflexive. I had no control over it."

"Of course not," Dr. Hartwell said. "What then?"

"I turned on the light to get a better look and... then it was gone."

"Disappeared?"

"Crazy, right?" Maggie said. "Probably something weird about the shadows in the room, like Janice said. But for those few moments before I turned on the lights, I could have sworn it—she was standing right there, between Gary and Denise. I don't know how to explain it, but I was scared—really scared—for the baby."

Dr. Hartwell nodded again.

Maggie continued to assume no one gave credence to

her story. She doubted she would have believed it coming from Nancy or Janice. *You had to be there,* she concluded. *Otherwise, nothing will convince you.*

But what Dr. Hartwell said next completely surprised her. "Let's have a look at the baby."

EIGHTEEN

In the morning, Sam, Dean and Castiel returned to the Holcomb house—site of the first murder—in the Impala, with Castiel following in his gold Lincoln in case they needed to split up at some point. On the way, Dean fiddled with the radio dial until he found a station wrapping up a block of Zeppelin with "Ramble On." As Dean swung over to the curb, Sam noticed a blue Dodge Ram 1500 that looked as if it had spent equal amounts of time off-road as on, parked in front of the house. Painted on the door panels of the pickup in slanted blue letters on a white oval was the company logo for Vargus Fabricators.

"Good timing," Dean said.

They'd come to talk to Sally about her husband's new job at the company to confirm or rule out a connection between Holcomb and Aidan Dufford's unemployed father. Rather than relying on second-hand information from Sally, it looked like they had an opportunity to question Stanley Vargus himself.

For this repeat visit, Sam and Dean had dressed down while Castiel, as always, wore his suit and overcoat. Though he looked the part of an FBI agent, the Winchesters led the way, and Sam stepped back as Dean rang the doorbell. Once again, Sally's grandmother Mary invited them inside.

Sally, who seemed oddly distracted but more composed than she had been the day before, sat in the middle of the sofa, with Ramon to her left and a tall man with a thick wave of black hair wearing a denim shirt, jeans and scuffed work boots on her right. The tall man held a bottle of Triple XXX Root Beer—taken from a cardboard six pack on the coffee table—by its long neck.

Sally started to stand with the tall man, but Sam told her, "Please, don't get up on our account."

She stood nonetheless and said, "Agents Rutherford, Banks and... Collins, wasn't it? This is Dave's friend, Stanley Vargus. Stan, they're with the FBI. They don't believe it was an animal attack."

After exchanging handshakes with the new arrivals, Vargus sat back down, along with Sally. Sam and Dean took the wingchairs while Castiel seemed content to stand between them.

"The police have their doubts too," Dean said. "But the medical examiner is clinging to the animal attack theory."

"What the hell kind of animal gu—attacks a man like that?" Vargus said, casting a quick apologetic glance at Sally for what he'd almost said. "No offense to the medical examiner."

"There have been other, similar attacks in Braden Heights," Sam said. "We don't believe an animal was involved or that the attacks were random. We're looking for a connection between the victims."

"We were hoping you could help with that, Mr. Vargus," Castiel said.

"Me?" Vargus replied. "I don't understand, Agent Collins. I'm here to support the family. Beyond that, how could I possibly help with your investigation?"

"The second victim was a young man named Aidan Dufford," Castiel said. "Does that name mean anything to you?"

"Aidan—oh, Dufford! That's Don Dufford's boy," he said. "I'm very sorry to hear that, Don is an employee—a former employee of mine."

"And Dave Holcomb was gonna be a future employee," Dean added.

"Not so," Vargus said. "I hired Dave already. Done deal. He hadn't officially started, but there were no conditions he hadn't met. He simply asked for some time to get things in order around here."

"Did Dave's hiring have anything to do with Donald's termination?"

"No, sir," Vargus said. "Donald was an hourly employee working in the plant. I let him go because I couldn't count on him to show up on a regular basis. Let me be clear, Vargus Fabricators is not some massive corporation. We have fewer than two hundred employees. I rely on them and they rely on each other. You know what they say about the chain only being as strong as the weakest link? Well, Donald got to the point recently where I felt I needed a fresh link in the chain."

"But that wasn't Dave?" Dean asked.

"Hell no," Vargus said emphatically. "One decision had nothing to do with the other. Besides, Dave was gonna be my night manager. I haven't figured out a way to not sleep at least once a day. My old night manager was set to retire. I asked him to stay on… until I can make other arrangements."

"No animosity between you and Mr. Dufford?" Castiel asked.

"Not on my side," Vargus said. "I know the man has some personal problems but I could only carry him for so long. But right about now, I can guess he's not my biggest fan." He shook his head and sighed, took a long pull from the bottle of root beer. "But I don't see how that weighs on what happened to Dave. If you're suggesting Don was out for revenge, I doubt those two ever met each other. Donald would more likely have punched me in the mouth than go after another Vargus employee. And if you think I would hurt a former employee's son for any damn reason, you're barking up the wrong tree."

"Understand, we need to follow up on any leads," Sam said.

"Certainly," Vargus said. "But this particular lead of yours is pure coincidence."

"Like the pregnancies," Dean said to Castiel.

Castiel nodded.

"Excuse me, Stan," Sally said abruptly, "are you finished with that bottle?"

He tilted the bottle side to side. "Would appear so."

"Let me take it out to the recycling container," she said, grabbing the bottle and rising.

Silent until now, Ramon placed his hand on her forearm. "I got it, sis," he said, reaching for the bottle. "Stay here."

Brushing away his hand, she shook her head. "No, I'm fine," she said, her voice strained again as her erstwhile composure slipped away. "I need to stretch my legs anyway."

Sam suspected her grief would continue to come in waves. One never knew what random reminder or emotional trigger would begin a new downward spiral.

Ramon seemed confused by his sister's reaction and started to rise, but sat back down when his grandmother, standing in the archway to the kitchen, shook her head at him. Sam thought she mouthed the words, "Not now."

Vargus leaned over and patted Ramon on the knee. "Son, rest assured I plan to help your sister however I can. Whatever she needs. I know she didn't sign up for this. She came all the way to Indiana to support her husband, my good friend, and I won't forget that. I'm sure she's told you, Dave and I go way back. I wanted good things for him, hoped to help him out here. If Sally chooses to stay here and keep this home, I'll find a good position for her with my company. Dave told me she was an administrative assistant back in California. I can arrange something similar here. And if she chooses to go back to San Bernardino, I'll give her whatever assistance I can." He leaned back. "Short term, if she needs help with funeral expenses, I've got it covered. What I'm trying to say is, she'll have options."

"Thank you, Mr. Vargus," Ramon said, genuinely moved. "I appreciate that."

"God knows, I'll miss Dave," Vargus said. "I can't even

imagine what this must be like for her…"

Sam noticed the grandmother's fleeting frown and looked at Dean, nodding slightly toward the old woman. When he stood, Dean rose with him. Castiel looked a question at them, but Sam shook him off. The angel nodded and remained standing between the wingchairs.

Vargus had segued into offering Ramon a job at his plant whether or not Sally chose to stay in Indiana. Ramon seemed to be considering the offer when Sally returned from the garage, passing through the kitchen. As she stepped past her grandmother, the old woman placed a hand on her upper arm and gave her a searching look. Sally nodded once and returned to the sofa. Sam thought maybe her eyes had become a bit raw since she'd stepped out.

Together he and Dean walked toward the kitchen.

"Could we speak in private?" Sam asked the grandmother as they passed her. She seemed to have been expecting this and wordlessly followed them into the kitchen. Reaching for glasses from a cupboard, she proceeded to fill them with chilled water from a dispenser in the door of the refrigerator.

"Mr. Vargus talks about options," the grandmother said. "But Sally decided to leave this morning. She's already making arrangements. David's parents want to see his body before it's moved, but that simply postpones the inevitable."

"Is everything okay with Sally?" Sam asked softly, so his voice wouldn't carry into the other room.

The grandmother shook her head. "Such a tragedy, especially with this latest news."

"What news?"

"She was sick again this morning," the old woman said, absently pushing the glasses across the countertop toward them. "She said she didn't want to know, that it was all too much. But this is different. It's not a house. Not something you can ignore or run away from. I finally convinced her to take the test."

"Test?" Dean asked.

"Yes," she said solemnly. "It was the plus."

Still confused, Dean looked a silent question at Sam.

But Sam felt the pieces coming together. Everything started to make sense. "Sally's pregnant."

NINETEEN

"Sally's"—Dean caught himself and lowered the volume of his voice—"Sally's pregnant."

The grandmother nodded. "Only a few weeks," she said. "But she will keep the child. That's why she made the decision to leave. She'll be a single mother, raising a child on her own. She wants to be near family. Mr. Vargus has offered to help her, but he is not family. He was close to David, but they hadn't seen each other in a while and Sally is not close to this man. Here, she is among strangers in a place which has only bad memories for her. And for her family."

"Found our connection," Dean said.

Sam nodded. "All the victims had some sort of relationship with a pregnant woman."

Unfortunately, each victim had a relationship with a different pregnant woman. There was no common denominator.

"Small problem," Dean said. "Until a few hours ago, nobody knew Sally was pregnant. Not even Sally."

"Please do not tell this news to anyone," Mary said. "Not even Ramon knows."

"We'll keep the information confidential," Sam assured her.

Dean downed his glass of water while imagining how much more refreshing a cold beer would have been. But he'd been trying to cut back, earn his choir boy badge in an attempt to keep the Mark's violent urges under control. With a sigh and a slight head shake, he placed the empty glass in the sink.

Through a gap in the curtains of the small window over the sink he could see the backyard of the Holcomb house and beyond, to the open space past their fence and the abandoned house on the far side of that lot. He remembered the field had been overgrown and the house had been visited by teenagers secretly indulging in alcohol and other controlled substances. But the condition of the connecting property had improved. Dean heard the buzz of the motor before he spotted the old man on the riding mower, trimming the weeds to a respectable height.

Dean recalled the stuffed plastic trash bags lined up by the front door of the house and wondered if the lawnmower man was the irregular caretaker of the place. If he'd been around at the time of Dave Holcomb's attack, he might have witnessed something that could help in the investigation. So far, the closest they'd come to having an eyewitness was Jesse Vetter and Olivia Krum, who had been in the same house but several rooms distant when the Perreault attack occurred.

"Gonna see a man about a mower," Dean said to Sam, pointing toward the caretaker visible through the window.

* * *

While Sam remained at the Holcomb residence with Castiel, Dean jumped in the Impala and followed the winding suburban street around to the curb of the vacant house. He parked opposite a GMC pickup from the late fifties; its red color had faded over time to a shade best described as rust. Hitched to the pickup was a single axle open trailer with a plywood bed and ramp that had a decidedly homemade quality. Or perhaps the original materials had been patched or replaced over the years with a dedicated DIY mentality. Neither truck nor trailer had a business sign on display, adding to the homebrew quality of the setup. If the old man on the riding mower was running a business he had avoided any attempt at marketing his services to the locals.

As Dean exited the Impala, the old man neared the back of the vacant house, his mowing grid taking him from the back of the property to the front. Dean estimated that he had less than fifteen minutes remaining to finish the job. The man made a turn at the right edge of the property line and rumbled back toward Dean, finally noticing the visitor.

The old man wore a grease- and grass-stained John Deere trucker hat, a threadbare red plaid shirt, naturally distressed jeans and scuffed, steel-toed boots. His face brought to mind prunes and old leather, with a touch of sunburn on his ears and the tip of his nose. A spotty gray beard swathed the bottom half of his face and the upper half of his neck, trimmed well enough to keep his thin lips visible but any attempt at precision grooming ended there.

When the riding mower came within arm's reach of Dean's

position, the old man switched off the power and sat there for a moment, silently squinting at him.

Though he hadn't donned his Fed suit, Dean had his fake FBI ID and flashed it for the old-timer. "Special Agent Banks, FBI."

The old man brought up some phlegm, turned his head to the side and spat an impressive distance before answering. "You don't say?"

He climbed off the riding mower with deliberate care, as if giving his old joints time to acclimate to a new alignment. With both feet on the ground, he pulled a rag out of his back pocket, wiped off his hands, tucked the rag away and held out his right hand. "Arthur Keating."

Dean shook the proffered hand and said, "I'm investigating a death on the property next door." Not wanting to panic the locals with tales of a serial killer on the loose in Braden Heights, he phrased the statement to conform to the official party line of an animal attack rather than a murder. He had no qualms about telling the family of victims he believed they were murdered, but telling the general public might annoy the police and end any pretense of cooperation and sharing of information. Moreover, their FBI credentials might not hold up to additional scrutiny. If Assistant Chief Cordero ever decided to call Washington to lodge a complaint about rogue agents, that day would not end well. "Hoping you can answer a few questions."

"Holcomb fella?"

"Got it in one," Dean said. "Know anything about it?"

"About as much as they put in the papers," he said. "And

what little I hear around town. Not one to trade in gossip but the stories going around these days certainly perk up the ears."

"I bet they do."

"Way I hear it, you got more than one of these guttings."

"There have been similar incidents."

"I'm no wildlife expert, Agent Banks," Keating said. "And I don't expect you are either."

"Not at all," Dean said.

"I'm at a loss what kind of animal might be responsible for all this."

"Some animals might surprise you," Dean said.

Keating flashed Dean a bit of knowing side-eye. "Suspect you're right," he said. "But I don't see how I can help."

"Answer a few questions."

"All right," he said. "I'd invite you inside, but there ain't no decent place to sit."

"Out here's fine," Dean said. "Do you own this property?"

"No, sir," Keating replied. "Look after it now and then. Long as someone pays for the privilege. Last owner died, left a contested will, tied up in the courts. I've been paid by the executor, usually after enough people complain about the state of the place."

"That why you're here today?"

"No, sir," Keating said again. "Real estate agent paid me to spruce up the grounds, make it presentable. Said she's putting the Holcomb place back on the market and doesn't want the neighborhood eyesore driving down the asking price."

"So you weren't working the grounds the day Holcomb was killed."

"No," Keating said. "And thank God I was nowhere near here. Could've been me gutted instead of Holcomb. Don't get me wrong, I've lived a long life—not always good or easy, but I don't have too many complaints—and Holcomb was a young fella, certainly not deserving of what he got, far as I know, but I ain't ready to give up the ghost yet. Suspect I have a few more years in these creaky bones."

Dean looked across the open field, mostly mowed, to the rotted fence Dave Holcomb had been attempting to repair when he was attacked. "Notice anything out of the ordinary back by the Holcomb property line?"

"Other than weeds?" Keating shook his head. "Couple fast food wrappers, garage sale flyer, few pages from a newspaper. Stuff I suspect the wind had a hand in depositing back there against the fence." He shrugged. "Of course, if there were shell casings or cigarette butts back there, I might have missed them."

"Good thing we're not looking for a sniper," Dean said.

"Wasn't always like this," Keating mused.

"How's that?"

"Braden Heights," Keating said. "Town's growing, for sure, but it's been a quiet growth, if you know what I mean. Not much trouble. Not real trouble anyway. Teenage mischief, broken windows here and there. But nothing to make you double-check your locks at night."

"That's good to know."

"I get the local monthly paper, *The Corner Press*," Keating said. "Hell, everyone does. It's free. As you'd expect, it's mostly local interest stuff, advertiser supported. But they also list the police blotter activity and it's mostly minor crimes; a comfort in a way, if you think about it. Live as long as I have, and you know how much worse that type of listing can get." He looked at the section of the yard he hadn't yet mowed and Dean imagined he wanted to get back to it. But he wasn't quite done. "As the town grows, as it becomes more successful, you know the bad stuff will come."

"But you didn't expect it to come so soon," Dean guessed.

"No, sir," Keating said. "I have days filled with gloom and doom thoughts, but I never imagined something this bad would come so soon."

"It's not normal," Dean said. "No matter how big the town. Sometimes bad things happen."

"Suspect you're right," Keating said. "Braden Heights had a good run, been quiet a long time. At least since they changed the name."

"Changed the name?"

"Of course, they had to," Keating explained. "After the tragedy."

TWENTY

Assuming Dean wouldn't need assistance with questioning a groundskeeper, Sam had stayed behind at the Holcomb residence with Castiel, but he was beginning to doubt he'd mine much more information out of the family or Vargus. Before Dean left, they'd established a pregnancy connection between the murders, but Sally's pregnancy remained an X factor. It seemed as if only Sally and her grandmother knew about the pregnancy, and then only for a day. But four male victims involved with four pregnant women was a bit much to chalk up to coincidence.

"Yes, moving to a new home is stressful," the grandmother said, in the kitchen with Sam. "But she hasn't really had time to settle in here. Better to think of it as an ongoing move."

"Won't be easy," Sam said. "Repacking everything."

The Winchesters traveled light and never had to consider packing up a lifetime of accumulated belongings. Until they'd found the bunker, they had no furniture at all. Every possession they had could fit in the trunk of the Impala, alongside their hunters' weapons cache.

From the other room, Sam detected a change in volume as Stanley Vargus said his goodbyes.

"Ramon will help, and the Holcombs," Mary said, walking from the kitchen before Vargus left. "I can't lift much, but I can pack plates, tape up boxes. We'll hire movers for most of it."

Stanley Vargus paused in the doorway facing Ramon, who held the door open for him, and Sally, who stood with her hands clasped before her, a polite smile flickering off and on as she struggled to retain her composure. Castiel hadn't strayed too far from the wingchairs.

"These aren't just words, Sally," Vargus said. "I mean to help out, however I can."

"Thanks," Sally said.

"I convinced Dave to come here. So I want to cover his funeral expenses. You don't need to worry about that."

"I appreciate that," Sally said, her lips trembling.

"Dave always called you Sally, but going through the paperwork to have a check cut, I noticed a different name listed for spouse…?"

"Oh, Sally is a nickname," she said. "Not my legal name."

"That's my fault," Ramon said. "When I was a kid, I couldn't pronounce Dalisay so I called her Sally instead. And it stuck."

"Why do you think these two insist on calling me Grandma Mary, instead of Marilag?"

"Well, I'm glad I've cleared that up," Vargus said. "I'll have a check sent over tomorrow if not later today."

"Thank you, Mr. Vargus," Mary said with a slight bow of her head. "Ramon and I appreciate the kindness and support you've shown our Sally."

"Believe me," Vargus said, clearly moved. "It's the least I can do. Dave was a good friend. And I feel somehow responsible for this whole situation."

"Don't be ridiculous," Sally said, wiping away a tear. "There's no way you could have known something like this… how this could happen."

He shook his head, at a loss for words.

Sally stepped forward and hugged him.

Vargus shook Ramon's hand. "Job offer stands, son." He took the grandmother's hand gently and thanked her for her hospitality. Then he turned to Sam and Castiel, who hung back a little from the group. "Find whoever took Dave away from us," he said grimly. "And lock the bastard up for the rest of his worthless life."

After he left, Ramon closed the door so it hardly made a sound.

Sally turned away and hugged herself, looking somewhat lost as she surveyed the house which hadn't yet become a home and now never would. "I don't know anymore," she said. "Sometimes I feel Dave's presence here. Maybe I *should* stay. Maybe I won't feel completely lost and alone…" She turned, facing the backyard but staring off into space. "But then I close my eyes and I see him out there, how I found him…"

"That will never change, Dalisay," the grandmother said. "You made the right decision. Best to leave as soon as possible."

Ramon shook his head. "You don't need to stay here, in

this house, sis," he said. "But you could stay in Indiana. Evansville, maybe."

Mary shook her head. "Too close," she said. "Start making new memories far from here."

"No matter where she goes," Ramon said, "she won't forget what happened here."

"This place is bad for her now," the grandmother said. "I wasn't sure before, but I am now. Bad omen."

"What's changed?" Ramon asked, looking back and forth between them. "How is it worse now than before?"

The old woman crossed her arms, her mouth clamped shut, but stared at Sally, not Ramon. Clearly, she felt the answer wasn't hers to give.

Sally sighed. "Because I'm pregnant, Ramon."

"What?"

"I suspected, but I only found out for sure this morning," she said. "As sure as I can be without seeing a doctor. But I didn't want Stanley to know."

"Why not? He could help!"

"He'd want me to stay," Sally said. "He feels guilty for some reason and wants to help. But I need to make this decision on my own. And I don't think I should stay—could stay."

"Good. Trust your instincts," Mary said. "Don't have the baby here. I believe this place is cursed for you."

"Cursed?" Castiel asked.

"Because of what happened to Dave?" Sam asked, not quite rhetorically, as he sensed something else factored into the old woman's newfound conviction that Sally should leave as soon as possible.

"Yes," she said and took a deep breath. "And because of what happened long ago."

"What are you talking about?" Sally asked.

The old woman walked over to the nearest wingchair and lowered herself into it, gripping the padded arms for support. "My aunt, Malaya Mercado," she said. "She left the Philippines before any of our family. Married an American G.I., a medic, after World War II and moved to Indiana."

"Aunt Malaya?" Sally said. "I never knew that. I remember someone in the family saying she left the Philippines when she was young, but not much else. She really lived in Indiana?"

"Briefly," the grandmother said solemnly. "Moved to her husband's hometown. When I heard you were moving here with David, I looked for it on a map. Somewhere in southern Indiana. Carson County—or maybe it was Carter City. Memory's not as sharp as it was. I thought the town might be close to Braden Heights, but couldn't find either of those names on the map."

"You mentioned she stayed in Indiana briefly," Sam said, hoping to steer the conversation toward the source of the old woman's misgivings.

"No, I said she lived in Indiana briefly."

"She died here," Castiel guessed.

Mary nodded. "Malaya was expecting when she came to Indiana," she said. "Hoped to start a new family here with her husband, but there were complications during childbirth. Hemorrhaging. She lost too much blood."

"And her baby?" Sam asked hesitantly, expecting the worst.

Mary smiled briefly. "Beautiful child, from the few pictures

I saw. But willful and disobedient, like she resented the hole in her life, not having a mother, and it angered her."

"What happened?" Sally asked.

"All we know is what little filtered back to us from her father," Mary said. "Riza never contacted anyone on our side of the family. We must have seemed half a world away, and I suppose we were. Anyway, her father told us she met a boy who was no good for her, from the wrong side of the tracks, as they used to say. He disapproved. Naturally, for a rebellious teenaged girl, that was all the encouragement she needed. One thing led to another and she got herself in a family way. Her father threatened to separate them, send her to live with us and never see that boy again. You can imagine what happened."

"She ran away," Sam guessed.

"Her and the boy," the old woman said. "Before she left, she promised him he would never see her again, or the baby. And she kept her word. I often wonder what happened to little Riza. If she eventually found happiness... or more heartache." She sighed, still gripping the padded armrests as she looked up at her standing granddaughter. "You see, Dalisay? That is why you must leave this cursed place. There is only death and sadness for pregnant Mercado women here. First Malaya, then Riza, and now losing your David... history is repeating itself. It's already started. If you stay, more sadness will come for you."

An uneasy silence fell across the room. Until Sam's cell phone rang. He excused himself and walked away from the group to take the call.

"This is Agent Rutherford."

"Hello, Agent," said a familiar woman's voice. Before he could identify the caller, she spared him the trouble. "This is Dr. Vanessa Hartwell from LMC."

"Hello, Dr. Hartwell," Sam said. "Of course, I remember you."

At the mention of the doctor's name, Castiel crossed the room to stand near Sam, a look of concern in his eyes.

"Agent, have you ever had the feeling that strange things were happening all around you without your knowledge?"

"All the time," Sam said honestly. "I don't like not knowing. That's why I got into this business. What's up?"

"Not sure if it relates to your case," Hartwell said mysteriously, "but there's something I need to tell you—well, show you. But I can't really show you because technically it's gone, but... I think it would be best if you could come here and see—or not see—for yourself."

"I'll go," Castiel said, having heard enough over the receiver to make his decision. "You stay here. Wait for De— Agent Banks."

Sam pressed the mute button. "You sure?"

"I'm sure," Castiel said. He turned to the others and excused himself, slipping quietly out the door before Ramon could open it for him.

Sam switched off mute. "Agent Collins is on his way there now."

"Thank you."

While Sam took the call, Sally had begun to pace behind the sofa, hugging herself as if to ward off a chill. As he rejoined the group, she asked, "Was that about Dave's attacker?"

"Maybe," Sam said. "It might be related."

She nodded in resignation, perhaps accepting the possibility she might never get closure for the murder of her husband. Looking toward her grandmother, she placed a hand on her abdomen and said, "Leaving here won't bring back David. Either way, this baby will never know her father. And there's already a hole in her life, before she's born. Just like Riza. Maybe it's too late…"

"That is dangerous thinking," Mary said. "You are this baby's hope and future. You must light the way for her—but not here. This place will always want to pull you into darkness."

"Maybe she's right, Sal," Ramon said. "You should go."

Sally looked at Sam, as if seeking an objective opinion from outside the family. Though Sam couldn't tell her what to do with her life, he could try to keep her safe from the immediate threat. "Look, I don't know if this place is cursed," Sam admitted, though he wouldn't rule it out. "But whoever is responsible for killing your husband is still out there. A real, tangible threat. If you want a fresh start, in this instance, a change of scenery might not be a bad thing."

Sally nodded thoughtfully and rubbed her palms together. "Guess I better start packing."

TWENTY-ONE

"So this town wasn't always called Braden Heights?" Dean asked groundskeeper-for-hire Arthur Keating.

"No, sir," Keating said, scratching the underside of his jaw through his patchy gray beard. "Probably have to go back to the late sixties, early seventies to find references to Braden Heights by its original name, Larkin's Korner. That's Korner with a K."

"That free local paper, *The Corner Press*," Dean said. "Named after the original town name?"

"Yes, sir," Keating said. "But you're not likely to find many in town make that connection. Second or third generation families. And some of those probably never knew, since the paper refused to adopt the K spelling. Original editor couldn't abide the intentional misspelling in the town name."

"Other than the goofy spelling," Dean said, "why'd they change the name? You mentioned a tragedy…?"

Having stood for a while, Keating took a step back to lean against the riding mower. He crossed his arms over his chest and nodded. "Most of the land around here was owned by Ruth Larkin's family. Still is, I imagine, except for some parcels of land they've sold to the town or private developers. The construction going on around town? Wherever you see that, you're most likely looking at lots the Larkin family owned previously. Was a time the Larkins were the prominent family in this area, but they cleared out in the early sixties, after the tragedy. But who could blame them?"

Dean contained his impatience. For a man who professed not to trade in gossip, Keating sure seemed to revel in the telling of it. "And this tragedy…?"

"Right," Keating said. "Ruth Larkin's son, Calvin Nodd, a doctor no less, snapped. Maybe it started in the war, after the things he saw over there. Heard he had regular nightmares, the wake up screaming and drenched in sweat type of night terrors. Or maybe the Larkin family played that stuff up later to garner sympathy for the man.

"Anyway, he came home in one piece, which was better than some. And he brought a new bride with him. For a while, he seemed happy. But he was home less than a year when his wife died in childbirth. Baby girl survived, though. Nodd became something of a hermit after that, avoiding contact with most folks, but he raised that girl on his own. Don't imagine he was a model father, damaged as he was. As you might expect, that little girl ran a bit wild. Years later, sixty-two it must have been, she gets herself knocked up and runs off with a drifter boyfriend. Rebels of a feather, I guess. Doc Nodd never heard from her again."

"Must have been hard for him."

"Yes, sir," Keating said. "Comes home from the war traumatized. Back then they didn't recognize PTSD or that kind of thing, but I imagine he had major head issues. Then his wife dies in childbirth less than a year after they're married. Finally, his daughter flips him the bird and runs off carrying a grandchild he'll never see. That there is one big downward spiral."

"A spiral that ended with him snapping?"

"Supposedly, he tried to strangle one of his patients, during childbirth no less. Almost killed her and the baby. Would have, if not for the attending nurse. Doc Nodd skipped town before the case went to trial. And just like his daughter, he was never heard from again."

"Why 'supposedly'?" Dean asked. "Isn't this a matter of record?"

"Well, some of it is and some of it isn't," Keating hedged. "Rumor had it the Larkins paid off the woman's family and the nurse and maybe a few others to keep quiet about the whole incident. And by 'paid' I mean paid handsomely. The papers published some vague nonsense about Doc Nodd having some kind of episode, war-related psychological damage overcoming him for one terrible moment. They brought up the death of his wife, abandonment by his only child, and so on. Mother and child were fine. Maybe her family even believed it was an unfortunate episode. They left soon after the incident so they wouldn't be around to answer any troubling questions."

"If the Larkins paid off everyone involved," Dean said, "how'd you find out this information?"

"Information might be too strong a word for what I know," Keating said. "Like I told you before, this is rumors, whispers passed around. You can't buy off a whole town's silence. So and so knew one bit of it, someone else knew another piece of it. You hear enough, you start to put those puzzle pieces together. It was an old-fashioned cover up, by all accounts, but it's not like the Larkins had to cover up an actual murder, although they might have tried, if it had come to that."

"That the end of it?"

"Once the dust settled, it seemed like the doctor and his entire family had dropped off the face of the earth, but the Larkins' sterling reputation had suffered a bit of tarnish. Wasn't much longer before they pulled up stakes. Still owned much of the land, mind you, but they were nowhere to be found. Heard at the time that they'd relocated to Europe, but that's about as specific a location as I ever heard. Few years later, the town changed its name. To honor a local war hero, or so they said. Only us old-timers know the real reason. It's taken all this time, but it looks like the Larkins—whoever is left among them and wherever they are these days—are finally selling off any land they still own around here."

Dean calculated that if the disappearing Doctor Nodd was still alive, he'd be ninety, possibly older. Certainly in no condition to brutally murder and eviscerate four healthy young men, even if he could have extricated himself from a fatal car crash unwitnessed. But he could be responsible for unleashing whatever had committed the murders. While his mental gears turned, Dean said, "That's quite a story."

"And every word of it true," Keating said. "Of course, we'll probably never know about the Riza copycats."

"Wait—copycats?"

"Five other local girls who got themselves in a family way and left town, just like the Doc's girl. Not sure if they thought it was a romantic notion, leaving behind the small town for the big city. Most folks blamed the recession, lack of jobs and opportunity. Rough times, certainly. Nobody could blame them for leaving, wanting something better. Of course, my own feeling on the matter is the big city's more likely to chew you up and spit you out. But there's a reason they got that expression, the grass is always greener on the other side of the fence. Some people got to find out for themselves different don't mean better."

"What happened to the copycats?"

"Their families never heard from those girls again. Not one of the five came crawling back. Damn poor odds, right? Always thought that was mighty peculiar."

"Yes," Dean said. "It is."

"Well, sir, if you don't mind, I need to finish up here."

"Thanks for your help, Arthur," Dean said, shaking the man's hand before he climbed back up on his riding mower.

The engine fired up as Dean hurried back to the Holcomb residence.

TWENTY-TWO

Exhausted, Melissa Barrows crept down the stairs and collapsed on the sofa beside her husband. "She's asleep," Melissa mumbled. "Finally."

He appeared equally wiped out, slouched on the cushions, one arm thrown over his head, TV remote balanced on his thigh, feet crossed on the coffee table—even though she'd asked him more times than she could count to keep them on the floor. But this time she was too tired to argue. Pick your battles, her mother had advised her before she got married. Same rule applied to raising kids. Of course, for the longest time, Melissa and Kevin feared they'd never have any kids to raise one way or the other.

"Thank God," Kevin sighed. "Hard to believe something so small has the energy to keep two grown adults up all night, night after night."

"We should patent her internal fuel cells," Melissa said, setting the baby monitor on the coffee table and adjusting the volume to the halfway mark. She imagined if she listened closely she could hear little Noelle breathing softly, but all she really heard was the blissful silence of a contented baby.

"You telling me we have a baby cyborg?" Kevin asked in mock surprise. "I specifically ordered the pure human model with a sixteen-hour sleep recharge cycle."

Melissa snuggled against his chest. "But the cyborg model was a free upgrade," she said. "And you know I can't resist a bargain."

For years they tried to get pregnant the old-fashioned way but had no luck. Rather than accept that a Barrows baby was not meant to be, they decided to get medical help, which led to fertility testing, which segued into several rounds of IVF at the Stanton Fertility Clinic before the stars finally aligned for them. Kevin once joked that the natural act of getting pregnant had taken on the complexity of a NASA mission, years in the making, followed by nine months until touchdown on Planet Newborn. And having Noelle presented a whole new world for them. But it was a world they were eager to explore for the rest of their lives.

"Okay, then," Kevin said. "I guess we'll keep her."

"That's good," Melissa said, starting to slur her words. "Because I accidentally threw away the receipt with her box."

"Jeez, now you're telling me she was delivered in a box by a truck," Kevin said. "Here I thought we ordered blanket and stork air mail shipping."

"Two-day box shipping was free," she mumbled. "And you know I can't resist…"

"You can't sleep yet!"

"Watch me."

"Thought we were finally going to binge-watch *Battlestar Galactica*."

"Binge-watching the back of my eyelids right now," Melissa said around a jaw-cracking yawn. "Fascinating stuff. You should try…"

"Shame to waste quiet-baby-time sleeping."

"You had… other ideas?"

"Besides *BSG*?" Kevin asked. "Maybe one or two."

"Such as…?" she asked, managing to raise an eyebrow high enough to show her interest was piqued without convincing him she had the requisite enthusiasm to follow through.

"Never mind," Kevin said. "Mind is willing, but the body is weak. Or is it the other way around? Maybe both."

"We may already be asleep and dreaming this conversation."

"Are you dreaming about me? Or am I dreaming about you?"

"Yes," she said. "Definitely."

The baby monitor squawked with a startled baby cry.

Melissa's eyes fluttered open, her head turned toward the speaker on the monitor, waiting.

Kevin tensed, hoping she'd calm herself and settle back into peaceful sleep, but ready for the wailing to commence. His turn to check on her if she woke. And at the moment, he felt like his body was glued to the sofa cushions.

"Should have sprung for the video monitor," Melissa mumbled.

"You'd watch her 24/7," Kevin said. "Big Mother."

"Maybe you should rephrase that."

"Oh, sorry," Kevin said, chuckling. "You know what I meant."

"Whatever. Don't like it."

Another baby cry, but this time it cut off abruptly.

"Kevin?"

"Yeah, I'm on it," Kevin said, suddenly invigorated with nervous energy. Perhaps they were overprotective—some of their friends thought so, especially those with multiple kids— but Noelle was their first child and they had gone through so much to bring her into their lives that any concern became a major concern. Neither one of them had to say the words out loud to know what the other was thinking: sudden infant death syndrome.

Kevin took the stairs two at a time, already regretting he'd only read about CPR and hadn't taken any classes. He'd always assumed he'd get around to it in his spare time, but now Noelle was here and he had a gap in life-saving knowledge. Probably too many to count. He wondered fleetingly if somebody published a baby survival guide he could purchase and study until he'd memorized every page. What to do in any infant emergency, indexed from A to Z. Melissa and he could grill each other with flashcards until every tip, trick and procedure was etched indelibly into their gray matter.

As expected, Melissa had closed the door to the nursery to prevent any minor sounds from disturbing the baby's seemingly infrequent sleep. Kevin had oiled the hinges to eliminate metallic creaking whenever they checked in on Noelle. On the chance she'd fallen asleep again, he turned the knob and opened the door slowly, intending to peek inside the room before entering. If she was awake but quiet, he didn't want her to see him and cry for him to come get her. He'd carefully slip back out unobserved.

Leaning through a ten-inch gap in the doorway, he never could have been prepared for what he saw. Instead of Noelle lying peacefully in her crib under the cartoon animal mobile, he saw only the hunched form of a pale woman with straggly black hair bent over the crib. She completely blocked his view of Noelle, which was probably why he next noticed a weird, pulsing appendage snaking from the nape of the woman's neck, over her shoulder and down out of view.

He threw the door open and charged into the room. As the woman shifted, half-turning to face him, he saw what he had feared. The glistening and pulsing appendage stretched into the crib and had clamped onto the back of his daughter's neck. Noelle's eyes were closed, her body limp and her lips slack.

"Get away from her, you freaky bitch!" he shouted.

"Kevin?" his wife called in alarm from below.

Fearing that his daughter was ill or had trouble breathing, he'd never thought to bring a weapon to the nursery. Not that he kept guns or hunting knives in the house, but he could have taken a knife from the kitchen or the old baseball bat from the downstairs closet. He hadn't even brought a cell phone to call the police. But none of that stopped him from rushing the intruder whose strange body mutation was harming his daughter.

Tangles of dark hair fell like a fetid veil in front of the strange woman's face so that he only glimpsed her feral eyes in their dark, sunken sockets. But as soon as he rushed toward her, the snake-like appendage released his daughter and retracted into the back of the woman's neck, leaving only a slimy, puckered orifice as evidence of its existence.

Kevin grabbed the woman's shoulders—covered in rank, tattered clothing—intending to pull her away from the crib, shove her into the hall, down the steps and out the front door, in one enraged motion if he could manage it. He'd worry about how she'd gotten into their house later. Right now, his priority was kicking her the hell out.

"Get out!" Kevin yelled at the woman as he pulled her away from the crib.

Her body had seemed frail, almost sickly, with a hunched posture and an enlarged abdomen, but the amount of force required to move her just a few inches surprised him. Before he could adjust his grip and try again, her hands, weirdly long—and clawed!—dug into his chest and shoved him backward, hurling him into the far wall.

He fell on all fours, stunned by the ferocity of her attack and the force of the impact. As he struggled to rise, the strange woman glided forward, an eerie inhuman movement whereby the minimal shifting of her legs belied how far and how fast she had come. With her left hand she grabbed him by the collar of his shirt, hoisted him off the floor and flung him into the corner. Another awkward spill, but this time blood flowed from gashes under his throat, where her claws had slashed his flesh.

Blood dripping down his shirt and staining the beige carpet, he scrambled to an upright position, unsteady on his feet.

She came for him a third time.

He sidestepped, stumbling away from her—but not fast enough—and grabbed the windowsill for support.

Once again, she clutched his throat in her left hand.

"Call the—!" he gasped. "Call the police!"

But this time, she didn't toss him aside. She held him still as her right hand ripped into his abdomen, pushing through the momentary resistance of skin and muscle to bore deep into his gut. As her arm burrowed deeper, her claws ripping and pulling, her unkempt hair shifted across her face, exposing her dark, sunken eyes. And they reminded him of a shark's eyes, black and merciless and almost alien.

A moment later she noticed him staring in horror at her face and eyes and she shrieked in rage, releasing the hand that had clutched his throat. But her grip had been the only thing supporting his weight. His legs felt numb and lifeless.

Her clawed left hand darted toward his face, toward his own eyes.

In a frozen moment, he saw Noelle, fully awake and staring in his direction, crying—how long had she been crying?— at the top of her lungs. And he realized his daughter was watching him die—watching his brutal murder. And after he was gone, the clawed woman with the snake-like mutation in her neck would return to his baby to finish whatever the hell she had started. Melissa couldn't stop her. The police would never arrive in time.

Then that moment shattered and he got to his feet, grabbed the demonic woman's arms and hurled himself and her—using her own force against her as she reached for his eyes—backward against the bedroom window. Their combined weight broke the glass and he continued to clutch the intruder against him in a literal death grip until gravity came to his rescue and they both tumbled from the second-story room toward the unforgiving sidewalk below.

Kevin had already begun to feel his hold on consciousness slipping before plunging out the window. The fading of the light had finally blunted the searing pain coursing through his midsection. All he'd needed was a last burst of adrenaline after seeing Noelle helpless in her crib to give him the strength to save her from imminent danger.

Grimacing as he plummeted to the ground, locked in a fatal embrace with the hideous woman, he strained to speak one final thought. He tried to say, *Taking you with me, bitch!* Instead, in a harsh whisper filled with pain, he managed to utter a single word before the back of his skull split open on the sidewalk. "…you…"

Once again he was too late. As he spoke, the woman vanished. And his hands clutched only air.

Lying on the sidewalk in a spreading pool of his own blood, he welcomed the numbing tide of darkness that lapped over him and pulled him under. As his heartbeat slowed, fading toward stillness, he sank deeper into its embrace. His last thoughts were gratitude that his sacrifice had saved his daughter's life.

At least he hadn't died for noth…

TWENTY-THREE

When Castiel heard Sam take the call from a worried Dr. Hartwell, his first thought was that Chloe Sikes was in danger. As the call progressed, with no mention of any particular patient in distress, least of all Chloe, Castiel couldn't shake the sense that the young woman might need his help. At that first meeting, he'd been struck by the uncanny physical resemblance between Chloe and Claire as well as their similar fashion sense, although Chloe's jeans were made with an elasticated waistline. Chloe lacked Claire's left-side braids in her blond hair, but she wore it back with a hairclip, revealing a collection of ear piercings reminiscent of Claire's.

Though the similarities went beyond height, build and eye color, Chloe's demeanor was, understandably, less troubled than Claire's, despite her teenaged pregnancy. Claire remained on her own, having lost her father, whose body Castiel inhabited alone now that Jimmy Novak's soul had departed, and having lost touch with her troubled mother. Chloe, on the other hand, had a support system in place with both parents. She was not alone and adrift in the world, at the mercy of strangers. Nevertheless, she had lost the father of her unborn child, a young man who may have shared a life with her. She may not have come to terms with that loss. Castiel doubted she could have. And the loss would only become more pronounced when her baby was born. In addition, Aidan's murderer remained on the loose and extremely dangerous with an unknown agenda. Chloe hadn't been a direct target yet; only men had been murdered so far. But that could change at any moment. They had no way of knowing where the killer would strike next.

Castiel drove to Lovering Maternity Center at a few miles above the posted speed limit in his gold Lincoln. Though he liked the car for what it was, sometimes his patience was tested by the need to cross every mile from one destination to the next. If he had his full Grace, he could have dropped in on Dr. Hartwell in seconds to satisfy his curiosity and allay his worry. For now and possibly until the end, he remained at the whim of stop signs and traffic lights and other drivers.

With a physical sense of relief, he parked the Lincoln in the LMC parking lot and hurried inside the lobby, assuring the seated receptionist Dr. Hartwell was expecting him and that he knew the way to her 321 North office. Compared to the stop-and-go drive to LMC, the wait for the elevator was a minor inconvenience.

On the ride up, he wondered about Claire again, knowing he would sense her if she needed him or, less likely, prayed to him. Okay, not likely at all. But he acknowledged the loopholes in that need for contact, desperate or surprise situations where she wouldn't have time to reach out to him. And even if he did hear her call, he couldn't simply pop in and help her. He had logistics to consider. He'd have to drive to her location or hop on a plane, depending on how far away she was at any given moment. Most likely she would be out of reach for hours, possibly an entire day or longer.

Now he seemed to have added Chloe to his list of concerns. She faced a more immediate threat and would not reach out to him personally, even if she were in danger. He wouldn't know until after the fact. And by then it might be too late to save her.

He stepped off the elevator and strode purposely toward Dr. Hartwell's office. His only recourse, until they figured out who or what was targeting the citizens of Braden Heights, was to stay as informed as possible about potential threats, whether signs, portents or gut feelings. Dr. Hartwell's concerned call possibly fell into the last category. And yet, at this point in the investigation, any lead was potentially an important one.

A young couple stepped out of Dr. Hartwell's suite, talking softly. The woman was about six months pregnant; her husband looked nine months anxious. Castiel wondered if fathers-to-be were so nervous because the process of carrying and delivering a baby was completely out of their control. They became helpless bystanders to one of the most important days in the couple's life. The woman suffered all the discomfort and examinations and the pains of childbirth while the man got off relatively scot-free, relegated to the role of supportive coach. Instead of feeling relief, the man suffered guilt and worry in his secondary role. Or maybe there was more to it than that. Castiel would never know.

Slipping past the departing couple, he entered Dr. Hartwell's suite and made a beeline to the reception desk, where the nurse-slash-receptionist transcribed scribbled patient updates from pages in a manila folder to a computer application.

"Special Agent Collins, here to see Dr. Hartwell."

Startled, the woman looked up at him. "Oh—yes, Agent Collins! She's expecting you."

Dr. Hartwell peeked out of her office, saw him and approached, wearing a fresh white lab coat with "Hartwell" stitched in dark blue letters over the right breast pocket. "Thank you for coming, Agent Collins."

"No problem," Castiel replied. "You said—Agent Rutherford told me you had something to show us, possibly related to the Aidan Dufford case." For some reason, Castiel didn't want her to think he'd been eavesdropping on their phone conversation. Seemed better—more professional—to say he'd been briefed about the situation by Sam.

"Well, I'm not sure if it's directly related to Aidan's… death, but it certainly is weird, in a very troubling way."

"Does it involve Cla—Chloe Sikes?"

"No, not directly," Dr. Hartwell said. "Why do you ask?"

"Just curious," Castiel said quickly. "We met her here after Aidan's death."

"Right."

"How is she, Doctor?" Castiel asked. "I imagine this has been difficult for her."

"You do realize I'm bound by doctor–patient confidentiality?"

"Of course, I just wondered if…" Castiel cleared his throat. "She reminds me of the daughter of a close friend."

With an understanding smile, Dr. Hartwell placed a hand on his elbow and directed him away from the reception desk until they stood just inside the door to the suite. Lowering her voice, she said, "Physically, Chloe is fine. Mentally? Psychologically? I'm not qualified to give a conclusive diagnosis. But I'm sure it is an emotionally devastating time for her, especially considering how near she is to her due date. Fortunately, her parents have been supportive throughout the process."

"Good," Castiel said. "We don't know if whoever killed Aidan and the other men will target the pregnant women left behind. I'm glad Chloe has people close who care about her."

"You needn't worry on that account."

"About that phone call…?"

"Right," Dr. Hartwell said. "It concerns another patient of mine. I believe you bumped into the couple on your way out, Denise and Gary Atherton. Denise had her baby, a boy, and all three of them were asleep in her birthing room when one of the night nurses, Maggie O'Brien, checked in on them."

"What happened?" Castiel asked, concerned, wondering how the doctor remained so calm if Gary Atherton had been eviscerated in one of her patient rooms.

"Nurse O'Brien saw something so strange and frightening, she screamed," Dr. Hartwell said. She held up her hands to forestall any questions. "Before you say anything, I must stress that Nurse O'Brien is the only one who saw this... person in the birthing room. Her scream woke the Athertons and when she turned on the light nobody else was in the room and there was no sign of an intruder. Except..."

"Yes?"

Dr. Hartwell seemed to fidget, almost as if she thought she'd said too much already. She shoved both hands into the pockets of her lab coat and heaved a sigh. "This is where it gets weird..."

Castiel strode from the lobby of Lovering Maternity Center, out from under the porte cochère emblazoned with its cursive LMC, to where he'd parked his Lincoln. He had another impatient drive ahead of him, but as he pulled out of the parking lot, he reached into his pocket. He could pass along the information he'd been given long before he physically arrived at the Holcomb house. He speed-dialed Dean's phone number.

"Cass? What've you got?"

"Dean, where are you?"

"Back at the Holcombs," Dean said. "Just walked in the door."

"Is Sam there?"

"Both here."

"Put me on speaker," Castiel said. "You should both hear this."

"Right," Dean said. "Hold on."

Castiel heard Dean tell Sam to follow him into the kitchen. Anticipating the nature of the information Castiel might have for them, Dean naturally didn't want the Holcombs to hear what he had discovered, at least not without a filter. The angel had to admit Dean's circumspection was, in this instance, a good call.

Castiel wouldn't want anyone who lacked the background and experience of a hunter to hear what he'd learned.

TWENTY-FOUR

"All right, Cass," Dean said. "Spill."

Castiel told them about Maggie O'Brien, a night nurse at LMC who witnessed an intruder in the Atherton birthing room the previous night, standing over the bed where mother and baby slept. Though the room was dark, the nurse described the intruder as a woman based on general build and her long straggly hair. The fact that an intruder had snuck into the Atherton room was unsettling enough, but the nurse had screamed in fright when she noticed the long appendage extending from the nape of the intruder's neck to the back of the sleeping infant's neck. "But after Nurse O'Brien screamed and turned on the lights, the intruder disappeared."

"Disappeared?" Sam repeated.

"When first discovered, she retreated to the darkest corner of the room. Then, before the lights came on, she vanished, as if she'd never been there."

"Anyone else see this intruder?" Dean wondered. He had to

at least consider the possibility of an unreliable witness. But his years as a hunter left him more inclined to give anyone the benefit of the doubt when it came to unbelievable stories.

"Only the nurse," Castiel said. "Other nurses heard her scream and checked the room. They found no trace of the intruder. Nurse O'Brien began to doubt what she'd seen."

"Understandable," Sam said. "But there's more to this, right?"

"Dr. Hartwell talked to the nurse after the incident," Castiel said. "She decided to examine the child. More specifically, the infant's neck."

"And?" Dean prodded.

"Dr. Hartwell discovered slight redness at the base of the infant's neck and a tiny ring of puncture wounds. She intended to run tests on these wounds, but within a few hours they had vanished and the skin appeared normal."

"Let me guess," Dean said. "Doctor thinks she imagined the whole thing, right? Power of suggestion and so on?"

"She might have," Castiel said. "If not for the picture she took with her cell phone."

"She has a photo?" Sam asked, intrigued.

"Yes, she showed me," Castiel said. "In the image, the wound looks like a rash, but some of the small punctures are clearly visible. I have a copy."

A photo would be their first solid piece of evidence about who or what was involved in the murders. Assuming the hospital intruder was also responsible for the four murders. Dean wondered if someone else took out the babies' fathers to leave the mother and infant vulnerable to the hospital intruder. "What about Gary Atherton?" Dean asked.

"Untouched," Castiel said. "The intruder targeted only the baby."

"At least until she was interrupted," Sam said.

Good point, Dean thought. *Who knows what she would have done if the nurse hadn't interrupted her—doing what?—with the baby?* They had no idea what the neck connection meant, for the baby or the intruder. A mental link? A transfer of... something? *A feeding?*

"How's the baby now?"

"Fine, according to Dr. Hartwell," Castiel said. "The baby was more upset by the nurse's scream than by anything else that happened that night. Hartwell's requested some lab work."

"All right, Cass," Dean said. "We'll catch you up later."

Dean ended the call and they walked into the living room where Sally sat with her brother Ramon and her grandmother, looking at them expectantly. He launched into a rundown on what Keating had told him about five missing pregnant women from the early sixties, back when Braden Heights was called Larkin's Korner.

"That's it," Mary said, attempting to snap her fingers, but then merely shook her hand up and down for emphasis, index finger pointed at Sam. "The name of the town I couldn't remember."

"No wonder you couldn't find it on a map, Grandma Mary," Ramon said. "It no longer exists!"

"Larkin's Korner is Braden Heights now," Sally said, letting the revelation sink in.

"Where your great grandaunt Malaya moved with her

American G.I., and also where she died in childbirth."

"So Malaya died here," Sally said and shivered. "In this town."

"I don't know the exact address," the old woman said. She looked up at Sam. "But it must have been close, right?"

Sam nodded. "Braden Heights isn't that big."

"This Malaya," Dean asked the old woman, recalling the beginning of Arthur Keating's story about the Larkin family leaving in disgrace. "Any chance she married a doctor? Name of Nodd?"

"Dr. Calvin Nodd," Mary said, surprised. "How did you know?"

"She married into a prominent family, owned a lot of land here," Dean said. "Nodd's mother was a Ruth Larkin. The town was named after the Larkin family. The heirs have been selling off the last of the lots."

"Where are they?" Sam asked.

"They pulled up stakes, headed for Europe, haven't been seen around here since," Dean said. "After Nodd's daughter skipped town, the not-so-good doctor snapped. Psychotic break. PTSD. Something. Nearly killed a patient during childbirth."

"Calvin did this?" Mary asked, stunned. "I never knew. After Malaya died we lost touch with him. Except for the few pictures of Riza he sent us before she ran away. After that, nothing. We wrote him, but received no answer. We respected his silence, to grieve in his own way. Sadly, with Malaya and Riza gone, nothing remained to connect us... except painful memories." Remorseful, she shook her head. "Maybe we should have tried harder to reach out to him."

"What happened to Nodd?" Sam asked Dean.

"Larkin family bought off the witnesses," Dean said. "He never stood trial. Bolted. Never heard from again."

"Lot of that going around," Sam mused.

Distracted during the conversation between the Winchesters and Mary, Sally became more agitated, lost in disturbing thoughts and connections. "If Malaya died here… and now Dave, over fifty years later." Her face grew taut in dawning horror, at the unlikelihood of mere coincidence. She looked down at her hands, both shaking uncontrollably, and pressed them to her chest. Ramon put his arm around her shoulder in an attempt to comfort her. "It doesn't make any sense."

Rising from her seat, her grandmother said, "Let me make you some tea, dear."

Sally said softly, "I need a shot of whiskey."

"Not in your condition, Dalisay!"

Sally gasped and dropped her hands to her lower abdomen, as if somehow, in all the revelations about Malaya's death and the runaway pregnant women, she'd forgotten she herself was pregnant. And maybe she had. But considering what had come to light, the fact that she was expecting had taken on a sinister aspect.

She looked at the Winchesters, her eyes darting feverishly back and forth between them. "Somebody *please* tell me what the hell is going on!"

"We don't know—yet," Sam said.

"But we're working on it," Dean assured her.

Hard to believe Malaya's death during childbirth and

the five young missing pregnant women from the early sixties—six if you counted Riza herself—were not somehow connected to what was happening in Braden Heights today. But what was the connection? Malaya's death had resulted from hemorrhaging, an apparent accidental death during a common medical procedure. And the missing women had run off to escape their circumstances during a local recession. Everything up to that point, Dean could rationalize. But none of those missing women were heard from again, as if they'd dropped off the face of the earth. And the first Braden Heights murder occurred when the Holcombs came to town, more specifically when Sally Holcomb arrived. And Sally had a familial connection to the Larkin family, which had practically owned the town when Malaya died and those women went missing.

Dean's cell phone rang. "Cordero," he told Sam after checking the display. "Agent Banks."

"Thought you'd want to know," Cordero said. "We got another one."

"Another murder?" Dean said, looking to Sam, who only heard his side of the conversation. "Same M.O.?"

"Somewhat," Cordero said. "Opposite Green situation. Gutted, but kept his eyes. And apparently this vic fought back. Not that it helped."

Dean took down the address. "On our way."

TWENTY-FIVE

While Dean drove the Impala to the Barrows address, Sam called Castiel to give him the latest development. The angel's gold Lincoln arrived less than two minutes after Dean parked the Impala several houses away from the crime scene. The BHPD had cordoned off nearly half the suburban block with a combination of police cruisers and yellow crime scene tape. Patrol officers checked IDs of residents before allowing them to pass through, while turning away random gawkers out for a closer look. But no one left. They merely gathered beyond the taped border, each asking and answering questions, with facts in short supply. Everyone seemed to agree that somebody had fallen out a second-story window. Comments from neighbors standing with bystanders supplied the victim's name in short order.

Dean flashed his FBI ID at the nearest patrol officer guarding the perimeter and was waved through, along with Sam and Castiel. Several steps inside the police line, Dean heard a woman whispering behind him, unnaturally close, her words unintelligible. Unnerved, he looked over his shoulder but saw only the people gathering at the police tape. Dismissing the odd sound, he looked away and caught movement at the periphery of his vision, a woman in a red dress walking briskly on the far side of the street. Briefly, she turned toward him, and his jaw dropped in recognition.

"Lisa?"

"Dean?" Sam said, stopping beside him.

"Hold on," Dean said, raising a hand to stop his brother or Castiel from following him as he strode across the street to investigate. He could've sworn he'd seen Lisa Braeden, but he'd looked away for a moment and lost track of her. *Why would she be here?* Dean wondered. She lived in Indiana, but Cicero was nearly two hundred miles away. And she wouldn't be looking for him. Even if Castiel hadn't wiped her memories of Dean at his request, she'd have no way of knowing he'd come to Braden Heights.

He caught a flash of dark movement shifting behind the trunk of a red maple, the roots of which had raised two sections of sidewalk into an inverted V, and he veered toward the tree. A moment later, he caught himself nervously rubbing his right forearm, where he bore the Mark. Stepping over the curb, he glanced around the tree, expecting to see someone who resembled Lisa rather than Lisa herself, but no one was there. A lost-dog flyer stapled to the tree trunk flapped in the breeze and for a second Dean imagined it sounded like a whispering voice. Had the whole episode been a vision triggered by the Mark? Best to put it out of his mind. He was in control. Not the other way around.

Shaking his head, he returned to the others.

Sam looked around, checking no one was within earshot. "Dean? What was that all about?"

"Nothing," Dean replied dismissively, making sure his left hand didn't stray again to the Mark. Sam already worried too much about the Mark's effect on him. No need to feed that fire. And that meant no mention of hallucinating Lisa. "Thought I saw… someone sneaking around."

"And?"

"Maybe a witness," Dean explained, spreading his arms. "Lost her. Probably a curious neighbor. Ducked inside her house when she saw me coming."

Sam seemed unconvinced by Dean's explanation, but Dean ignored the lingering doubt in his brother's gaze, and resumed his path to the crime scene.

Due to limited parking, several emergency vehicles clogged the street at various angles, some obstructing driveways, others double-parked. The trio weaved their way through police cruisers, the medical examiner's SUV, a black crime scene unit van and a white EMT van, parked closest to the Barrows residence.

At the front door, Assistant Chief Cordero talked to a sobbing woman in her mid to late thirties. An older woman holding a crying infant stood on her right, an older man to her left. The wife's parents, Dean guessed, based on the resemblance between the two women.

Looking up, Dean saw bright yellow curtains fluttering through a shattered window. He noticed a few splashes of red, equally bright, on the flapping material. Beneath the window, on the sidewalk below, four police officers stood in a loose circle, intentionally obstructing the view of a supine corpse lying in a pool of congealing blood.

Within the ring of cops, the medical examiner—who'd been squatting next to the body—stood up with a grunt of discomfort and tugged off a pair of blue latex gloves, signaling the end of his official on-scene examination of the body.

Once again, Dean flashed his fake ID, this time to the cop with a military style crew-cut standing nearest the remains of Kevin Barrows. The man nodded, raising no objection when Dean, Sam and Castiel moved forward to examine the body.

Two pools of blood formed a grim solid figure eight under the corpse, the top half by the head, where the skull had split open on impact, and another larger circle around the abdomen which had been ripped open, through shredded clothes, to reveal the slashed devastation of the man's liver, stomach and intestines. Besides the intact eyes, which seemed to stare at everything and nothing at once, something else seemed at odds with the other victims Dean had examined. Breathing through his mouth to avoid the stench of human fecal matter, Dean leaned forward. "This is different."

"You noticed, huh?" Dr. Trumble, the medical examiner said, impressed.

"Abandoned your animal attack theory?"

"Not at all," Trumble said, annoyed once again. "Clearly these slash marks were inflicted by animal claws. The difference you've noticed is the organs."

Sam leaned forward, wrinkling his nose as he caught a whiff from the perforated bowel. "They're slashed too."

"They're present," Castiel said. "All the organs. And intestines."

"Give the man a prize," Trumble said. "Apparently, the fall from the second-story window frightened the animal enough that it ran off without consuming any of the exposed flesh or organs." He leaned over, pointing. "Note the transverse colon. Pulled completely out of the abdominal cavity, yet despite significant trauma, there are no bite marks or missing pieces." He chuckled and, with a bit of gallows humor, said, "*Consummatio interruptus,* you might say."

"Pretty sure none of us would say that, Doc," Dean replied.

Castiel glanced up at the sobbing wife and crying infant then looked back at Trumble. "I find nothing about this situation amusing."

With a dismissive wave before he walked away from them, the medical examiner said, "Give it time, agent man. Give it time."

Trumble signaled for one of the EMTs hovering nearby. Turning his back to the Barrows widow, he instructed the young man to fetch a body bag and a gurney to take the corpse to the morgue. With the help of a female EMT, the first one wheeled the gurney from their van to a position beside the body. The widow looked on in shock, her eyes impossibly wide as she pressed a hand to her mouth. She shook her head, turned and retreated into the house. Her mother said something to Cordero before following her daughter inside. The wife's father rubbed his grizzled jaw as he stared across the street without seeming to focus on anything in particular. Dean thought maybe the older man needed to look anywhere but at the body the EMTs were settling into the unzipped body bag.

Sam had stood with his back to the corpse, but glanced down at the sound of the zipper sealing the ravaged remains of Kevin Barrows inside. The EMTs gripped the bag by its side straps and, on the count of three, transferred it to the lowered gurney.

"We need to find out what the wife knows," Sam said and strode toward the front door.

Dean and Castiel followed in his wake.

Sam listened as Cordero briefed him on Melissa Barrows' account of the attack, but was determined to talk to the woman himself. Though she was in a fragile state at the moment, he needed to question her while her memory of the incident was fresh. Unfortunately, that meant the emotions were still raw. But any little detail might give them the clue they needed to stop the attacker. He had to focus on that for now.

Melissa had retreated into the kitchen, staring out the window at the backyard while her mother stood nearby holding baby Noelle, who had stopped crying but fidgeted in the older woman's arms.

Dean and Castiel had followed him inside the house but hung back beyond the archway into the kitchen, giving both women some space.

Sam stepped forward. "Mrs. Barrows, I'm Special Agent Rutherford, with the FBI," he said. "I'm sorry for your loss."

Without turning to face him, she plucked several tissues

from a cardboard box on the table and dabbed her eyes with them. She nodded slightly and said softly, "Thank you."

"I'd like to ask you a few questions."

Her mother heaved a frustrated sigh. "Everyone has a thousand questions," she said. "My daughter just lost her husband! Can't you see she's grieving?"

"I know, ma'am," Sam said. "But we're trying to catch whoever did this."

"Well, look around," she said bitterly. "He's certainly not here!"

"She," Melissa Barrows said softly. "The attacker was a woman."

"Mrs. Barrows?" Sam said, edging around the table in an attempt to make eye contact. "I was told you didn't see the attacker."

"No."

"You heard her, then?"

"No," Melissa said, sniffling. She swiped at her nose, as if she were annoyed at herself. "Static."

Confused, Sam canted his head. Though convinced she had information he needed, he had to tread lightly. She'd suffered a devastating loss and might shut him down at any moment if the situation became overwhelming for her. "You heard static?"

"On the baby monitor," she said. "After Kevin went up to the nursery. I had put Noelle down, finally gotten her to sleep. I was exhausted. And it was his turn, when we heard her. Wasn't much... just a little cry." She held her thumb and index finger an inch apart as a way of indicating brevity.

"But we worried about every little thing. Double-checked and triple-checked. We obsessed about her safety because it took so long to bring her into our lives. One of us had to check, don't you see?" She fought a sob, pressing the wad of tissues to her mouth. "It could have been me," she said. "Then maybe Kevin would... would still be here."

"You don't know that, Melissa," her mother said. "He— she could have come after him next. Kevin sacrificed himself to save you and this precious little girl."

"I know... I know he did," Melissa said. "I called the police but they... it was over before they got here."

"You heard Noelle cry on the baby monitor and Kevin went up to investigate?"

Melissa nodded. "But once he entered the nursery, the monitor... the sounds changed. Filled with static. I heard him yell and then lots of static."

"If you didn't hear her or see her upstairs or after—the fall," Sam said, "how do you know it was a woman?"

"Because, when Kevin yelled, he said, 'Get away from her, you freaky bitch!'" She finally turned around to stare at Sam, clutching the back of the nearest kitchen chair for support, almost as if she dared him to dispute her conclusion. "Would he say something like that if it wasn't a woman?"

"No," Sam said, but thought it only proved that Kevin believed it was a woman. Appearances, especially in a hunter's line of work, could be deceiving. "Did you hear him say anything else?"

"Not really," she said. "With all the static, I could hear him better from the stairwell, telling me to call the police.

He fought with her… Kevin wasn't a small man. He played college football. But she… she slammed him into the wall—so hard the house shook. And she never made a sound."

"Do you have any idea how this woman could have gotten into your home?"

Melissa shook her head. "We were home all day," she said. "With a newborn, we don't get out much. I never saw any sign of an intruder."

"You need to find this woman before she tries to steal another baby," Melissa's mother said. "Whoever she is, she's a menace. And a murderer."

"Why do you think she came to steal the child?" Castiel asked.

The woman startled, as if she'd forgotten Dean and Castiel stood a few feet away.

"Isn't it obvious?" she said. "Kevin didn't find her rooting through a jewelry box or looking for a wall safe. She was sneaking around in the damn nursery."

Castiel came forward while the woman talked and took advantage of his proximity to examine the fussing baby. "Beautiful child," he said, smiling.

The older woman returned the smile reflexively, with a grandmother's pride. "She certainly is, aren't you, dear?"

Sam noticed Castiel's gaze shift toward the back of the infant's neck. His smile faded abruptly and he caught Sam's eye. "A word, Agent Rutherford?"

Nodding, Sam excused himself to both women and joined Castiel and Dean in the adjoining room. Castiel had taken out his phone and brought up a photo of another baby. Sam noticed what appeared to be a round rash on the nape of the infant's neck, and closer inspection revealed several tiny puncture wounds, forming a partial circle outlining the rash. They'd already begun to heal by the time Dr. Hartwell had taken the photo.

"I haven't had a chance to send you this image yet," Castiel explained, his voice low enough that neither Melissa nor her mother could hear what he said. "The Barrows child has the same rash and marks on the back of her neck."

"Whoever this woman is," Dean said, "we now know she's responsible for the murders *and* the attack on the Atherton baby."

Before they left, Sam wanted to examine the nursery. Leaning through the archway into the kitchen he asked Melissa if she had any objections to them checking the room.

She shook her head, but added, "You won't find anything. I don't know how she got into the nursery, but she never came out through the door. I stood near the bottom of the stairs while Kevin… while he stopped her. She had to have gone out the window with… when he fell."

Sam led the way up the steps. After Melissa rescued her infant daughter from the nursery, the police had blocked access to the room with an "X" of crime scene tape across the open doorway. From the hallway, they could see indentations where Kevin had been thrown bodily against the drywall, and blood splatter on the floor and curtains. But the crib was across the room. Ducking, Sam stepped through a gap in the tape and crossed the nursery, careful not to step in any blood stains.

He examined the mattress pad and the floor under the crib,

looking for anything the intruder might have left behind—a slimy residue, a broken tooth—but other than a few strands of fine hair, his search proved fruitless. The baby monitor sat on a dresser facing the empty crib.

Sam spread his arms. "So she came here to what? Feed on the baby somehow while both parents were downstairs?"

"But didn't notice the baby monitor," Dean said. "They hear something."

"The father interrupts… whatever she's up to, and she guts him instead?"

"He defended his child," Castiel said. "The woman fought back."

"But he manages to wrestle her out the window," Dean said. "Assuming Melissa's correct and that's how she exited the house."

"So this time," Sam said, "the attacker herself was surprised."

"She must have a trigger," Dean said. "The father was in the house, but instead of attacking and feeding on him, she goes after the baby."

"She attacks the fathers when the mothers are still pregnant," Sam said. "After childbirth, the babies become her target."

"Or she has two options once the baby is born," Dean said.

"Both times she's… attached herself to an infant," Castiel said, "the infant has survived."

"She was interrupted both times," Sam reminded him.

"You assume she's only done this twice," Castiel said ominously. "She may have attached herself to other infants without getting caught in the act."

"You saying she means them no harm?" Dean asked.

"The rash and puncture wounds prove she is harming them," Castiel said. "But somehow those wounds are healed within hours."

"It's a form of concealment," Sam said. "If her visits go undetected, it allows her to return multiple times."

"She kills the men," Dean said. "But we have no idea what her endgame is with the babies."

They descended the stairs, continuing their discussion in lowered voices as they approached the kitchen. Sam turned to Castiel. "Dr. Hartwell found nothing wrong with the Atherton boy, right?"

"Correct," Castiel said. "Other than the rash and punctures that healed by morning. If she hadn't stopped by to hear the nurse's account, she never would have known about them."

"Whatever she's up to, it ain't good," Dean insisted. He lowered his voice further after a quick glance toward the kitchen. "In my book, if a cannibal freak attaches its spine tentacle to a baby's neck, you assume the worst."

Sam returned to the kitchen to find Melissa holding her baby, smiling at the child though her eyes were puffy and red-rimmed from crying. "Excuse me again," Sam said. "I was wondering if Noelle's doctor has stopped by to check on her."

"Not yet," Melissa said, tracing the infant's face with her index finger. "Thank God Kevin stopped that woman before she could hurt my little baby."

"Dr. Hartwell's on her way," Melissa's mother informed

them. "Called her as soon as I heard what happened."

"Good," Sam said. "I'm familiar with Dr. Hartwell."

Since Hartwell had already seen the rash and punctures on the Atherton baby, she might have some insight on how Noelle's wounds compared. In both incidents, it appeared that the mystery woman hadn't had much time to harm either child. Castiel was correct to suggest other attacks could have happened without anyone's knowledge, but Sam wondered how both babies would have fared if the woman hadn't been interrupted.

Sam heard activity at the front door.

Melissa's father ushered in Dr. Vanessa Hartwell. "I'm so sorry about Kevin," she said as she walked purposely toward the kitchen with him. "They have to stop this person." She spotted the baby. "But my little patient is okay?"

"She's upset," Melissa's father said. "But that's natural, I guess."

Castiel caught the OB/GYN by the arm and whispered in her ear.

She nodded, her features shifting from personal sympathy to professional concern. "Thanks. I'll check."

Sam left the kitchen after Hartwell entered. She placed her medical bag on the kitchen table, then stood beside Melissa as she began a cursory visual inspection of Noelle. She placed a finger at the top of the child's onesie and gently pulled it down enough to examine the nape of the baby's neck. She looked up toward Castiel and nodded. A moment later, Melissa passed the infant into Dr. Hartwell's arms.

"She's fine, isn't she, Dr. Hartwell?"

"I think she's incredible," Dr. Hartwell said, smiling at the baby. "Let's have a look…"

Unless the doctor found something other than the fading rash and puncture wounds, Sam decided they'd learn nothing more from Melissa and her child. He led the way out to the front walk.

Overhead lights flashing but silent, the EMT van left the scene with the remains of Kevin Barrows. Trumble wrapped up a final conversation with Cordero, climbed into his dark SUV and left in the same direction as the van. The patrol officers who had stood guard over the body had returned to the street, now grouped by one of the patrol cars, talking among themselves.

Sam turned to Dean and Castiel. "This is connected to Nodd and those disappearances in the sixties," he said. "Sally's arrival in this town must have triggered something that's been dormant until now."

"Sally and Riza are related by blood," Dean said. "Maybe Riza came back when Sally moved here."

"Maybe Riza never left," Sam said, although he couldn't imagine how she could have stayed hidden in town all these years. With her boyfriend and a child in tow? She could have changed her appearance, assumed a false identity. Even so… "She would be seventy years old now."

"Her child would be in his or her fifties," Castiel said.

"Nobody in town, not even the old-timers, would recognize that child," Dean said. "He or she could have come back any time, unnoticed."

The front door opened and Dr. Hartwell hurried outside.

Sam caught her attention. "Something wrong with Noelle?"

"She seems fine, but I'm ordering a comprehensive metabolic panel, to be sure," she said. "My service just called—twice in two minutes. Just when I think nothing else strange can happen…"

"More strange?" Dean asked.

"Two of my patients have gone into premature labor," she said. "I believe you've spoken with both of them in relation to these attacks. Olivia Krum and Chloe Sikes."

As she strode to a silver Lexus GS hybrid parked beyond the police perimeter and drove away, Sam frowned. One more weird coincidence in a string of unlikely coincidences involving pregnant women in Braden Heights dating back to the early sixties. Back then pregnant women went missing, never to be heard from again, and now the fathers of their children were being murdered while the newborns themselves had become prey.

TWENTY-SIX

As Dean and Castiel wove through the remaining emergency vehicles and edged their way past the crowd gathered at the edge of the crime scene tape, Sam veered off to speak with Assistant Chief Cordero. He waited while Cordero sent some of his patrol cops on their way, keeping a few around to maintain order while the crime scene unit wrapped up.

Once Sam had Cordero's full attention, he said, "Getting out of the office more than usual these days?"

"Only wish it were under better circumstances," Cordero said. "Chasing a phantom serial murderer has everyone rattled."

"Trumble's sticking with his wild animal attack theory," Sam said.

"He's like a dog with a bone," Cordero replied, shaking his head. "But until one of us proves the other wrong, we'll keep telling the press these are suspected animal attacks. At this point, I'd rather have the public fearful than panicked. Lesser of two evils, basically. I assume you didn't stop by just to check the status of our public relations efforts."

"Any eyewitnesses?"

"To the attack?" Cordero shook his head. "Melissa was downstairs. Heard the commotion; didn't see squat."

"To the fall," Sam said, pointing toward the broken second-story window. "Neighbors outside see anything? Passing motorists?"

"What's it take to fall from that height?" Cordero asked. "A second? Maybe less?" Again, he shook his head. "Had a few officers canvass the street. Nobody saw him fall. Several heard the crash, saw the aftermath."

"But no wild animal sightings?"

"Not one," Cordero said. "All anybody saw was that poor bastard lying on the sidewalk with a cracked skull and his guts ripped open. Unfortunately. Nightmare fuel."

"Melissa didn't see the intruder come out of the nursery," Sam said. "And nobody saw the woman fall from the window."

"Say Barrows broke her fall so she's not hurt much. She'd only need a few seconds to duck between houses, cross a backyard. Not unreasonable."

"But unlikely."

"Maybe so," Cordero said. "But that's our working theory. Unless you got a better one…?"

I could suggest a few, Sam thought, *but you'd never believe me.* "Not yet."

Unwilling to share his own speculations with Cordero, Sam left the marked crime scene area, ducking under the police tape in one of the less crowded areas. Almost half the gawkers had departed when the EMT van took Barrows' corpse to the morgue. As the minutes ticked by with no further developments, others began to disperse, their morbid curiosity mostly unsatisfied. Sam noticed a woman in a red dress, standing by herself on the far side of the street. As he looked toward her, she returned his gaze and a jolt of recognition startled him.

"Amelia?" he whispered.

Amelia Richardson? Here? Why...?

He started walking to her, about to call out, to ask her what she was doing in Braden Heights—

An elderly couple crossed his path. He'd been so distracted by the sight of his old flame, he'd nearly run into them. "Excuse me," he said, flashing a friendly and, he hoped, apologetic smile for almost bowling them over in his haste.

"Quite all right, young man," the woman said. "Old as we are, you'd think we'd look both ways before crossing—well, walking down the middle of the street."

Sam smiled politely at her attempt at humor.

After they passed him, he looked up, Amelia's name again on his lips. But this time he didn't say it aloud. She was gone. He looked left and right.

How far could she have gone?

The crowd had thinned considerably, so she'd definitely stand out in that red dress, but he couldn't locate her. For a split-second, he glimpsed an older, hunched woman who looked like she'd never been exposed to the sun, drifting behind several onlookers, but his gaze swept past her, seeking the red dress, and when he looked back the other way, the old woman had disappeared as well. If one more person dropped out of view as suddenly, he'd begin to suspect open manhole covers lined the street.

After a slow 360 turn came up empty, he had to chalk the sighting up to a trick of his imagination. Stress induced? Lack of sleep? Had he been thinking about Amelia? They'd gotten pretty serious—at least until she found out her husband hadn't been killed overseas. But Sam's relationship with her had been a while ago. He'd put it behind him. At least he'd thought he had…

He worried about Dean and his Mark-induced visions. So now wasn't a great time for both Winchester brothers to get distracted by hallucinations. He shook off the incident and strode toward the Impala.

Fortunately, Dean had been talking with Castiel and hadn't seen Sam bumbling around, looking confused, so he had no need to explain himself. As Sam approached the front passenger door, Castiel climbed into his Lincoln and made a U-turn.

Before Dean climbed into the driver's seat he looked across the roof of the car at Sam. "Ready?"

"Cass in a rush?"

"Volunteered to check on Chloe and Olivia," Dean said. "They're probably safe for now. At least until the babies are born. Tentacle Tessa doesn't target pregnant women."

Dean slipped into the Impala and started the engine. As soon as it roared to life, Dean flipped through the town's rock stations, settling on CCR's "Who'll Stop the Rain."

After one last glimpse back to where he thought he'd seen Amelia, Sam opened the passenger side door and climbed in. "She's branching out, Dean," he said. "First the boyfriends and husbands of the pregnant women. Now the babies. We don't know what's next."

"So let's find out."

Back at the motel, Dean flopped on his bed, grumbling about the lumpy mattress as he stared at the ceiling. Sam opened his laptop and, with unmoving fingers resting on the keyboard, stared at the screen. Not a productive start by any means. *Maybe Castiel had the right idea,* Sam thought. *At least he has a clear task.*

Without the crutch of the bunker's vast library of hunter lore, they had to go about the hunt the old-fashioned way. They had multiple victims, a few clues, and a definite, if still emerging pattern.

As tempting as it was to cast suspicion on Riza Nodd's illegitimate adult child, whoever he or she might be, they couldn't ignore all the evidence pointing to a supernatural entity. A human may have set the monster on its murderous course, but the monster was what they needed to stop. And to stop it, they needed to identify it and learn its weaknesses.

Problem was, monsters weren't listed in the phone book, in print or online. But if the murders were triggered by Sally's arrival in Braden Heights because of her relationship to the Larkin family, then maybe that was where he had to start. He took out a pen and legal pad and started making notes on property records and sales dating back from when the town was called Larkin's Korner to the present day. Finally, he pushed the laptop aside as he pored over those notes.

"Mind if I use that?" Dean asked, indicating the laptop.

"Go ahead," Sam said.

"I have an idea," Dean said, turning the computer around to face him and opening the web browser. After a few minutes, he seemed engrossed in his search.

"So the Larkin heirs are in London," Sam said. "One parcel of untended farmland recently sold to a developer building single family homes, currently under construction as... Coventry Crossing. Another recent sale was for a lot with a farmhouse and barn. From the photo I saw, they were in bad shape. That land is adjacent to the Stanton Fertility Clinic. Plans are to raze the farmhouse and barn."

"Stanton," Dean repeated. "That's next to LMC. Where we met Chloe Sikes."

"Right," Sam said. "We drove by the construction."

"For the expanded parking lot," Dean said.

"Before we talked to Melissa," Sam said, "Cordero mentioned the Barrows used Stanton for their IVF cycles."

"Think I got something, Sammy," Dean said.

"What?"

"Checked into a Philippines angle," Dean said. "Since Calvin Nodd met Malaya there before they came to Nodd's hometown."

"Right," Sam said, curious.

"Take a look," Dean said, turning the laptop around again to face Sam. "It talks about disembowelments, sucking out eyeballs."

Sam set down his notes and scanned the browser windows Dean had opened. "There's information here about a pontianak... and some overlapping stuff about a langsuir.

Created when a woman dies in childbirth." He looked up at Dean. "Like Malaya?"

"Keep reading."

"Preys on men," Sam read from the screen. "That fits… Sucks out the eyeballs if you stare at it directly… This also talks about the langsuir sucking the blood of infants, like a tiny vampire. You know she's nearby if you hear a crying baby or smell a pleasant aroma."

"Like fresh baked pies?" Dean wondered aloud, as if the tradeoff would be worth the inconvenience of a subsequent disembowelment.

"She can appear… as a beautiful woman," Sam read and paused.

"I missed that," Dean said, craning his neck for a better view of the screen. "Any beautiful woman?"

Sam's mind jumped back to the Barrows crime scene. He thought he'd seen Amelia when there was no possible reason for her to be in Braden Heights. But later, he'd seen a hunched woman dressed in black slip into the crowd and disappear. Was that second sighting closer to her true appearance? And had she been watching them at the scene? A predator recognizing a hunter? Or like an arsonist who hangs around to watch his handiwork?

Was it too late to confess his hallucination of Amelia? If he told Dean now, he'd have to admit concealing it previously. And they'd made an effort to stop keeping secrets from each other. The information—the pontianak's ability—was out there now. Dean would know to look for it. Maybe that was good enough.

"Doesn't say," Sam told him. "Probably. But, uh, it also

says she can separate her head from her body."

"Saw the illustration," Dean said. "Raises the freaky quotient. So how do we gank it?"

Sam scrolled down, skimming the information in both windows. "Putting a nail in the hole in her neck puts her down."

"Guess that's the tentacle hole."

"But if you remove the nail, she's back in business," Sam said. "Like it only puts her to sleep or into some sort of supernatural coma. But she's scared of thorns and sharp objects."

"Forget thorns," Dean said. "We have no shortage of sharp objects."

"We can put her to sleep long enough to figure out how to end her," Sam said. "But first we have to find her."

"Those recent Larkin land sales and construction?" Dean said. "Probably not a coincidence."

"Makes sense," Sam said. "What if the pontianak is somehow... locked to Larkin land? What if she has been since Malaya died here?"

"So when she's not gutting fathers-to-be and feeding off the blood of infants, she heads back to her little Pontiac lair."

Sam was about to correct the mispronunciation, but guessed it was deliberate on Dean's part. At least he'd stopped calling her Tentacle Tessa. "Far as we know, she's been inactive for the past fifty-odd years... some kind of hibernation, maybe?"

"But Sally's arrival or the new construction on former Larkin land woke her up."

"For her, it might seem as if no time has passed."

* * *

Castiel attributed more than coincidence to Chloe and Olivia going into labor at the same time. As soon as Dr. Hartwell mentioned the calls from her service, Castiel became concerned for the safety of both women. Maybe in another place and under different circumstances, coincidence would be sufficient explanation. But in Braden Heights, coincidences involving pregnant women had proved disturbing in the case of the newborns and fatal for their fathers.

Before they left the Barrows scene, Castiel volunteered to keep an eye on both women. The Winchesters didn't need him for research and Castiel couldn't help wondering if this was the moment of Chloe's greatest danger. Maybe the connection he'd felt to her, seeing her as Claire during their brief introduction, had been some sort of premonition telling Castiel he would need to be there for Chloe the same way he hoped to be there should Claire ever need him. Based upon the evidence they'd collected, the clawed monster targeted the men before the babies were born and preyed on the newborns soon after birth. But what about the pregnant women during childbirth? That's when they would be most vulnerable. At this point, they were still guessing about the identity and motives of the cannibal woman.

Though he'd offered to keep an eye on Chloe and Olivia, he had neither the home address of the former, nor the hotel address for the latter. He doubted Jesse Vetter would check his baby's surrogate mother into a low-quality motel, which left a couple of mid-range options and a luxury hotel in the heart of the downtown district. Three, possibly four addresses to check. Chloe, on the other hand, lived with her parents and would have had no reason to change locations. He dialed Captain Sands, identified himself with his FBI alias, and requested Chloe's home address. Less than ten minutes later, he drove down the Sikes' street. As he scanned the house numbers, he spotted Chloe's father loading a pink and white striped duffel bag into the back of a blue Ford Escape. Chloe was already in the front seat of the car, her mother in the back.

Castiel pulled into the nearest parking space, engine idling, waiting until they drove past the Lincoln to follow them to Lovering Maternity Center at a discreet distance. They might recognize him from their prior meeting and he didn't wish to alarm them. Chloe could be safe from danger but she was already dealing with the tragic death of her baby's father. On top of that, she had to endure hours of difficult labor pains. Castiel wouldn't compound her anxiety without cause. He could be overly cautious without alarming her—or Olivia Krum. But if the danger became real and immediate, he would be on hand to intervene.

At Lovering Maternity Center, Castiel parked in the visitor lot in a space where he had a view of the porte cochère. The blue Escape stopped at the lobby entrance. Chloe's mother hurried inside and returned less than a minute later with a wheelchair she steered to the front passenger door. After Chloe situated herself in the chair, left hand clutching the armrest, right hand nervously rubbing her round abdomen, her mother pushed her toward the lobby doors. Meanwhile, her father unloaded the duffel bag and parked the SUV.

Castiel left his Lincoln and walked slowly toward the

lobby, looking left and right for anything unusual. Would the monster attack out in the open? She seemed to prefer isolated targets, the men and infants alike.

A flash of unnaturally fast movement caught his attention.

A pale green Prius sped toward the lobby entrance as Chloe and her parents made their way inside. The hybrid's driver traveled at a speed much too fast for a parking lot frequented by slow-moving pregnant women and recent mothers shepherding newborns home. Frowning, Castiel picked up his pace, almost running to intercept the vehicle. Though he doubted the driver would be the monster they sought, a human agent might also be involved in the murders.

With barely a glance back at the reckless driver's car, Chloe and her parents entered the maternity center.

Castiel slowed when he saw the driver emerge from the car.

Jesse Vetter hurried around to the passenger side of the Prius, then stood patiently as the woman inside rolled down her window, said something calmly and pointed toward the building. Jesse pressed both palms to his face, shook his head, seemed to take several deep breaths, then walked to the back of the car, opened the trunk to remove a suitcase only to set it down in front of the car. Darting inside the building, he too returned with a wheelchair and helped Olivia into it. She grimaced in pain—*probably experiencing a contraction,* Castiel thought—as he wheeled her to the lobby entrance and set the suitcase down beside her.

Leaving Olivia there, he returned to the car. In his nervous haste, he nearly clipped the bumper of a Dodge Durango, but managed to squeeze the Prius into a tight spot before rushing back to her. A moment later, they too had entered the maternity center without incident.

Castiel took his time crossing the parking lot, examining his surroundings for anything unusual. Ostensibly, he looked for a strange woman with clawed hands—he doubted he'd see the exposed tentacle sprouting from the nape of her neck—but he also examined the cars he passed to determine if anyone was lurking in the area. Since he'd arrived behind the Sikes family, the only car to enter the lot had been the Prius. But as he made his deliberate way to the automatic lobby doors, two other cars arrived and parked. Visitors bearing helium balloons, stuffed animals and boxes of candy. Nothing to arouse suspicion.

With one last sweeping look across the parking lot, he walked into the lobby and approached the familiar middle-aged receptionist at the U-shaped desk.

"Can I help you?" she said with a cheery smile.

"Agent Collins, FBI," Castiel said, once again trotting out the false identity. "I need to check on two of Dr. Hartwell's patients. Chloe Sikes and Olivia Krum."

"Chloe and Olivia," she said. "Oh, my! They both came in minutes ago. Literally."

"I'm aware of that."

She typed on her computer keyboard, checking information on the monitor. "They're both in labor, waters broken, both admitted... I don't see birthing room assignments. Let me call up there." She reached for her phone, made a quick call and jotted down information on a notepad. "They're on the second floor of the tower. Chloe is in birthing room 7, Olivia in room 9. Dr. Hartwell arrived a few minutes ago. She's up there already. Is she expecting you?"

"No," Castiel said.

He circled around the reception desk and walked to the center bank of elevators.

The receptionist spun around in her chair to follow his progress. "Should I call and let her know you're coming?"

Castiel pressed the UP button. "Only if it's necessary."

"It's… well… she might want to…" the receptionist said. "I should call."

The elevator doors opened. Castiel stepped inside and pressed the button for the second floor. Dr. Hartwell might question why he'd come to the maternity center, but he wasn't sure he had a good answer. His only acknowledged reason was the vague sense of unease he'd experienced when he learned of the simultaneous labor. For now, he'd prefer to wait nearby, in the background, on the off chance something happened. At the same time, he understood that maternity wards might have security concerns over strangers lurking in the hallways. Yet another reason to flash the ID for his fake persona. And at that point, Dr. Hartwell might as well know he was present.

He hadn't taken more than a dozen steps on the second floor when a nurse intercepted him to ask if he needed help. After identifying himself and stating his intention to see Dr. Hartwell, he continued for another two dozen steps before a male doctor with gray-streaked hair and horn-rimmed glasses stopped him and asked which patient he had come to see.

"Patients," Castiel said.

"Patients? Plural?"

"Sikes and Krum."

"Two? You're not the—never mind," he said, shaking his head as if to rid himself of a distracting thought. "This is most unusual."

"I need to talk to Dr. Hartwell," Castiel said.

"Agent Collins!" From behind the older doctor, Vanessa Hartwell waved and approached. "I've got this, George."

"Very well," Dr. George said. "He's here to see two, he says."

"Yes, George, thanks."

After he backed away and moved out of earshot, Dr. Hartwell said, "I wasn't expecting you. Is there a problem with the case?"

"I wanted to check that everything is… normal with Chloe and Olivia."

"Other than both of them going into labor minutes apart, everything is normal," she said. "Why wouldn't it be?"

"The trauma," Castiel said instead of discussing any supernatural control over the pregnancies. "They've both lost someone close to them."

"Of course," she said. "Well, at this point, nature takes over. I've only checked in with them briefly. But I'll be here monitoring everything, just in case there are any complications."

"Has anyone reported seeing the strange woman?"

"Oh, no! I would have called immediately," she said. "And security has been notified to look for anyone matching her description. Granted, a vague description, but it should be sufficient. After the Atherton incident, they're on high alert, believe me. We have security cameras covering the public areas. Nothing in the patient rooms, obviously. Privacy concerns. Otherwise, everything about the pregnancies is fine and normal."

Everything seemed under control, but Castiel couldn't shake his unease. How could he ask this woman to report anything that defied reason without losing his credibility? Still, he couldn't leave without trying. "Agents Rutherford, Banks and I are concerned that whoever is responsible for the murders may try to… interfere with the birthing process."

"That's not possible," she said. "I'm very familiar with everyone on staff here today. If I see any strangers, I will report them to security, but we have everything under control. If they—I don't know—cut power to the building, we have backup generators. Don't worry, Agent. We do this every day. It's our specialty."

"You'll call us if anything… strange happens?"

"Okay," she said, smiling indulgently. "Anything weird, I call."

"Thank you."

He started the walk back to the elevators when she called out to him, "Oh, Agent!"

Stopping, he turned to face her.

"Chloe's fine," she said. "I'll take good care of her."

Castiel nodded.

As he returned to his Lincoln, he told himself that Denise Atherton had given birth without incident, as had Melissa Barrows and Brianne Green. There was no reason to think that the monster would interrupt or try to influence the birth of either child. For now, they both seemed safe. At each red light on the way back to the motel, he pulled out his phone to check that it was working, that the battery hadn't died, that he had a good signal.

Despite his initial misgivings, a call for help never came.

TWENTY-SEVEN

While Castiel checked on Chloe Sikes and Olivia Krum at Lovering Maternity Center, Sam and Dean made trips to the county recorder's office and the county assessor's office to check deeds and get maps for any properties previously or currently owned by members of the Larkin and Nodd families. Though current information was available online, the records from when the town was known as Larkin's Korner were spotty, as the conversion to digital was incomplete. At the assessor's office they printed copies of property maps, focusing on lots involved in recent sales.

They also checked any properties owned by either family and zoned for residential use from the mid-forties to the mid-sixties. That timeframe included Calvin Nodd's return from the war with Malaya, his Filipino bride, as well as Riza Nodd's life in Larkin's Korner through the time of her pregnancy and departure with her rebel boyfriend and, finally, Nodd's last days in town culminating in a physical assault of one of his patients and his flight from town.

"If the pontianak arose or winked into existence—or however one is created—after Malaya's death during childbirth and attached itself to any of the Larkin properties," Sam reasoned as they climbed out of the Impala and returned to their motel room, "we'll have a record of that land here. And we should be able to find her."

Looking at the thick stack of printouts Sam carried from the car, Dean shook his head in doubt. "Good old Arthur Keating wasn't kidding about the Larkin family owning most of the freakin' town."

He opened the motel room door.

Across the room, Castiel rose from the chair where he'd been sitting. "Good. You're back."

"Everything okay at LMC?" Dean asked.

"Nothing unusual," Castiel said. "Both women should be in labor for at least several hours. Dr. Hartwell promised to call if anything unusual happens."

Sam laid the pile of records and maps on the table, completely overwhelming the small surface area. While he sorted the information to place the maps of recent property sales on top, Dean drove to a diner a few blocks from the motel to pick up an order of burgers, chicken sandwiches, a salad and fries.

While he was gone, Sam told Castiel they believed they were hunting a pontianak, created when Malaya Nodd died giving birth to Riza, and how they planned to stop it. He then recounted their search of Larkin and Nodd property records going back to the post-war era.

As Sam finished the abbreviated debriefing, Dean returned

with the food and, since the round work table overflowed with photocopies, lined up the wrapped sandwich options on top of the dresser.

Sam grabbed a chicken sandwich and salad. "The working assumption is that either Sally's arrival in town or the new construction on former Larkin land somehow awakened the pontianak."

"So we check the land involved in the recent sales?" Castiel asked, taking one of the burgers.

"We have a bunch of recent sales here," Sam replied. "But only a couple of those properties have gone under construction during the timeframe of all four murders, which narrows the search considerably."

Castiel looked from one brother to the other. "Any idea what we're searching for?"

Dean smirked. "No freakin' clue."

Sam cleared his throat. "Anything unusual, obviously," he said. "Sigils, a shrine, human organs as trophies…"

"Trust me," Dean said. "He has no clue."

"Or the pontianak herself," Sam continued, ignoring Dean's jibe. "Her lair or nest, wherever she concealed herself for the past fifty years."

"Maybe she's like a bear," Dean suggested. "Hibernates in a cave."

Dean unwrapped a cheeseburger, seemed to think about it a long time before pushing it aside and taking a bite of a chicken sandwich. Another test of his control, forgoing his indulgences, at least those involving red meat and alcohol.

"Who knows?" Sam said. "But these properties give us

a place to start." He looked from Dean to Castiel. "Unless someone has a better suggestion."

"Should've bought the pecan pie," Dean lamented. "Damn it."

"I meant about—"

"I know what you meant."

"If we knew her next target," Castiel said, "we could wait for her to attack."

"A stakeout?" Dean asked, distracted as he joylessly worked his way through the chicken sandwich. "Only if there's pie."

"That's the problem," Sam said. "We can't predict her next move."

"Wonder if they deliver."

"Forget it," Sam said. "We're leaving."

Of all the recent sales of Larkin land, the two with ongoing construction represented their best chance of discovering the pontianak. Sam asked Castiel to check the Coventry Crossing development, while he and Dean took the farmhouse and barn on the large property adjoining the Stanton Fertility Clinic. Sam figured he and Dean could split up and check the two buildings separately, while the Coventry Crossing development was nearly complete, so Castiel wouldn't have a large area to cover on his own. With luck, they would either find the pontianak's resting place or rule out both locations before Chloe or Olivia gave birth. The monster's connection to both women meant their unborn children would be in danger, through no fault of their own, soon after they came into the world.

Before splitting up to conduct their individual searches, they made a pit stop at On Track Locomotive Repair outside Evansville for a specialty item not sold by the local hardware stores. Then Castiel left for Coventry Crossing, while Sam and Dean drove in the opposite direction to check out the farmland.

The sun dipped below the tree line as Dean drove past a street-level billboard promoting the arrival of the Braden Heights Outlet Mall, COMING TO THIS LOCATION EARLY NEXT YEAR!

"We're close, Dean," Sam said. "The east end of the property was sold for the Stanton Fertility Center parking lot expansion. The west end was rezoned for commercial use for those outlet stores."

Dean nodded, tapped the brake and swung the Impala onto the entrance of the gravel driveway of the old Larkin farm but stopped short. A rusty chain at the foot of the driveway hung between weather-beaten wooden posts on either side, blocking casual access to the property. High grass, a sea of weeds and wildflowers covered most of the land. Up a long, gradual incline, at the crest of a gentle hill, Sam saw the sprawling farmhouse and, beyond that in deeper shadows, the long rectangular shape of the barn. In the dying light, the red paint on the abandoned structures had faded to a rusty brown. At this distance, their lack of structural integrity was suggested rather than confirmed. Far beyond the farmhouse rose the silhouettes of modern buildings bathed in a haze of artificial light cast by office windows and streetlights. Somewhere on the far side of the expansive property, the

Stanton Fertility Clinic's parking lot had already begun to encroach on former Larkin Land.

AC/DC's "Hells Bells" came on the radio as Sam exited the car to unhook the chain from an eye bolt. No padlock, obviating the need for bolt cutters. The small metal sign nailed to the left post—PRIVATE PROPERTY – NO TRESPASSING— substituted for tighter security. After Sam climbed back in the car, Dean drove up the long driveway, frowning as gravel crunched and popped under the Impala's tires. Anyone within a few hundred feet would've heard their approach.

"So much for the element of surprise."

At the top of the hill, the gravel driveway transitioned to cracked and crumbling blacktop, with weeds sprouting at every fault. Dean parked between the two dilapidated buildings. At this distance, their lack of structural integrity was no longer a matter of conjecture. Most of the farmhouse windows were shattered, the main door—under a covered porch—hung precariously from one failing hinge, and the roof sported at least two jagged holes. The barn's long slanted roof sagged past the point of condemnation. Beyond the barn stood the blackened ruin of a grain silo, reduced to a waist-high ring of charred wood. Whether the fire had been the result of a lightning strike, vandalism or arson, a search of what remained required little more than a sweeping glance.

Dean switched off the headlights and killed the engine. "I'll take the barn."

"Okay," Sam said. "I've got the farmhouse."

From the trunk of the Impala, they grabbed flashlights and weapons. Sam picked up a shotgun loaded with rock salt rounds. A deterrent for angry spirits, the rounds forced them to dissipate briefly. He also grabbed an EMF meter.

"Remember," Dean said and patted his jacket pocket, "she hates pointy things."

Nodding, Sam also grabbed a hunting knife.

Dean reached further back in the trunk and pulled out a machete, holding it up to examine its edge, then cast a sidelong glance at Sam's dagger. "Mine's bigger."

"Compensating," Sam replied and turned toward the farmhouse, smiling.

Behind him, Dean slammed the trunk and proceeded toward the barn.

Through the broken windows, Sam saw only darkness inside, no electric or candle light. Not a surprise. Judging from the exterior, he doubted the place had been occupied by anything other than wild animals in at least a decade. He climbed up three wide, creaking and sagging steps onto the covered porch that ran the entire length of the house on the side facing the barn. Originally, four narrow posts supported the porch roof, but the two closest to the door had been split in half with an axe or hatchet. As a result, the middle of the roof had buckled, forcing Sam to duck beneath a hanging brass light fixture.

As a sick joke or an ambiguous warning, someone had nailed the carcass of a raccoon to the front door. This bit of vandalism was recent, judging by the clump of writhing maggots in the animal's gaping neck wound. The property had probably garnered renewed attention with the posting of the outlet mall billboard.

Even though the strike plate had been kicked out of the doorjamb, Sam reached for the door handle to open the door. As soon as he tugged on the door, the screws on the remaining hinge pulled free of the rotted wood, and the door fell toward him. Jumping back, he whacked his head on the light fixture a moment before the raccoon carcass slipped off its nail and dumped a load of agitated maggots on his boots.

Cursing under his breath, he heaved the door aside. Its weight struck and broke through a section of hand railing, and a whole row of balusters fell like tenpins. He stomped his feet to scatter the maggots.

"Sammy?"

"I'm fine, Dean!" Sam called. *Mostly,* he thought as he rubbed the growing knot on the back of his head and winced.

He took a deep breath then removed his flashlight from his jacket pocket and shone the beam of light into the interior of the farmhouse. He swept the light across the floor before stepping inside.

As he proceeded through the foyer, into the dining room and through the kitchen, each step was accompanied by a creak of yielding wood. The rooms, with the exception of a round wooden table on its side, held no furniture; the walls were bare, save for a few nails and picture hooks left behind after personal items had been removed. A downstairs bathroom had been gutted, sink ripped from the wall, missing toilet evidenced by a drain hole in the floor. With one fateful step, wood cracked and split beneath him and his boot sank into the jagged hole, momentarily pinning him in place. A startled rat bolted out of the narrow linen closet and ambled past him into the darkness. Another rat surged over the rim of the toilet drain pipe and scampered between Sam's feet before joining its compatriot. Sam tugged his foot back and forth until it came free.

With his shotgun pinned under one arm, and the flashlight under the other, pointing forward, he took out the EMF meter and checked for any spikes. Nothing. Between the great room and the kitchen, a staircase with a ninety-degree turn led to the second floor. Sam tested each tread on the staircase before committing his weight to it. He avoided the rickety handrail altogether. The landing at the turn of the staircase was split down the middle, so he kept close to the edge as he cautiously continued upstairs.

One by one, he checked the bedrooms, not surprised to find all the furniture gone, along with any personal effects and decorations. The doorjamb on the smallest bedroom had small notches carved in the wood, a testament to a child's growth over the years, though the identity of that child was lost in time. Again the EMF meter gave no indication of an angry or vengeful spirit on the premises. The flooring by the broken windows, subject to countless rainstorms, seemed especially hazardous. Each time he tried to approach a window to look toward the barn, the creaking of the wood increased in proportion to the sagging he felt beneath his feet. He might not fall through to the first floor, but he had no desire to risk it.

The ceiling above the hallway featured an abundance of water stains in Rorschachian patterns. Within the ring of stains, a frayed pull cord revealed a set of folding stairs.

Though the hinges were rusted and the insubstantial steps creaked under his weight, Sam climbed high enough to shine his flashlight beam around a narrow attic with slanted walls. The beam revealed a freestanding lamp with a broken bulb, an old baby carriage and a moldy child's car seat in the otherwise empty space. Two unsightly holes in the ceiling accounted for significant water damage to the flooring. Bits of the wood crumbled in Sam's hands so he decided against walking on the surface. Placing his shotgun on the floor beside his head with the flashlight next to it, Sam performed a quick EMF scan before descending the rickety stairs.

If the pontianak nested or hibernated in the farmhouse, he'd found no evidence to indicate a prolonged presence by anything other than common vermin. Taking as much care descending the stairs as he had on his way up, he reached the ground floor without incident, but as he turned through the great room toward the foyer, the darkness seemed to press in on all sides, overwhelming the now feeble flashlight beam. *Probably dying batteries,* he thought, but despite evidence to the contrary, he sensed a silent menace nearby.

Outside, he circled the house and found a pair of padlocked cellar doors on the side opposite the barn. One last place to check. But he'd left the bolt cutters in the Impala. Instead of returning to the car, he decided to check the condition of the wooden doors. Gripping a steel handle he tugged and felt some give. Yanking the handle side to side, he needed half a minute to wrench the screws out of the rotted wood. With the handle clear, the chain and padlock hung uselessly to the side. The rusty hinges elicited a squeal as he pulled the doors open. Descending the steep wooden steps, he used the tip of the shotgun to part a thick veil of cobwebs. He stepped down onto a dirt floor and swept the flashlight beam around the confined space. *Probably a root cellar,* Sam thought. Crude shelving made from untreated wood stood against the side opposite the stairs. The flashlight beam gleamed on fresh spider webs slung between the right angles of the shelving. The remains of a dozen shattered mason jars littered the floor, the shine of glass dulled by a thick coating of dust. In the corner, the flashlight beam revealed an overturned red wheelbarrow, its lone wheel missing.

One last EMF scan, this one underground but with the same negative results. As Sam packed the device away and climbed the wooden stairs to the surface, a fleeting darkness rippled before the framed evening sky above. Then a stiff breeze rattled the open cellar doors and, for a moment, he expected them to slam shut. But the breeze passed, and the brief darkness was probably nothing more than a scudding cloud blotting out the moonlight.

Closing the cellar doors behind him, he walked toward the barn.

Dean decided to circle the long horse barn before entering. But he'd hardly taken a dozen steps when he heard a crash from the farmhouse. He'd thought that hanging door looked dicey, but Sam said he was okay, so Dean shrugged and continued his search.

Besides wide doors on each of the barn's narrow ends for leading a horse in and out, and smaller doors on the longer sides, he found several holes in the walls, big enough to allow the passage of small animals, such as groundhogs, foxes, or wild dogs. Some of the holes were the result of wear and rot in addition to accumulated clawing and chewing, while others owed a debt to random acts of vandalism.

Dean entered the narrow passage separating the feed room, tool storage and horse shower on the left, and the tack room on the right. All three rooms had been cleaned out. On the opposite side, he searched the office on the right and the kitchen and break room on the left. The former held a desk with missing drawers and a broken leg, the latter nothing but a bare countertop. Adjacent to the kitchen, the bathroom no longer featured a toilet, but a small sink with rusty, nonfunctioning spigots remained. On either side of the office, kitchen and storage rooms were twenty horse stalls, ten on each side of the wide central passageway. Beside the kitchen, a staircase led up to the open hayloft on one side of the barn, while a crude wooden ladder provided access to the other side.

First Dean checked the horse stalls, each with its own Dutch door. The top halves of the doors had been left open, revealing empty spaces within. He dutifully checked each enclosure for anything other than the bits of trampled hay and petrified droppings revealed by his flashlight. Finally, he climbed the creaky staircase to the loft and walked the length. A few bales of hay remained close to the eaves, but that was all. Next, he climbed the ladder to the opposite loft and found nothing of note, but part of the roof hung dangerously low on that side. He ducked as he proceeded cautiously, worried that at any moment it would all come crashing down on top of him, the feeling reinforced when a strong breeze swept through the barn, rattling loose boards and causing the compromised ceiling to moan above him. He held his breath until the wind eased, realizing he'd been prepared to dive off the edge of the loft at the first sound of cracking wood above him. After a steadying breath, he continued his inspection.

Every footfall was met with the creaking of wood and, as he stepped on one particularly noisy plank, a dozen mice scattered around him in all directions. Otherwise, his visual search had come up empty and the EMF detector had offered no encouragement that he was on the right track. As the minutes ticked by, he'd become convinced they were on a snipe hunt.

Descending the ladder to the barn floor, he swept the flashlight beam around, trying to determine if he'd missed anything. Even though he had no idea about the preferences of a hibernating pontianak, he doubted the drafty barn would make for a comfortable lair.

About to head to the farmhouse to assist Sam, he heard his brother walking down the passage between the feed and tack rooms, flashlight beam flashing back and forth in front of him.

"Dean?"

"Here," Dean said, walking toward the light.

"Anything?"

"Whole lot of nothing," Dean said. "You?"

"Same," Sam said. His flashlight flickered until he whacked

his palm against the side. "House, attic, and root cellar cleaned out. What's left isn't worth anything. And the whole house is one strong storm away from collapsing."

Dean told Sam he'd searched all the rooms, empty horse stalls and the loft and found only a few bales of hay and a family of mice. "And some of the stalls—the ones closest to the office and break room—show no signs of use."

"Makes sense," Sam said, walking toward the break room entrance beside the stairs. "Keep the horses away from the noise, and the smell away from the office."

He peeked in the break room, flashlight raised.

"Already checked," Dean said. "They cleared out all the snacks."

Sam turned away from the office toward the staircase, its base enclosed on all sides. Running the beam from the top to the bottom, he seemed to look for a door knob or latch. Maybe he thought they used the space for storage. But Dean had checked already and had found no access.

Dean's phone rang, pulling his attention away from Sam's poking and prodding. He'd been expecting Castiel to call with an update. Probably more of the same. Convinced they had followed a dead end and prepared to commiserate with the angel about the lost time, he glanced at the number on the phone and didn't recognize it.

"Agent Banks," he answered, curious.

At first, he couldn't make out the voice speaking to him. In the background a woman shrieked in anger, her cries punctuated by intermittent crashing sounds.

"Hello?"

The voice spoke louder, sounded desperate. "Agent Banks, this is Malik! Brianna's brother. Man, I need your help now! She's freaking out."

Another crash sounded, alarmingly close to the speaker.

"Damn! She almost took my head off with that one!" Malik exclaimed. "How soon can you get here?"

"Malik," Dean said. "What the hell is going on?"

"It's Brianna, man," Malik said. "She's gone crazy."

Dean looked up and Sam was missing.

"Tell me," Dean said, walking toward the staircase. "What happened?"

"She asked me to check on the baby," Malik said. "Kiki was sleeping fine. But when I came down, Brianna was waiting for me with a butcher's knife."

"What?" Dean asked, stunned.

He saw a flashlight beam darting around the horse stall next to the staircase, so he walked that way. The bottom half of the Dutch door stood ajar and Sam was poking around in the stall, his shotgun leaning against the back wall.

Malik kept talking hastily, rapid-fire sentences to get everything out as quickly as he could while under attack. "Slashed my forearm before I got the knife away from her. Then she collapsed. Like she fainted. Thought she had some kind of seizure. Carried her to the sofa. Checked Kiki. Still asleep. Brianna woke up, seemed fine, couldn't remember anything. Then—"

"Then what?"

"Bree—stop! Don't!"

Dean heard glass shattering.

"Just chucked a glass vase at me," Malik said, breathless.

Sam rapped his knuckles against the near wall of the horse stall. They made a hollow sound. Looking up at Dean he held his hands about twenty inches apart. Dean hadn't noticed before but the wall between the stall and the staircase seemed thicker than the wall between the other stalls. And now that he examined it closely, the previously unused stall wasn't as wide as the others.

"Five minutes after she woke up, she tried to claw my eyes out. Minute later, she dropped again. Out cold. And the baby? Still asleep. Can't wake Kiki up even with all the racket. But Bree wakes up, is chill for about five minutes, then goes ballistic again."

Sam found a gap between boards, and ran his hand along it down to the floor and back. After a moment, he paused and frowned, reaching for something and pulling. With the creaking protest of a rusty hinge, a tall panel of rotting wood swung inward—a makeshift door—revealing a coal-dark space under the adjoining staircase.

"Don't want to call the police on Brianna, but I'm lost, man. What do I do?"

Retrieving his shotgun, Sam shone his flashlight into the darkness and down. Standing beside him, Dean saw the top of a crude staircase descending into darkness. Obviously whoever built those stairs and installed the hidden door panel wanted the underground space kept secret.

As Sam took the first step into the darkness, planting his foot on the top tread, his flashlight flickered and died. This time, no amount of whacking or shaking brought it back to life. He gestured for Dean to hand over his and began his descent.

"Agent Banks!"

"Malik, don't leave the baby alone," Dean said quickly. His phone display now provided the only source of illumination in the barn as Sam sank into the gloom. "I'll send someone as soon as possible."

"What about"—another loud crash—"Brianna?"

"Keep ducking," Dean said. "Next time she's out, tie her up."

"Tie her—what?"

"To stop her from hurting you or the baby next time she wakes up," Dean said. "Until we figure this out."

"I don't know, man, that's—!"

Dean heard a loud clang of metal, followed by a pained curse from Malik.

"Okay—okay, I'll tie her up," Malik said. "Get here quick!"

Dean called Castiel then followed Sam into the deeper darkness beneath the Larkin barn.

TWENTY-EIGHT

Castiel had a longer drive than the Winchesters, but judging by the maps and the status of the Coventry Crossing development, potentially a smaller area to investigate. Only the far section of the development remained under construction. Any building or remnants of the former Larkin land would be in that confined area. If the pontianak had been in any other section, her hibernation would have been interrupted long before the Holcombs arrived in Braden Heights.

Spotting a decorative sign up ahead, Castiel tapped the brake of the Lincoln to confirm he had arrived. Fronting a section of well-maintained landscaping on the near side of the development's entrance, the sign proclaimed COVENTRY CROSSING in bright green script letters. Beneath the wooden sign, a white vinyl banner billowing in the breeze advised, FINAL PHASE – HURRY BEFORE THEY'RE ALL GONE!

As Castiel entered the development, he looked left and right, seeing nothing but completed and occupied homes,

windows aglow in amber light. From the plans, he recalled
that the homes lined the paths of two mirrored S curves on
either side of a gazebo overlooking a drainage pond, with a
few outlying cul-de-sacs for deluxe units.

The snaking roadway was wide enough for two lanes
of traffic and parking on either side. By the time Castiel
reached the last loop of the second S, the finished homes
were replaced by wooden frameworks, skeletal houses in
various states of construction, and the blacktop gave way to
stretches of gravel and packed dirt between loose mounds
of overturned earth. Beyond a dark construction trailer and
two portable toilets, a backhoe and a bulldozer had been left
near the entrance to the last planned cul-de-sac. The land for
these last few homes hadn't been entirely cleared of trees and
brush. And some uprooted trees remained, cast aside on top
of and beside excavated mounds of earth.

The last of the streetlights illuminated little beyond the
construction vehicles, the fallen trees suggested by their
silhouettes. Castiel flicked on his high beams and drove in a
slow arc, revealing a thin line of trees beyond the planned cul-
de-sac, trees that would likely survive to offer shade for future
homeowners. The halogen lights stabbed into the darkness
and cast stark shadows of the fallen trees and branches on
the standing trees behind them. As the twin beams swept
from one side to the other, the branches seemed to twist and
contort, as if the trees struggled to right themselves but fell
quiescent with the return of darkness.

Castiel had hoped to see an old manmade structure left
over from the previous landowners, maybe a rundown

house or a storage shed, anything that could have survived and offered shelter for the past fifty years. Unfortunately, he saw nothing other than trees beyond the edges of the fresh construction. Parking by the construction trailer, he switched off the engine and proceeded on foot, carrying a flashlight to check his footing as he left the dirt path and strode toward the tree line. Maybe he'd find a dilapidated groundskeeper's shack among the trees, unpainted wood that blended into the background.

He climbed the first earthen mound, his shoes sinking into the dirt and knotted roots just enough to compromise his balance. Recovering enough to avoid a spill, he worked his way to the top and shone his flashlight into the overturned brush beyond. Here and there, broken branches erupted from the loose soil as if they had grown independently at tortured angles. Some were dark, others long dead and stripped of bark, a few unnaturally pale and grouped together, possibly the white branches of a fallen sycamore.

As he was about to descend the mound and continue deeper into the brush, his cell phone rang. He expected a call from Dean or Sam, but frowned in alarm when he answered and heard Dr. Hartwell's frantic voice.

"You said to call if anything strange happened," Dr. Hartwell said urgently. "Well, something strange is happening now!"

Claire!

"Chloe? Is she in danger?"

Castiel had already begun to retreat, descending the earthen mound and hurrying to his Lincoln, frustrated again that he could no longer teleport himself where he was needed.

"It's Chloe *and* Olivia," Dr. Hartwell said. "In the middle of labor, they both fell into a comatose state. Near as I can determine, it happened to both simultaneously. It makes no sense."

"Tell me exactly what happened," Castiel said as he pulled open his car door.

"One minute they were both in labor, everything normal," she said. "Then, while I was checking on Chloe, she started coughing and gagging—but she'd only had a few ice chips. Barely had time to check that her airway was clear when one of the nurses rushed into Chloe's room to tell me Olivia was choking. That's when I saw spontaneous bruising appear on Chloe's throat."

"Bruising?"

Castiel had started the Lincoln, took a wide turn and drove back onto the finished roadway toward the development's exit.

"I can't explain it," Dr. Hartwell said. "As if invisible hands were strangling her right there in the bed. Olivia exhibits the same bruising on her throat. Less than a minute later, Chloe's eyes rolled back in her head and she collapsed into unconsciousness. She's been unresponsive ever since. From what I can tell, the same thing happened to Olivia at the same time. Neither will respond to stimuli. Worse, their heart rates are slowly dropping."

"Was the strange woman spotted during any of this?"

"Who—? No! No one has seen her and she certainly hasn't been in my birthing rooms."

"And the babies?"

"The whole labor process is… again, I'm at a loss for words," she said, frustrated. "Frozen. Like someone hit a pause button. Contractions have ceased. The babies don't appear to be in distress, but I'm not sure how much longer I can wait before attempting C-sections on both of them."

"I see," Castiel said grimly. He leaned over the dash, checked traffic on the highway before darting out.

"What is this?" she demanded.

"I'm afraid I don't understand the question."

"My patients," she said, exasperated. "What in hell is happening to my patients?"

"I don't know," Castiel said. Whatever the pontianak intended, this was new and completely unexpected. Her intentions, while definitely malicious, remained a mystery. "But I'm on my way."

He disconnected the call as he raced to Lovering Maternity Center, weaving around slow moving vehicles when necessary, despite the risk of police interference. He'd rely on the false FBI identity if they tried to stop him, though he had no intention of pulling over to flash it. His bigger concern was what he could do once he arrived at LMC that a trained doctor could not.

His cell phone rang again.

Staring intently at the road in front of him, he answered without checking the display and assumed Dr. Hartwell was calling with an update. "Doctor, what's—?"

"Cass, it's Dean. Where are you?"

"I had to leave Coventry Crossing," Castiel said. "Dr. Hartwell called. There's an emergency at LMC."

"What kind of emergency?"

Castiel relayed the information he'd received from the OB/GYN.

"Forget that," Dean said. "I have a bigger emergency."

Castiel doubted that. Four lives were at stake at LMC. "Dean, I don't—!"

Dean launched into a quick explanation of Malik's call. "You need to get over there before she hurts Malik or the baby."

"But four lives are—"

"Cass, you can't help them," Dean said. "Without your full Grace, you can't heal anyone." He was silent for a moment, waiting. When Castiel didn't respond, Dean continued in a more sympathetic tone. "You can help with Brianna. And what if this spreads to the other new moms? Cass, something big is happening now. Sam and I may have located the lair. We'll stop her but you need to help these people. Let Dr. Hartwell handle her patients."

Castiel sighed. "Dean…"

He kept picturing Claire in danger, Claire in a coma and slowly dying, and he couldn't help her. But Chloe wasn't Claire. And even if it was Claire unconscious in that hospital bed, Castiel couldn't help her in his present condition. Dean was right. He'd been thinking the same thing before the call. If he gave in to his selfish need to be present at the hospital, he would be of no help to anybody.

"You know I'm right."

After a long moment of silence, Castiel said softly, "Yes."

"Okay," Dean said. "Here's the Greens' address."

At the next intersection, Castiel drove through a gas station driveway, startling one of the attendants as he shot across the lot to the cross street. He made a left turn at the light and headed back the way he'd come.

In the undeveloped section of Coventry Crossing, beyond the yellow construction vehicles and the dirt mound upon which Castiel had stood to shine his flashlight into the darkness beyond the toppled trees, the clump of white branches he'd observed poking through the dirt at odd angles began to move, jerking spastically to free themselves from the tangle of roots and grass, and the cold weight of dirt and stone. Human arms and legs, rather than broken tree limbs. Bowed backs heaved upward out of the muck, revealing pale faces, with mottled skin drawn taut as drum skin over broken jaws and split skulls. Each of the five desiccated bodies lurched upright, revealing swollen abdomens. Five young women killed in their prime, buried in shallow graves fifty years ago, only to rise again upon hearing the insistent call.

They climbed and staggered their way over the loose mounds of dirt and broken trees, silent as death but unwavering. With each agonizing step, their bones knit, rends in their dried flesh sealed, and they began to resemble the young women they had been long ago, rather than the skeletal remains they had become over the span of five decades.

But the repairs to the ruined human forms went beyond restoration to transformation. Fingernails that grew back soon thickened and elongated into claws. Teeth extended downward to form fangs.

They were needed so they answered the call, and because

they answered the call, they were rewarded with a second chance. Wrath flowed like venom through their now-inhuman veins. Reborn as vengeful predators, they would never again be victims.

TWENTY-NINE

Gary Atherton stood in the hallway outside the nursery as Denise lowered Gabriel, freshly fed, changed, and finally asleep, into his crib. A low-level headache, sign of his own lack of sleep lately, throbbed behind his brow. When he dozed, he dreamt of freshly brewed coffee. Never decaff. Sometimes he felt as if caffeine was the only thing that kept him going.

Denise and he had tried to have a child through their late twenties and thirties but it never happened for them. And they decided to let nature take its course—or not. If it wasn't meant to be, they wouldn't force the issue with tests and interventions. Once Denise turned forty, they assumed fate had decided for them: childless couple. Three years later, long after they'd given up on the idea of shepherding a new Atherton generation through the trials and tribulations of life, Denise became pregnant. Just having that news confirmed was quite a mental adjustment for both of them. Suddenly the life together they had come to accept demanded a complete revision with a nine-month deadline. Rather, eight months, counting from the time the news finally sunk in. And while the mind was more than willing, the body was not always able.

Gary tried not to think too far ahead. Knowing he would be in his mid-sixties when his son graduated from high school in no way prepared him for changing diapers at 3AM today. Of course, Denise was more sanguine about the whole affair, insisting they take things one day a time, and that having a young child in their lives would keep them young at heart. But then, Denise was always a glass-half-full person, which was one of the things he loved about her. Gary would admit the glass was half full, but understood that water evaporated and glass itself was fragile. Almost four years Denise's senior, Gary felt that extra mileage entitled him to a bit of skepticism. Nevertheless, he loved Denise and he loved little Gabriel. So what could go wrong?

Denise backed out of the room and closed the door so softly he never heard it click shut. Gabriel continued to sleep. Gary debated a nap versus a ginormous mug of coffee. If he could take a power nap while absorbing coffee intravenously, that would be ideal, but neither he nor Denise had the medical chops to rig a DIY IV java drip.

Denise turned toward him, smiling. She whispered, "Rocking chair worked like a charm."

"We shall have one in every room of the house," Gary declared sotto voce as they walked toward the staircase.

He started down the stairs ahead of her, paused to look back and said, "You know what else—?"

Denise stood above him, her eyelids fluttering as her eyes rolled upward, showing nearly all whites.

"Denise, are you—?"

She gritted her teeth and spoke angrily, "You bastard!"

"What—?"

She shoved him hard.

Flung backward, he reached for the hand rail, missed, wrenching his arm as it slipped between two balusters before popping free, and tumbled down the stairs. Fortunately, the stairs were carpeted, a deep pile that cushioned each impact as he rolled down to the landing.

"Denise! What the hell—?"

She stormed down the stairs after him, her face contorted in rage.

He scrambled to his feet and stood there dumbfounded as she charged him. When she struck him with her fists, he tried to catch her wrists and missed. Then she tried to claw out his eyes with her fingernails, spittle flying from her mouth. It was as if someone had flipped a switch in her brain to turn her into a raving lunatic. With his forearm he shielded his eyes and backed away from the continuing assault. Everything happened so fast, he couldn't process the information and think of an appropriate course of action, other than defending himself.

Finally, he shoved her sideways, onto the sofa. But she rebounded off the cushions and jumped onto the glass coffee table to launch herself at him. As she pushed off, the inset glass panel cracked and collapsed. Her slipper-covered foot dropped through the break and she fell face first on the other side of the table, struggling to get up.

"Son of a bitch!" she raged. "I'll never forgive you!"

"What the hell, Denise?" Gary asked. "Have you gone completely insane?"

As she pulled her trapped foot free, a wicked smile appeared on her face. She lunged backward and grabbed a wedge-shaped piece of broken glass, holding it like a dagger, but so tightly her palm bled around the edges.

"Worthless piece of crap," she hissed. "I'll cut your throat!"

"Jesus!" Gary said, backing away, hands raised. "What's wrong with you?"

"You're what's wrong with me, Ronnie!"

"Ronnie?"

"Coward! Rotten piece of filth!"

She lunged, swinging the broken glass at his throat, as promised. Expecting the attack, Gary managed to block it with his hand, but the sharp edge sliced his left palm from the base of his little finger to his wrist. "Christ, Denise! That hurts!"

"Don't worry," she said. "Nothing hurts when you're dead!"

At the last word, she lunged again, this time stabbing the glass at his abdomen. The pointed tip of the glass struck his metal belt buckle and snapped off. Denise stumbled and fell into his arms, and this time he managed to catch her wrist and hold it clear of his body. But she struggled fiercely, as if her life depended on freeing herself and killing him.

With a frustrated roar, she lunged forward and sank her teeth into his shoulder, biting through the cloth of his flannel shirt and undershirt into his flesh. At first he felt pressure but as she continued to bear down her teeth punctured his flesh. Grunting in pain, he redoubled his effort to keep her right hand away from him but felt his grip slipping as he lost more blood through the lacerated palm.

"Denise—stop!"

And again, like a switch flipped in her brain, all the ferocity in her tensed body vanished. He looked at her face and her eyes appeared normal, if confused. She looked back and forth, seemed to register that he had both her wrists pinned and frowned at him. "Gary? What's going on? Are you bleed—?"

Her body went limp.

She collapsed in his arms, as if she'd fainted. He'd never witnessed anyone faint before, but he didn't think she was faking it. Sweeping her up in his arms, he laid her on the couch, then grabbed a kitchen towel to wrap his bleeding palm until he could bandage it properly. For a minute, he sat staring at her, unconscious—sleeping?—on the sofa, looking so peaceful and relaxed. If not for the shattered coffee table and his bloody hand, he might almost believe he'd imagined her vicious attack.

He'd read all the baby books for new mothers and fathers along with Denise, but he couldn't recall reading a chapter in any of them about one of the parents turning into a homicidal maniac. He'd thought nothing could prepare you—truly prepare you—for becoming a parent, other than becoming one. And, slowly, he was adapting to a new worldview with a helpless infant at the center of it. But what had just happened to him was something he would never understand because there could be no rational explanation.

Had Denise experienced some kind of psychotic break? She had no history of psychosis or any mental problems.

Or was there a dire medical reason for the violent episode? Could a brain tumor turn a normal forty-something woman into a murderer?

Answers were beyond him, so he picked up the phone and called 911.

As soon as he hung up, Denise awoke, pushed herself up and looked at the broken coffee table before focusing on him. "I had the weirdest dream… did I have an accident?"

"What do you remember?"

"Putting Gabriel to sleep—oh, no! I hear him crying."

Lost in thought, the sound hadn't registered with Gary. But it was Gabriel's displeased cry, not his five-alarm-fire come-get-me-now hysterical shrieking, so Gary had to cut himself some slack. He stared at Denise. "You don't remember shoving me down the stairs?"

"What!?"

"Or cutting my hand with broken glass?" he asked, raising the bloody towel wrapped around his hand as evidence.

"No!" Denise stood up, looked at her own hands, the trickles of blood on her own palm from gripping the glass tightly as she fought him. "How did I—? Gary, what's going on?"

She hurried to the downstairs bathroom and grabbed the first aid kit.

"You had some kind of… episode," he said. "Like a seizure, but violent."

She wrapped gauze around her own hand after applying antibacterial ointment, then she looked at his more severe wound, grimaced in sympathetic pain, and began to apply ointment and gauze.

When she was done, she stood and glanced toward the stairs. "I should get Gabriel," she said. "Might need to be changed again."

"No!" Gary said abruptly. The thought of her flipping into her Mrs. Hyde persona while caring for their child terrified him. "I'll take care of him."

"I'm perfectly capable of—"

The doorbell rang. "Emergency services!"

"It's okay, I called them…" Gary's voice trailed off as he saw Denise's eyelids fluttering, nothing but the whites of her eyes showing. "Come in!" he called frantically. "It's happening again!"

Several miles away, Alan Crane, Melissa Barrows' father, opened the door to her house and urged Assistant Chief Cordero to come inside. The older man had a knot on his forehead and a split lip. "I really don't know what's gotten into her," Alan said. "She's never been violent a day in her life."

"She attacked your wife?"

"Both of us," Alan said. "We were sitting at the kitchen table, talking about arrangements for Kevin's funeral. Not a pleasant topic, to be sure, but then she stood up so abruptly she knocked over her chair. She grabbed a ceramic cookie jar off the table and… and smashed it against Barbara's head." He pointed to the lump on his forehead. "Got this when she chucked a drinking glass at me. I was too stunned to duck."

"Where is Barbara—Melissa's mother—now?"

"On the sofa. She was dazed. I put a cold compress on her head. Worried she might have a concussion."

"Melissa?"

"On the floor," Alan said, chagrined. "She passed out. I made her comfortable. Put a pillow under her head. But she's had two of these episodes. I don't know what to do. Fortunately, Noelle—the baby—is upstairs, out of harm's way. For now."

They walked into the living room.

Mrs. Crane waved at Cordero. "Pardon me for not getting up," she said. "Still feel a bit woozy."

"That's fine, ma'am," he said. "I'll call an ambulance. You'll need an X-ray, possibly a CT scan."

As expected, Melissa Barrows was unconscious on the floor, but she had begun to stir. In a moment, she would be fully awake. Instinctively, Cordero's palm fell to the butt of his gun. Frowning, he moved his hand away. He was not about to shoot a recent widow with a newborn child in her care. Instead, he unsnapped the leather pouch on his belt that secured his handcuffs.

"If it's like last time, she'll be normal for a couple minutes," Alan said. "Then something happens to her eyes and they roll back. First time, I thought she was about to faint, but then she attacked."

"No warning otherwise?"

"Just screaming and cursing at us," Alan said. "Weird thing

is… well, it's all been weird, but when she threw that glass at me, she called me Ronnie."

"Who's Ronnie?" Cordero asked.

"I have no idea."

When Castiel arrived at the Green residence, he raised his fist to knock on the front door but heard a baby crying, a man and woman yelling and the sound of glass and ceramic shattering. He tried the doorknob, but the door was locked. Though it was within the powers of his remaining Grace to blast the door off its hinges, he couldn't risk injuring Brianna, Malik and baby Kiara. Instead, he thrust his elbow through the windowpane closest to the deadbolt, unlocked the door and entered the house.

"Malik," he called, "Agent Collins, FBI."

"In here!"

The angel followed the sound of his voice, crossing through the dining room and edging through the archway to peer into the living room.

Malik crouched behind the sofa, which faced the open kitchen, huddled over his crying niece, who was bordered by a ring of throw pillows and mostly covered by a baby blanket with a rainbow design.

Brianna stood behind an island counter in the kitchen, grabbing ceramic plates from an open cabinet and hurling them at her brother. Most of the plates had smashed into the wall behind him, but one had hit its mark, judging by the cut on his cheek. "Son of a bitch!" she yelled and flung a ceramic teacup at him. He dipped his head to the left and the cup struck the wall and broke on the hardwood floor.

"What happened?"

"Agent Banks said tie her up next time she passed out," Malik said, unable to look away from his sister lest she hit her target when he was distracted. "Found clothesline in the garage and tied her hands. Kiki finally woke up while Bree was out cold and started screaming, so I got her. Bree woke up and went berserk sooner than before, found a knife and cut herself loose before I came down."

"Bastard!"

A saucer shattered above his head.

Face twisted in rage, Brianna's eyes had rolled back in her head, showing only the whites, no pupils. In that state, she couldn't see anything. Something or someone else guided her hands—with dangerous precision.

"I had the baby with me, man," he said. "Ducked behind here to wait for help."

Brianna noticed Castiel peering into the living room and swiveled, hurling a full-sized plate at him. Her aim was true. If Castiel hadn't whipped his head back at the last instant, the plate would have shattered on his skull rather than the side of the archway.

"One of your stupid friends, Ronnie?" she yelled.

Castiel looked at Malik. "Her behavior is irrational."

"Was that your first clue?" Malik said, eyebrow arched. "We gotta get this situation under control before she hurts Kiki. She'd never forgive herself."

"How long do these episodes last?"

"Never this long," Malik said. "She's getting worse."

Having run out of plates, saucers, glasses and cups, Brianna grabbed a blender off the countertop, yanked the power plug from the wall and raised it over her head with both hands. Before she took aim at her brother, Castiel noticed her nose had started to bleed.

When Dean first stared down into the darkness, he had the odd sensation that he gazed into a bottomless pit, an abyss that consumed the souls of all who entered. But the disturbing thought was fleeting, the product of an imagination so often exceeded by the terrifying reality of a hunter's life. He followed Sam down the steep staircase and almost sighed in relief when he realized the passageway was only fifteen feet underground. The walls and ceiling were made of plywood painted a dull red—though maybe the red had been bright crimson once but faded over time—with loose boards on an earthen floor. A secret passageway carved in the earth and supported with the simplest DIY building materials.

With his shotgun resting against his right shoulder, Sam swung the flashlight in his left hand back and forth to expose any side passageways that might branch off from the main one, which was almost wide enough for two people to walk abreast. Nevertheless, Dean brought up the rear, armed with the machete in case anything came at them from behind while their attention was directed forward.

He took out his cell phone, but not simply for the extra illumination. Before they went any deeper underground, he called Cordero to warn him the new mothers might exhibit violent tendencies. Castiel was headed to the Green house, but he couldn't be everywhere at once. And if one new mother had flown into a murderous rage, Dean had a feeling the others might follow suit.

Cordero knew about the bouts of temporary rage and was currently dealing with Melissa Barrows, who had attacked and injured her own parents. Moreover, Cordero told him Captain Sands had gone to the Atherton house to stop Denise from trying to kill her husband.

"When will this stop, Agent?"

"Soon," Dean said. "One way or another, this stops soon."

Next Dean called Dr. Hartwell, to check on Chloe and Olivia, since he'd directed Castiel away from LMC, and to tell her about the attacks by the new mothers.

"Nothing's changed here," she said, clearly worried. "No response from Chloe or Olivia to any stimuli, their labor is arrested, and their heart rates are slowing down. They're not reacting to any treatment. As I told Agent Collins, I may need to perform C-sections on both women the minute I detect any distress in the babies."

"Agent Collins had to respond to another emergency," Dean said. He described what was happening with the other women: bouts of rage, followed by a period of brief unconsciousness and calm, followed by another bout of homicidal rage. "All patients at LMC. Were they given any kind of experimental drug? Anything with side effects? Like the world's worst case of postpartum depression? That might explain…?"

"No," she said definitively. "Nothing like that. I don't experiment on my patients with unknown or dangerous drugs."

"Didn't think so," Dean said, all but convinced the episodes were also linked to the pontianak, which was not something he could explain to a medical doctor.

"It's curious, the timing of these violent episodes," Dr. Hartwell said.

"Curious how?"

"Think about it," she said. "A period of rage, followed by a period of calm, coming in waves, one after another."

"Labor pains," Dean said, nodding. "The violence is the contraction, followed by the calm between contractions."

"But why?" she wondered. "Obviously these women aren't pregnant anymore."

"No."

"Women in labor may curse and scream, but…"

"They don't become homicidal."

"Dean," Sam called. "I've got something."

"Gotta go, Doc," Dean said.

"Agent Banks," she said before he could disconnect. "These women are slowly dying. If we can't discover the cause I won't let their babies die with them. Time is running out."

THIRTY

Dean tucked his cell phone back in his pocket and looked ahead to where Sam shone the flashlight beam. Unlike the crude underground passage braced with planks and plywood, the door at the end of the passage could have been found inside a typical home—except that it had been painted black.

Taking a moment, Dean looked up at the boarded passageway ceiling and tried to visualize how far and in which direction they'd walked since descending under the barn. "We're under the burnt silo."

Now Sam paused, pointing the flashlight toward the crude stairs and back again, making the mental calculation. "Maybe that fire wasn't an accident," he said. "Debris left to conceal the excavation."

"Of what?" Dean wondered.

"Whatever's behind this," Sam said as he redirected the light forward to examine the door. Over time, the doorjamb had warped, pinching the top right and bottom left corners of the door. Sam passed the flashlight back to

Dean, turned the knob and pushed to no effect.

"Locked?"

"Stuck," Sam said. "Back up."

They both took a step back. Sam raised his right foot and struck the door. It shuddered but held. A second kick and the lock popped free of the dislodged strike plate. With a squeal of protesting hinges the door swung inward, revealing an open space much wider than the passageway. Since Dean held the flashlight, he took the lead, shining the beam back and forth, up and down.

After the makeshift red passageway and the ominous black door, Dean had not expected to find a large room, painted white, approximately twelve feet wide and fifteen feet deep. Though the hallway appeared haphazard and unfinished—a means to an end—this room was relatively complete, though the construction was basic, consisting of sections of plywood nailed to a two-by-four framework, judging by the give in the floor. Utilitarian and quick to assemble once the space was excavated. In its original condition, nothing other than the lack of windows would have hinted that the room was underground, a space carved out of dirt. Since then, somebody had smashed through the bottom of the back wall, while years of moisture, mold and rot had taken their toll on the untreated surfaces of the wood. Here and there, sections of plywood bulged where the rotted wood had popped free of nails, and the lines of the room seemed out of true, though the floor remained level.

In the center of the room, at a skewed angle, stood a narrow, military-style hospital bed with low side rails and two welded IV drip poles rising from the head rail. At the foot of the bed, permanently welded to the frame, were two crude gynecological stirrups. The thin mattress, pillow and bedding were all stained and moldy. Dean suspected the darker stains were blood. The flashlight beam illuminated a metal ring attached to the side rail.

"Sammy," he said. "Look."

Sam stepped around him and lifted up the other dangling metal ring attached to the first by a short length of chain, rusty but easily recognizable. "Handcuffs."

"They don't leave until they pay the bill," Dean said, walking around the other side of the creepy hospital bed.

The right side of the room looked as if it had been struck by a whirlwind. A metal stool lay on its side, along with a large bucket, and pieces of a shattered enamel wash basin spread out from an overturned small table. In the near right corner, also on its side, near a severely cracked section of plywood, lay a wheeled baby crib. The metal tubing was mangled, with two wheels missing, the crib split in half.

Against the back wall, a large wooden cabinet had toppled over, leaning away from the wall at an awkward angle, one leg broken, shattered door panels scattered, along with broken jars, an assortment of pills decades past their use-by dates, and medical instruments, including a stethoscope, blood pressure cuff, a half-dozen crushed syringes, a black handheld inhaler that looked like a small gas mask to cover the nose and mouth, and freaky obstetrical forceps. Pinned under the forceps was a torn paper chart depicting Friedman's curve for estimating cervical dilation over time.

Dean moved on, inspecting the hole in the corner of the back wall. The broken section of plywood had burst into the room, as if something from beyond the wall had crashed inside. And what he found beyond the wall looked like a small addition to the original room, an unfinished storage area with some tattered black cloth in a hole about the size of a...

"Shallow grave," Dean said. "Somebody was buried here."

"Dean—I got something," Sam called. "Under the cabinet."

Sam laid his shotgun on the hospital bed. He crouched, gripped the front edge of the cabinet and lifted it upright, but not before a drawer fell out and dumped a worn leather-bound journal on the floor. The shattered cabinet balanced precariously on three intact legs, but the Winchesters directed their attention downward, at what—or who—had been under it.

The flashlight beam revealed the desiccated corpse of a tall man in a torn white lab coat, brown trousers and black leather shoes. Most of his dark hair had fallen out and what remained looked like a fright wig. His face was gaunt, stretched into a horrified rictus. The skin around both eyes had been shredded, the bone underneath scored, the sockets dark and empty. Further down, the body's midsection had been ripped open, ribs shattered, pelvis cracked. Dark stains discolored the white lab coat from the corpse's sternum all the way down.

"Grave you found over there wasn't his," Sam concluded. "Looks like he was thrown against the cabinet, killed right here and left to rot."

"Pontianak victim zero," Dean said. "My money's on Calvin Nodd." He kneeled beside the body, checked the pockets, and came up with a billfold containing forty-two dollars and a faded Indiana driver's license. "Bingo! Doctor Nodd never left town."

Sam glanced toward the shallow grave. "Was the pontianak here all along?"

"She rises from the grave and kills Nodd. But why?"

"Dean, she was returning the favor," Sam guessed. "He handcuffed patients to that bed. This was his kill room."

"Why the operating room if he planned to kill them?"

Sam picked up the leather-bound journal, opened the cover and read a name. "This belonged to Nodd," he said and started flipping through the early pages. "He's writing about events that happened during the war, when he was in the Philippines… It's a recitation of atrocities Nodd witnessed directly or after the fact. Dean, I think this journal was his attempt at self-therapy."

"Lot of good it did."

Sam shook his head. "Brutal stuff. Whole families and villages—men, women and children—massacred by machine-gun fire… weak and injured prisoners were bayoneted, then beheaded and dumped in mass graves. Others doused in petrol and burned alive."

"Saw a documentary on the Bataan Death March. Nasty stuff."

After reading several sections in a hushed whisper, Sam flipped through more pages, skipping ahead, seeking answers about what could have happened fifty years ago to spawn a pontianak terrorizing Braden Heights today.

"Yeah," Sam said. "It gets worse."

"Not surprised."

"Apparently Nodd was captured by the Japanese," Sam said. "His writing is a mess, almost illegible, like he struggled to put some of this on paper, reliving the horror... says he never told anyone about this stuff, not even Malaya. Nobody in the service ever knew he'd been captured..."

"How is that possible?"

Sam shook his head and kept reading. "He was forced by a Japanese doctor—Kurokawa, but sometimes he calls him Dr. Smiles—to assist in wartime experiments... he's talking about amputations and vivisections of healthy civilians captured during the occupation... Nodd's writing... he's almost incoherent at this point... the victims were alive during these surgeries and Kurokawa refused to use sedation on any of them. When he finished with a subject, assuming they were still alive, he would bob his head and smile broadly, then slice their throats open."

"A nightmare clown college graduate."

"Kurokawa removed limbs, eyes, genitalia... he would cut them open and remove organs... all in the name of science, testing endurance, survival times... and nutrition..."

"Do I even want to know?"

"Looks like he fed human flesh and organs to the other prisoners," Sam said, shaking his head in disgust. "Something about alternative food sources in times of severe rationing. He cut up men, women—and children... to test the quality of the meat. And Kurokawa made Nodd participate in all of this, acted like he was Nodd's mentor. Nodd finally guessed that Kurokawa was testing his psychological limits, to see how far he could push him on penalty of torture and death before Nodd would refuse."

"Did he?" Dean asked. "Stop?"

"Nodd didn't stop," Sam said. "He snapped. Happened around the time Kurokawa started cutting up children and feeding them to other prisoners. Nodd acted like he was going along with it, very helpful… until he gained Kurokawa's trust or at least inattention—he was never sure—long enough to conceal a scalpel. He picked his moment, when the two guards who were always present were distracted. Nodd flew into a rage, sliced open Kurokawa's carotid artery, then jumped the nearest guard, cut his throat and killed the other guard with the first guard's gun. He escaped in the night with minor physical wounds… told everyone afterward that he'd been injured and pinned down in enemy occupied territory until it was safe to get away… the whole ordeal messed with his head…"

Dean exhaled as if he'd been holding his breath during the entire recitation. "I can imagine."

"Whole pages about how he knew he'd be punished… cursed for what he did, killing the innocents… until he met Malaya—Riza's mother—while recovering from his physical injuries. When he writes about her, his whole tone changes… as if he rediscovered hope again, the doom and gloom forgotten. Says he's found peace in himself. Looks like it ends there…"

Sam flipped through several blank pages… and then the

writing continued in a cramped hand, condensed and angry in the force of the letters on the paper.

"That doesn't look good," Dean commented.

"This section… it's after Malaya died during childbirth. Convinced he's being punished, that the hope was false and his life is cursed. A cruel trick of fate to make him think he escaped retribution for wartime atrocities… He knows he has to raise Riza alone and there's no joy in it… he's convinced it's another trick. Love his daughter and she will die because he's cursed. Or detach himself and she will become an agent of his punishment. Thinks he's doomed no matter what he does."

"His kid never stood a chance."

"That's the last he wrote… for years."

"What happened?"

"Riza hooked up with a drifter, Ronald Deluzio… Nodd forbade her from seeing him, so naturally Riza—rebelling against her emotionally absent father—couldn't resist Ronnie. Ends up pregnant, which infuriates Nodd. Like she's making a mockery of her mother's death. Squandering the life her mother's sacrifice gave her. Says he blames the hospital for killing her mother. His mistake was letting others control what happened to her. Riza has always thought her life would have been so much better if her father had died instead."

"With Nodd as her old man," Dean said, "kid has a point."

"So he convinces Riza to have her child at home," Sam said. "Ah, here's why. Apparently Ronnie couldn't handle the idea of fatherhood at his age. Nodd writes, 'I told her the last thing she wanted to hear, but it proves I was right all along and that's reason enough. She must have had her own doubts because she now believes, as I have always warned her, that Ronnie ran off and left her to take care of the child alone.'" Sam paused, frowned. "Okay, this takes a turn…"

"What now?"

"Riza, devastated by Ronnie's abandonment, agreed to the at-home birth and Nodd made the preparations, had everything he needed. This time he was in control… but during Riza's labor, he was filled with rage and disgust at how Riza had wasted the life her mother gave her in death. Riza was screaming in pain. Nodd decided against drugs because they would take control from him, and he started berating her, blaming her for the pain, blaming her for killing her mother. And then he… Dean, he strangled his daughter to death during labor."

Her face contorted with rage, Brianna raised the blender over her head in a two-handed grip. For a second or two, she paused, hands trembling, as if an internal struggle raged for control of her body. But the hesitation was fleeting and she hurled the appliance at her brother.

"Duck!" Castiel told Malik who had, a moment before, leaned down to check on Kiara.

When Malik hunkered down behind the sofa, Castiel raised a hand and sent a small wave of force to redirect the blender sideways, where it struck and toppled a flatscreen TV.

"The hell was that?"

"A blender," Castiel said. "And a television."

Before this latest attack, Castiel had noted the onset of a nosebleed from Brianna's left nostril. Whatever force possessed her and triggered the cyclical bouts of rage apparently caused physical damage to the host body. Either that, or her internal struggle for control was not without its own cost. Lacking his angelic ability to heal, Castiel needed to subdue Brianna before she suffered serious or permanent damage.

"This is beyond crazy, man!" Malik said.

Removing the necessity for her to fight the murderous possession might alleviate the physical toll it was taking. Until they discovered how to stop the recurring violent episodes, restraint remained the best option not only to protect potential victims of the attacks but the host body as well.

"The rope?" Castiel asked.

"Fell off the coffee table."

Castiel spotted the discarded clothesline, coiled between the front of the sofa and the coffee table. "Next time she passes out, take the infant upstairs. I will subdue Brianna."

"Don't hurt her, man," Malik said. "She's my sister."

Brianna yanked out the kitchen drawers one by one, then paused and smiled. When her hand rose from the last drawer, she held a long serrated knife. This time her hand was eerily steady. "I'll carve your face off," she shouted as she walked out from behind the counter. "You hear me, Ronnie? I'll carve your lying face off and shove it down your throat."

Castiel decided he couldn't wait for her to pass out.

"Run," he told Malik. "Now!"

"So Nodd killed his own daughter," Dean said, the ramifications sinking in. "Explains why nobody ever heard from Riza again."

Shaking his head in disbelief, Sam returned his attention to the horrors revealed in the journal. "Nodd says Riza must share some of the blame for her own death, that there's justice in her dying in a way similar to how she killed her mother. But Riza died before she could give birth. At first Nodd says this is fine because he won't get attached to a grandchild who would only die or punish him later in life, as Riza had." He flipped through some pages. "Oh… I was expecting remorse… but this is almost the opposite. He talks about the unexpected power he felt in taking a life at the moment of birth—short-circuiting creation—that it made him feel invincible. Total control."

"Doctor with a warped Old Testament god complex."

Sam paged through more of the journal, his look of disgust growing more pronounced. "He's talking about other girls now…"

"Right," Dean said, realization dawning. "The copycats."

Sam nodded. "He talks about other wayward girls very close to their due date, how he offers them and their boyfriends money for a fresh start in a new town, under the strict condition they tell nobody about his generosity. Reason he gives them is he doesn't want 'beggars lining up at his door looking for handouts.'"

"Free money, no strings attached," Dean said. "What's not to like?"

"Plenty," Sam said. "So these couples tell their close friends they're leaving town for a better life. Maybe they compare themselves to Riza and Ronnie, but they leave the promised bankroll from Nodd out of those conversations. Once their friends expect them to run away, Nodd kills the young men and holds the women captive until they go into labor."

"And strangles them," Dean said. "So nobody left Larkin's Korner."

"Five couples," Sam said. "He killed them all." Sam turned a few more pages, nearing the end of the journal. "Until he had the 'lapse of judgment' at the hospital where he worked, which was his professional undoing. Knowing nothing about his homicidal hobby, his wealthy and powerful family swoop in to protect one of their own. As far as they're concerned, he was traumatized by his war experience—without even knowing the full extent of it—then lost his wife and all contact with his only child and future grandchild. Taking full advantage of the sympathy card, Nodd was plotting his escape—from Larkin's Korner and, more importantly, from suspicion and scrutiny. From what he's written here, he planned to continue his killing spree..."

Sam paused, shaking his head in disbelief at what he was reading. "He now believes Kurokawa—Dr. Smiles—really was a mentor, but at the time Nodd couldn't see the power the man was offering him. He rambles about that for... a long time." Sam turned the few last pages. "He's made a checklist of everything he needs to do before he leaves town... pack up his equipment, destroy any evidence in his underground 'workshop'... says he's not worried about anyone discovering the bodies of the boyfriends, which he weighted and dumped in a remote lake fifty miles outside of town, but he buried the pregnant women in the woods on Larkin land and worries they'll be found, decides it's not worth the risk. But he says,

'Riza's situation is another matter altogether.'" Sam flipped back and forth between two pages. "Doesn't say where her body is buried... The next entry is about finding a new place to continue after he assumes a false identity. That's where it ends."

"Riza was the first," Dean said.

"She was special to him," Sam added. "Not for who she was. But for getting him hooked on the power high from snuffing out life."

"Special enough to want her close?" Dean asked, turning the flashlight beam toward the shallow grave in the corner.

"Dean, maybe we got this wrong," Sam said. "We assumed Malaya dying in childbirth triggered the appearance of the pontianak. But that was an accident. What if it happened sixteen years later, when Nodd killed his own daughter during childbirth?"

"He comes down here to dispose of the body, again—"

"—and Riza somehow comes back to life *as* a pontianak."

"With a major score to settle against dear old Dad."

"Makes sense," Sam said. "The man she loves abandons her and her unborn baby to an overbearing father who has been emotionally absent her whole life, which ends when he murders her and the unborn child."

"As a pontianak, she makes it her mission to kill the men around other pregnant women before they have a chance to betray or hurt them."

"Far as she's concerned," Sam said, "they're all worthless and unreliable."

"Should update Cass," Dean said. "Let him know what we've found."

He took out his cell phone, checked the signal: one bar. He tried walking out into the passageway. Not great, but he had to try. He dialed Castiel and waited three indistinct rings before the angel picked up. First thing he heard was a crash.

"Dean?"

"Cass? What's happening?"

"I'm at the Greens'," Castiel said. "I'm... assessing the situation."

Sounded like he had his hands full. Dean gave him a brief rundown of what they'd found in Nodd's secret underground room and in his journal. "So Nodd killed his daughter and those copycat couples. Then Riza came back to after-life as a pontianak."

"And killed her... father," Castiel said. Another crash sounded. "Now any man close to a pregnant woman is fair game."

The connection was faint, with occasional drops of audio. Dean hunched over, eyes closed and a finger pressed to his left ear to focus on the call. "Kill them all," he said. "Let God sort them out."

"God never participated in... a sorting process," Castiel explained in all seriousness.

"Don't think she's losing any sleep over it."

"Dean," Sam called.

"Just a second."

"Dean!" Sam said insistently. "Riza."

Dean looked up from his call. "What about R—?"

"She's here."

THIRTY-ONE

At Castiel's urging, Malik had run upstairs with a swaddled Kiara in his arms.

Brianna was determined to kill Malik, her own brother, but in his absence, she seemed perfectly willing to accept Castiel as an amuse-bouche before moving on to her fratricidal entrée. She rushed him from the kitchen, clutching a long serrated knife in her right hand.

Before taking the baby to safety, Malik had made Castiel promise not to hurt his sister. Even without that request, Castiel had not planned on harming Brianna, but refusing to created a tactical problem. How does one peacefully stop a person consumed by a fit of uncontrolled, irrational rage?

Castiel waited until she was an arm's length away from him—knife raised high to plunge it into his chest—then grabbed a throw pillow from a chair next to him. Gripping the pillow between both hands, he held it firmly in front of him to intercept the blow. The tip of the knife ripped through the embroidered fabric and the polyester fiber within, emerging from the near side, inches from his chest but trapped. He twisted his arms to wrench the blade from her grasp.

"Brianna," Castiel said in a calming tone, "you don't want to do this."

Shrieking in frustration over the loss of her lethal weapon, she grabbed a ceramic lamp from the table beside the chair and smashed it across the side of Castiel's head.

The unexpected blow stunned him. He found himself on one knee as he regained his senses. And Brianna had returned to the kitchen in search of more makeshift weapons.

Unless he could pin her down and wait for the next dormant period in her cycle, he would have to endure the nonstop assault that had trapped Malik behind the sofa. He dabbed at his scalp to see if he was bleeding, but his hand came away clean. He stuffed the bundle of unused clothesline in his jacket pocket and started toward the kitchen, determined to subdue the frenzied woman.

She grabbed an iron skillet out of a cabinet and threw it at him overhand, like an ax. Castiel raised his hand, palm out, then flicked it sideways with a push of force, and the skillet veered away in midair, smashing into several staircase balusters. A moment later, the tempered glass carafe from a coffee maker spun toward him. He flicked his wrist in the opposite direction and the carafe shattered against the wall.

Dean chose that moment to call and update him on what he and Sam had found under the old Larkin barn. The angel took in the information about Nodd being a serial killer and his daughter becoming the vengeful force known as a pontianak while dodging kitchen projectiles hurled with deadly force. Brianna had shifted her attention to the pantry and a plentiful row of canned goods.

Castiel heard Sam say the chilling words, "She's here."

And then the connection died.

Even if Castiel had his full Grace and could instantly appear next to the Winchesters, he would not have done so. The brothers could take care of themselves. He wasn't so sure Malik, with a newborn in his care, would survive five more minutes with his homicidal sister. The angel was needed here, at this moment.

The closer he came to Brianna, the more desperately she flung cans at him. He dodged some, redirected others, and continued to close the gap. When her supply of canned goods was exhausted and she cast about for something heavier than cereal boxes filled with bran flakes or uncooked pasta shells to hurl at him, he caught her wrists in his hands.

"Stop this," he said in his most commanding voice.

She screamed and kicked him in the shins.

He winced in pain just as she lunged forward, teeth bared to bite his face—

—and she fell limp, dangling by her wrists.

Wasting no time, he carried her to the nearest kitchen chair, sat her down and tied her hands behind her back. He cut another two sections of rope and tied her ankles to the crossbar between the chair legs. If the rope held she would awaken confused but sedate, enough time to convince her why she needed to be restrained before the unreasoning rage took hold again.

For now, Malik and Kiara were safe, but Castiel needed to check on the families of Melissa Barrows and Denise Atherton. Once they were safe, he could aid the Winchesters. And yet, he still wondered about Chloe and Olivia. If Sam and Dean stopped the pontianak, the women might recover, but how long could they and their unborn babies be left in a non-responsive state, with the mothers' heart rates steadily dropping?

Assistant Chief Cordero dropped to one knee beside Melissa Barrows as she regained consciousness on the living room floor of her home. He helped her sit up, left hand supporting her back, while his right held his handcuffs. Melissa looked around the room, confused. Then her eyes located her mother lying on the sofa with a cold compress on her forehead.

"Mom? Are you okay? What happened?"

"I'll be fine, dear," Barbara Crane said.

"You've had an… episode," Cordero said in a soothing tone to keep her calm long enough to restrain her.

"Episode? What's going on?"

"I'd like to put these handcuffs on you before—"

"Handcuffs? Are you serious? You're arresting me? Mom? Dad? What's happening?"

"I'm not arresting you," Cordero said. "This is strictly precau—"

Melissa's eyelids fluttered.

"Look out!" Alan said. "That happens right before—"

Suddenly, Melissa punched Cordero in the mouth, splitting his lip.

Momentarily stunned, he almost fell over as she launched herself at him, trying to claw his face with her fingernails. "Bastard!" she screamed.

Fortunately, Cordero had spent years dealing with unruly suspects and angry drunks before getting promoted to glorified desk jockey at BHPD. With a deft move, he slipped a cuff over her left wrist, snapped it shut, and pulled her arm behind her back. She was practically hissing and spitting in anger as he locked the other ring around her right wrist, and she continued to kick. "Don't make me use the Taser," he said, hoping the threat would be sufficient deterrent.

"No!" Barbara said, horrified at the thought.

"You can't reason with her," Alan said. "Not when she's like this."

"Give me a hand," Cordero said. Cordero carried leg irons in the trunk of his police cruiser, but had a simpler solution right in his belt: nylon cable ties. He couldn't transport her with them, but he only needed to get her under control for now. He grabbed her flailing ankles and pinned them together with both hands. Then he had Alan wrap a long cable tie around them and zip it snug.

She twisted and strained against the metal and nylon restraints, but as long as he only saw the whites of her eyes, he had no other option. "Truly sorry about this, Mrs. Barrows," he said, even though she couldn't process the apology.

He called Captain Sands at the Atherton home. She and Gary Atherton had managed to restrain Denise in a similar fashion, although Jaime said she'd likely have one hell of a black eye courtesy of Mrs. Atherton.

"Holding an ice pack on my eye as we speak."

"Split lip here," Cordero said. "No ice yet."

"So… What now?"

"Ice seems like a good idea."

"I meant about these women?"

Cordero looked down at Melissa Barrows, straining and cursing every few seconds. This was beyond anything he'd ever encountered in his law enforcement career. Hell, it was beyond anything he'd ever heard about. He shook his head, realized she couldn't see the gesture over the phone and said, "I don't know, Jaime." Then, because he was supposed to be the one with the answers, even when no answers appeared forthcoming, he added, "We'll think of something."

If he was a betting man, he'd put all his chips on the FBI agents finding a solution because, as much as he hated to admit it to himself, he doubted he'd ever know how to resolve a situation this bizarre.

THIRTY-TWO

Riza Nodd, murdered and reborn as a wrathful pontianak over fifty years ago, appeared beside her former shallow grave.

At the moment of her arrival, Sam felt a sudden chill and a brief displacement in the air as a sweet-smelling breeze washed over him. But he didn't see her. Not at first.

His attention had been focused on Dean, on the far side of the military hospital bed speaking to Castiel. Before making that call, Dean had laid his machete at the foot of the bed, but he still held the flashlight in his left hand, which he had pressed to his left ear. As he talked and turned at random, the beam of light played about the interior of the underground workroom, splashing against the warped plywood walls, gleaming off the bed rails, exposing the ruin of the supply cabinet but without dipping low enough to highlight Calvin Nodd's shattered ribs and ruined eye sockets.

As he swiveled to face the bed, Sam turned away from the bright beam and saw her standing there, less than three feet behind him, motionless as a rotting statue.

Caught off-guard by her sudden appearance, Sam froze as well. She gave the impression of coiled menace. Like a startled snake, she might strike at the slightest provocation. He was uncomfortably aware that he and Dean had invaded her lair. She might as well have posted a sign on the black door: TRESPASSERS WILL BE DISEMBOWELED.

Without looking her directly in the eyes—a surefire provocation—he examined her in that long moment before either one of them reacted to the presence of the other. With her head bowed, her long straggly black hair falling forward, her pale face was mostly hidden. Thin to the point of emaciation, she wore the tattered remnants of a black burial dress that left her dirt-smeared arms and most of her legs and bare feet exposed. Her narrow frame made her swollen abdomen appear even more pronounced—damning evidence of the child never born. But his gaze settled on her long fingers ending in thick, hooked claws with sharp points. Once he noticed them, the fingers twitched, as if she couldn't wait to rip him open.

"Dean."

"Just a second."

Her head turned ever so slightly.

Sam followed the line of her gaze to—Calvin Nodd's body.

Even through the stringy veil of her black hair, Sam saw her wicked smile at the sight of her dead father. Worse, the broad smile stretched wide to reveal a fearsome row of pointed teeth.

"Dean!" Sam called. With Riza about to attack, Sam needed to act fast and Dean had no idea all hell was about to break loose. "Riza."

Finally, Dean looked up from his call. "What about R—?" But now he could see for himself.

"She's here."

Dean shoved his phone in his pocket, his gaze darting to the machete he'd left at the foot of the bed, currently out of arm's reach. And he, like Sam, must have had the sense that any sudden movement would trigger an attack.

"Avoid direct eye contact," Sam said softly to Dean, reminding him of her trigger. Then Sam looked toward the pontianak, his eyes hooded a bit, focused on a spot beneath her chin, peripherally aware that she still stared at her father's withered corpse. "He deserved it," Sam said, addressing her directly. "For what he did to you and the others."

A sound halfway between a groan and a sigh rose from her throat, which Sam interpreted as assent.

"But the others didn't," Sam continued. "The men you killed were innocent. You have to stop—now. Whatever you're doing at the hospital, you're killing mothers and unborn babies."

The strangled growl that erupted from her throat was ripe with disagreement. She had no intention of stopping anything. The guttural sound was the only warning Sam had of her impending attack. All the ominous energy brimming beneath the surface of her inhuman exterior exploded in a sudden lunge, claws extended, fangs bared.

With practiced ease, Sam swung his shotgun in front of her and fired a rock salt round at close range—to no effect. If she'd been an angry spirit, the salt would have forced her to dissipate briefly, but her rebirth as a pontianak had repurposed her flesh and bones, and different rules applied. Nevertheless, Sam worked the slide to eject the spent shell casing and pump a fresh round in the chamber, firing again just to keep her at bay.

Dean whipped his Beretta semi-automatic handgun out from the back of his waistband and emptied the magazine into her, almost every round striking home. The bullets ripped into her decayed flesh, most passing through her body to gouge holes in the plywood walls behind her. But no blood flowed from the wounds, the damage strictly cosmetic. Obviously, the force animating her body had little if any need for flowing blood or functioning internal organs.

She tilted her head to the side, almost as if to ask, *Is that all you got?*

With the slight motion, a clump of stringy hair shifted away from her dark, sunken eyes and Sam caught a brief glimpse of them—completely dark and inhuman—an instant before she lunged at him for the second time. Instead of shooting her with a harmless blast of rock salt, he held the shotgun up in both hands to block her vicious claws from gutting him. But the force of the blow staggered him, sending shockwaves down his arms.

She grabbed the shotgun in her long hands and hurled him against the broken cabinet. His body struck the front, lengthwise, and it fell on top of him, pinning him against Nodd's desiccated corpse. Sam felt several of Nodd's remaining ribs crack under the pressure.

Riza pounced on top of the cabinet, landing heavily despite her frail-looking form, and her added weight drove Sam further into Nodd's corpse. With a loud crack, his sternum gave way, and the remaining ribs broke and crumbled in rapid succession. Sam's weight squashed what was left of the corpse's shriveled organs. Trapped between a reanimated corpse and a long-dead one, Sam turned his head to the side, trying to escape the overpowering stench of decay. But he had a more immediate concern.

Riza lashed out with her powerful claws, smashing her way through the back of the cabinet, ripping out whole sections of wood, to reach Sam's flesh in the most direct way possible.

Trapped under the cabinet, Sam glimpsed Dean's legs moving to the foot of the military hospital bed, no doubt to try his luck with the machete since bullets had failed to slow her down. As Dean rushed toward Sam's position, the smashing over his head stopped. Riza had seen Dean's approach. Sam heard the blade of the machete whistle through the air, punctuated by Dean's grunt of effort. He was swinging for the fences, but the pontianak must have caught his forearm mid-strike. A moment later, the flashlight dropped to the floor as Dean's feet abruptly rose from the ground, and this time Riza grunted with the effort of hurling Dean across the room. A thunderous impact followed, as if someone had set off a small bomb behind one of the plywood walls.

Dean's body slumped to the wooden floor, pieces of rotted plywood scattered around his legs. As Dean groaned, the handle of the machete slipped from his hand, and his body, what little Sam could see of it from his restricted view, seemed to fall backward into the gap behind the shattered wall. Sam stared, helpless but hopeful. Unfortunately, Dean lay still, apparently unconscious.

A moment later, the destruction of the cabinet over his head resumed. After one powerful blow, Sam felt the cabinet shift above him. Wood cracked and split. The weight atop him seemed to ease. The cabinet had been split down the middle and, as Riza's weight shifted, each side slid away from Sam's pinned body.

Perched on the cabinet half to his left, Riza Nodd crouched above him, head leaning over the gap, her hair hanging down around her death-pale face and soulless black eyes. Her mouth opened wide, exposing rows of pointed teeth, and a wet hiss rose from the back of her throat. Saliva hung from her lower lip and chin in viscous strands. Raising her right forearm beside her face, she opened and closed her hand one finger at a time, either admiring her claws or savoring the moment before she disemboweled him.

She'd forgotten one minor detail. Sam still gripped the shotgun in both hands and, no longer pinned under the weight of the cabinet, he could finally move his arms again. With a rapid motion, he worked the shotgun's slide and blasted a round of rock salt into her black eyes at point blank range. In an instant, the flesh around her eyes was scoured away. The eyes themselves appeared pitted and cloudy, shifting from obsidian to milky white. Howling, she leapt off the smashed cabinet.

Freeing his legs, Sam scrambled away on all fours, desperately trying to put some distance between them. Blinded or not, she came after him, her bare feet slapping lightly against the cold wooden floor. He rolled over, shoving the shotgun barrel crosswise over his head, barely in time to block her claws. Parrying a second and a third blow, his arms grew numb from the sheer force of her attacks.

A fourth blow dislodged the shotgun from his grasp and she swatted it aside. It struck the black door then fell to the floor, far out of reach. She oriented on Sam's breathing, waiting a moment as the white film seemed to evaporate from her eyes, restoring them to pure black. Flashing her wicked, pointy-toothed smile, she raised her arms and pounced.

Sam rolled under the bed, avoiding the swipe of claws, which raked deep furrows in the wooden floor inches from his leg. With a frustrated roar, she backhanded the hospital bed, sending it sailing across the workroom, trailing its rotted mattress, pillow and stained bed covers before it crashed into the far corner of the room.

Gulping breaths of the fetid air, Sam sat on the floor with his knees drawn up, arms outstretched behind him, palms pressed to the floor for support.

Riza loomed over him, claws twitching at her side, ready to counter any move he made, seconds away from gutting him like a fish and feasting on his organs. He had to wonder if she'd gouge out his eyes before or after.

THIRTY-THREE

Once Castiel confirmed that both Assistant Chief Cordero and Captain Sands had the Barrows and Atherton situations under control, he assured Malik he and his two fellow FBI agents would have a solution soon. Promising to call when it was safe to release Brianna from her bonds, Castiel left the Green home and drove his Lincoln Continental Mark V to the old Larkin farmhouse with little regard for posted speed limits. Calls to Sam's and Dean's phones went to voicemail. Either they'd lost their cell signal underground or, more likely, close proximity to the pontianak interfered with reception.

If the Winchesters had defeated the creature, he would have heard from them by now. Their continued silence meant they were in danger or they had...

No sense dwelling on what might have happened.

Flicking on his high beams to illuminate the dark country road ahead, he pressed the accelerator pedal to the floor and the large car roared through the night. When he passed the billboard announcing the strip mall outlet stores, he hit the brake and spotted the gravel driveway leading up to the dark farmhouse and barn.

His tires rolled over the lowered chain and crunched along the gravel incline until he noticed the silhouette of the Impala at the top of the gentle hill. After parking beside the Chevy, Castiel strode purposely toward the barn, his flashlight sweeping back and forth to light the way. Entering through the open side door that faced the farmhouse, he proceeded down the short hallway between the feed and tack rooms. A few moments later, he located the formerly hidden doorway panel that led to the underground passage. About to descend, he paused at the sound of shuffling. It seemed to be coming from both ends of the wide corridor that ran the length of the barn.

"Sam? Dean?" Castiel called. "Are you injured?"

Out of the darkness, shambling shapes resolved as silhouettes, two approaching from one side, three from the other. All five of the hunched shapes belonged to women, their features cloaked in shadow, out of range of the flashlight.

"Five…"

The number was significant.

Calvin Nodd murdered five pregnant young women after Riza.

Another few steps, and his flashlight revealed their pale forms as they formed a circle around him. Each wore tattered clothing, caked with dirt from their shallow graves. Mud-streaked, their bare limbs reminded him of something. Another moment and it came to him. The fleeting memory of white sycamore limbs poking out of the loose mounds of earth at the Coventry Crossing construction site. Had he been that close to finding them? And while he helped Malik fend off his sister's attacks, had they somehow arisen and walked through the night? As a pontianak, Riza Nodd must have reanimated them and called them to her.

To defend her? Or to kill for her? Or both.

He examined them with the flashlight beam, one by one. They were hunched and decayed, faces obscured by matted hair, but had more flesh on their bones than he would have expected after five decades. Each had a large, rounded abdomen, as they continued to carry the rotted husks of their unborn children long after their deaths.

A moment later, he noticed that they were changing, evolving. In addition to regaining flesh lost to death and decay, claws visibly grew at the end of their elongated fingers and crooked grins revealed pointed teeth bursting through anemic gums. They were themselves transforming into pontianaks.

Determined to stop the growing threat they represented, Castiel belatedly realized they had him surrounded, cut off from the door to the underground passageway. One swiped at him with her newfound claws. He ducked to the side to avoid the blow, but another shoved him from behind with enough force to knock him down.

Soon they'll have the full strength of a pontianak.

They stared down at him, inching forward, their circle contracting. In the pale wash of his flashlight, their dark eyes seemed to glow with a cold fire. If they were evolving into the form of pontianaks, he knew of one way to put them down. He reached for the heavy metal weapon in his jacket pocket. If he'd known then what he knew now, he would have brought four more.

One at a time, he told himself.

Then the one standing directly in front of him shimmered and resolved into a new form. At first, he thought the change represented a stage in the human-to-pontianak transformation but she looked more human now, not less; different, but more than familiar to him. Whoever she had been before death, that identity had vanished, replaced by another. He blinked several times, but the face defied logic.

The face belonged to Claire Novak.

THIRTY-FOUR

Dean shook off the mental cobwebs, unsure how long he'd been out cold.

But a loud crash had brought him back to struggling consciousness.

Last thing he remembered was taking a violent, overhand swing at the pontianak, coming in at an angle sure to lop off her foul-smelling head, but she'd caught his wrist and tossed him across the room like a rag doll. As he shifted his position, he noticed all the broken, crumbly plywood around his legs and on his jeans. Remarkably, the flashlight still worked, spreading a wan illumination across the room. His upper torso was wedged into a hole in the wall his own body had created on impact. He had an inkling what it might feel like to be Wile E. Coyote.

Another muddled moment passed before he realized he'd broken through a false wall into a hidden compartment. To his left, he saw the overturned hospital bed in the corner. In the center of the room, Riza Nodd stood over Sam—who'd

lost the shotgun, not that it had done him much good—
and looked about one hot second away from gutting him
or snatching his eyeballs. Maybe the indecision about which
assault to commit first was the only thing holding her back.

Dean's machete lay just out of reach. He'd need to lunge
forward to grab it. But if he didn't distract Riza pronto, Sam
was a goner.

He tried to rise, felt resistance and heaved himself upward.

Something rattled and shifted behind him.

Glancing up, Dean startled at the sight of a withered
corpse, little more than a skeleton. "Whoa!"

Riza surged forward, taking a swipe at Sam, who dropped
flat on his back to evade her claws. At the same time, he raised
his legs and struck her in the abdomen with the soles of his
boots. She staggered back a few steps, not nearly far enough.

Dean lurched upward to pry himself out of the gap in the
false wall, while half expecting the skeleton to reanimate and
throttle him with its bony hands. His violent movement
jarred the skeleton again, and this time the skull—with
scattered patches of shoulder-length blond hair and a paper-
thin sheath of skin stretched taut over the bone—broke free,
striking Dean in the chest before falling into the main room
and rolling unevenly toward Riza.

Pausing in her attack on Sam, Riza fixed on the displaced
skull, sensing… something.

Sam looked over his shoulder, staring at the headless
skeleton as Dean pried himself free and snatched the
machete by the handle. Glancing back to see what had
caught Sam's attention, he noticed the corpse in the wall

wore the remnants of a black leather jacket.

Sam pointed at the skeleton, but turned to face the pontianak.

"That's him…" Sam said. "That's Ronnie. He never abandoned you, Riza. It was your father. He killed Ronnie and lied to you about it."

Riza stared at the skull. Then her head slowly rose to stare at the body hidden in the wall all these years, in her own lair. She'd never known.

Sam eased out of her line of sight and climbed gradually to his feet, his motions slow and deliberate, nothing to startle her or trigger a reflexive attack. A single swipe of her claws could gut him or rip out his throat.

Riza Nodd trembled with indecision.

Perhaps questioning her purpose: Her reason for vengeance had been built on half-truths and lies. Her father had been the cause of all her misery, her death and the death of the man she loved and thought had abandoned her.

Dean crouched, watching and waiting as Sam eased around Riza. His brother's hand had slipped into his jacket pocket. Dean's hand drifted to the metal object in his own jacket, one of the railroad spikes they purchased at On Track Locomotive Repair before coming to the farmhouse. Despite Riza's indecision, Sam had to know other lives were still in danger. He couldn't wait. There was still only one way for this to end. No mercy. Sam had to put her down.

Impatience surged within Dean. The need to act, to attack, to take the decision out of Sam's hands and kill her himself verged on overwhelming. When his impatience transformed into a simmering anger, he caught himself. Branded on his forearm, the Mark of Cain had begun to itch and throb, almost a burning sensation, goading him into a reckless assault. With considerable effort, he restrained the urge. The rational side of him knew that if he charged the pontianak now, he risked not just his own life, but Sam's.

Riza's hands twitched.

Maybe she sensed Sam removing the railroad spike from his pocket, holding it concealed in his hand, inching behind her. If she turned now…

A battle raged silently within Dean as he struggled not only to ignore the siren call of rage from the Mark, burning with the heat of white phosphorus, but to remain utterly still while suppressing it. A sheen of sweat dampened his brow. He couldn't attack her but—

"Your father," Dean called out, loud enough for her to hear without startling her. As he'd hoped, her gaze darted to her left, toward him and further away from Sam. "Real Edgar Allan Poe fan. Except plywood instead of bricks."

Still, Sam hesitated.

Don't let this go sideways…

Finally, Dean couldn't wait any longer. "Do it, Sammy!"

THIRTY-FIVE

With the railroad spike gripped in his right hand, flashlight in his left, Castiel climbed to his feet and backed away from the Claire doppelganger, unwilling to strike her down, even though he knew her appearance was a lie.

"You're not Claire."

It took him another moment or two to see through his own misperception. The evolving pontianak hadn't taken on Claire's appearance. She'd become the spitting image of Chloe. In the darkness, lit by the darting beam of the flashlight, his eyes had deceived him once again. How could he trust himself to determine who really stood before him? The recent mothers had been consumed by homicidal rages. Chloe and Olivia had slipped into a comatose state. In light of those events, he could imagine a situation where Chloe had left her maternity bed and made her way out here. What if he was looking at the real Chloe Sikes now, not a reanimated corpse that had taken on her likeness? Could he risk killing her?

One of the other newborn pontianaks struck him from behind, a powerful and painful blow with her fresh claws, slicing through his coat and raking his flesh. Wincing in pain, he drove his forearm into the collarbone of the pontianak on his left and slammed her into the walk next to the Dutch door of a horse stall.

He raised the railroad spike next to his ear, a moment away from driving the crude point deep into the newly formed hole at the nape of her neck. But she shimmered underneath his forearm, becoming another Chloe doppelganger—unless *she* was the real Chloe—and he stayed his hand.

Hissing, the four other pontianaks closed ranks around him.

By switching his grip, he wrapped his left arm around the throat of the second doppelganger and opened the bottom half of the Dutch door to back her into the stall. His captive reached up and clawed his arm, shredding his coat, her claws nicking his flesh, gradually slicing deeper.

One by one, the other three pontianaks shimmered and then they too took on Chloe's appearance. He faced four of her, tenuously holding a fifth. He was running out of options. Girding himself, he raised the railroad spike again, ready to strike down his captive.

Unable to cast his doubt aside, he accepted it and whispered, "Forgive me."

THIRTY-SIX

Confronted with the evidence of Ronnie's murder at her father's hand, Riza was forced to doubt her reason for existence as a pontianak. Her black eyes rolled up in her head, revealing a coronal rim of white, and her tremors became more violent, her entire body thrashing as if it might tear itself apart.

Sam must have sensed a turning point. If she recovered from the seizure convinced that she must remain on her murderous path, despite evidence that Ronnie had had no intention of abandoning her and the baby, they might lose their only chance to defeat her.

Leaping forward, Sam grabbed a clump of her hair and pulled her head down. He drove the point of the railroad spike into the hole in the back of her neck and jumped back.

Riza shrieked in agony, whirled around to face Sam, arms spread wide, the claws on every finger twitching uncontrollably. According to the lore, the spike should have stopped her, even if it wasn't enough to kill her on its own.

Apparently, the lore's wrong, Dean thought. *Wouldn't be the first time.*

But the frenzied moment passed, and the pontianak froze on the spot.

Clutching his machete, Dean circled around the perimeter of the room, edging closer to Sam in case his brother needed his assistance with whatever happened next.

A low moan escaped Riza's throat then faded to silence as her abdomen began to pulse and ripple. She flinched, as if struck by an invisible hand. Then, with a wet tearing sound, her abdomen ripped open from the inside, flesh splitting apart along jagged lines, flaps of raw skin pushing outward.

Slowly, a large, misshapen black mass emerged, rotting flesh spouting a thick umbilical cord, with a lamprey-like mouth, its glistening length surrounded by waving filaments like nerve endings seeking a connection. Straining against the fleshy confines of the pontianak's womb, it pulled free of its mother's body.

The fleshy tentacle darted toward Sam, the quivering lamprey mouth straining, seeking a connection to exposed flesh.

Wary, Sam stepped out of reach of the sucking mouth.

Dean approached from the side, machete raised. "Here's a sharp object."

A deft swing of the blade chopped off Riza's head, less than an inch above the embedded railroad spike. Her body toppled sideways, little more than a dried husk. But the large mass inside plopped out onto the wood floor, and immediately skittered on stunted limbs toward Sam, its blood-sucking tentacle waving back and forth, the lamprey mouth—ringed with needle-teeth—ever-seeking.

Dean tossed the machete to Sam, hilt first.

Sam snagged it out of the air without taking his eyes off the pulsating monster making its unerring way toward him. With a quick sideways slice of the blade, he lopped off the waving cord. Then, gripping the hilt in both hands, he drove the point of the machete straight down, through the misshapen head of the langsuir, pinning it to the wooden floor.

The creature twitched for a second or two, a seemingly involuntary response, then the stump of its tentacle drooped to the side, oozing a viscous black fluid. And it was over.

Satisfied, Dean looked at Sam. "Salt all four bodies and burn the place down?"

"Sounds like a plan."

Castiel's hand came forward, driving the spike toward the hole in the back of the doppelganger's neck. But an instant before the tip struck home, all five of the pontianaks went limp and collapsed. He felt the tension evaporate from the one he held by the throat. Stepping back, he let her fall to the ground.

None of them looked remotely like Chloe anymore.

Within seconds, they decayed at an accelerated rate. Skin and muscle dissolved—along with the rotted contents of their wombs, lost forever now—exposing pale bones. Less than a minute after that, the bones began to collapse under their own weight, forming white piles of ash on the dirt floor. A swirling breeze, ushered in through the open barn door, scattered the ashes in a haze of dust.

And soon the haze was gone as well.

THIRTY-SEVEN

In the end, no rational explanation would suffice. But sometimes it was enough to know the nightmare had ended and would never return. The Winchesters owed them that much.

Dean and Sam paid brief visits to Melissa Barrows and her parents, Malik and Brianna Green, and the Athertons to tell them their particular nightmares were over, that they could return to their normal lives, or what passed for normal for Melissa and Brianna, who grieved the loss of their husbands.

The women showed no further signs of rage seizures. Obviously, injured family members wouldn't press charges, with Melissa and Denise particularly relieved that Assistant Chief Cordero and Captain Sands had no plans to charge them with assaulting a police officer. Sam got the impression from Cordero that the BHPD was all too willing to put the whole bizarre series of events—along with the strange underground fire at the old Larkin farmhouse—in a case file marked "unsolved" and get back to routine law enforcement matters.

The Winchesters returned to the Holcomb house—never a home—to discover Sally had made her final decision. She would return to San Bernardino, closer to family who would welcome her and her baby with open arms, far from the place that had claimed the life of her husband. The house was lined with boxes of all sizes. Furniture awaited the movers, scheduled to come the next morning.

As she handed a box labeled "Special Occasion Plates" to her brother Ramon to take into the hallway, Sally turned to the Winchesters. "You caught the person who killed Dave?"

"We stopped the killer," Dean said without further explanation.

Sally wrapped her arms around herself, as if to ward off a chill. "Will I need to come back for the trial?"

"No trial," Sam assured her. He cleared his throat. "I'm afraid the details of the case are classified."

Sally nodded, taking their word that justice had been served.

"Why?" she asked. "Why David?"

Dean and Sam had decided ahead of time that no good would come from telling Sally her arrival in Braden Heights along with her unexpected pregnancy had unleashed the pontianak on a killing spree. They couldn't know for certain if the construction projects alone—disturbing her lair and displacing the remains of the other murdered women— would have been enough to awaken the dormant creature. So why dump the burden on Sally?

"A case of mistaken identity," Sam replied. "Brought on by extreme psychosis."

Again, she nodded, thanked them quietly for everything and showed them out.

As they walked toward the Impala, Mary—Marilag—hurried after them and caught Sam by the arm. Dean stopped as Sam turned to face the old woman.

"Was I right to tell her to leave?" she asked, her gaze flitting back and forth between them. On some level, she knew they'd kept some information from Sally, to spare her. "This place is cursed, *diba*?"

"It was," Sam admitted. "In a way. But not anymore."

"Not that she should stay," Dean added. "She made the right decision."

"Good," the old woman said, her voice quivering with emotion. "If only my memory about this town…"

Sam took her hand. "Don't punish yourself. Nobody could have known what was here."

"I'll try, young man." She forced a smile. "I'll certainly try."

"Soon you'll have a great grandchild to spoil," Dean said.

This time her smile was wide and heartfelt. "Yes, I will, won't I?"

While the Winchesters made their rounds, Castiel stopped at Lovering Maternity Center and waited in the third-floor hallway. He'd discovered that Chloe and Olivia awoke from their comatose states within seconds of each other, with no ill effects. Based on the timing, they recovered and their labor resumed shortly after the destruction of the demon. Chloe had given birth to a healthy seven-pound, five-ounce baby boy. Surrogate mother Olivia delivered a healthy girl, weighing in at eight pounds even.

Dr. Hartwell saw Castiel standing with his back to the wall and joined him.

"It's over? All of the madness?"

"Yes," he said. "All of it."

"I'd ask but…"

"You wouldn't believe me if I told you."

She looked up at him, with the hint of a smile. "After what I've witnessed, don't be so sure." She looked down, her hands clasped together around a metal clipboard. "That said, I have a feeling I don't really want to know."

"That's probably for the best."

She left him and walked to Chloe's birthing room as Chloe and her parents emerged. Her father Edward pushed the wheelchair, her mother walking beside her. Chloe held the swaddled infant to her chest, uttering a series of cooing sounds to soothe him.

Castiel nodded as they passed.

Chloe saluted him, then stuck her tongue out and smiled wistfully. "Bye, bye, FBI," she said. "Say hi to Claire for me."

Castiel returned the smile, if not the salute and the extruded tongue.

"I will." But she was already out of earshot.

At the time, he'd regretted his inability to come to her aid, though he knew logically he couldn't have helped her, couldn't have healed her out of a coma. Nevertheless, she had survived without his presence. She and her baby were healthy. He had to learn to accept his limitations and not let anxiety rule him. But he would never be completely free of its effect.

Chloe had the support of two involved parents, while Claire remained alone. But he had promised to be there for her if she needed him. And she knew that. For now, that was good enough.

As agreed, Dean and Sam waited for Castiel in the parking lot of the Blue Castle Lodge, even though they'd checked out hours ago.

Dean leaned against the Impala, arms crossed over his chest. In control. Sam had suggested the hunt as a distraction from all the fruitless searches for a cure. And it had certainly succeeded on that level, providing a healthy outlet for Dean's pent-up frustration. But it had also been a test of Dean's continued control. He knew there would always be tests. The best he could do was to pass them, one at a time. That's all that mattered.

He'd restrained himself in the pontianak's lair when it counted most. To keep Sam safe. To complete the hunt. When any unreasoned action would have meant failure, he'd remained rational, master of his own actions.

In Dean's book, that counted as a win.

Sam looked up as Castiel's Lincoln approached, maneuvering into the herringboned parking space next to the Impala, on the passenger side.

Sam glanced at Dean, careful not to stare. His brother seemed totally relaxed, so Sam counted the hunt a success. It had kept Dean occupied with something other than endless hours of research and dark thoughts of what the Mark would eventually cost him.

Though Dean had held back in the pontianak's lair, allowing Sam to ease into striking position and stop Riza, Sam had noticed the strain of Dean's effort to control the Mark.

After they emerged from the underground room, Dean had commented, "Took you long enough."

"Had to line up the perfect shot," Sam countered.

"Excuses."

"Hey, it worked."

After all, even Dean couldn't argue with success.

In the cold light of day, Sam knew Dean's battle wouldn't end well. They hadn't postponed the inevitable, they'd only ignored its approach for a few days. For now, Dean seemed happy to win the battles, but Sam intended to win the war. However, noble intentions only went so far. Eventually, time would run out, and with each failure to find a solution, the probability of defeat became more certain.

Castiel opened his door and stood up, close enough to Sam to read his solemn facial expression.

With a frowning glance at the cheap motel behind them, Dean slapped the hood of the Impala and said, "Let's go, gentlemen. It's bunker time."

When Dean climbed into the Impala and started the engine, Castiel caught Sam's arm and said, "We won't give up, Sam."

"No," Sam said, nodding in agreement. "We never do."

But sometimes, not giving up was not good enough.

Not by a long shot.

ACKNOWLEDGMENTS

An author spends a lot of time writing alone, but a book doesn't happen solely by his efforts. With that in mind, I am indebted to the following people:

At Titan Books, thanks to my editor, Natalie Laverick, for welcoming me back, for her support and patience, and for helping guide *Supernatural: Cold Fire* through the publishing process. At Warner Bros. Entertainment Inc., my gratitude goes out to Chris Cerasi and Victoria Selover for their feedback and suggestions.

For providing timely insight into childbirth during the early sixties, thanks to Randi Hutter Epstein, M.D., M.P.H.

At home, thanks to Emma Passarella and Luke Passarella for saving me precious time and tedium by gathering notes I needed for my writing process.

My enduring gratitude goes out to Greg Schauer with best wishes for Between Books 2.0. We need you!

Book after book, I remain grateful to Tangerine Dream for providing the soundtrack to my writing zone.

Finally, thanks to Eric Kripke for creating *Supernatural,* and special thanks to Jared Padalecki, Jensen Ackles and Misha Collins for bringing these characters to life so well that for a short time they can live inside my head.

ABOUT THE AUTHOR

John Passarella won the Horror Writers Association's prestigious Bram Stoker Award for Superior Achievement in a First Novel for the coauthored *Wither*. Columbia Pictures purchased the feature film rights to *Wither* in a prepublication, preemptive bid.

John's other novels include *Wither's Rain*, *Wither's Legacy*, *Kindred Spirit*, *Shimmer* and the original media tie-in novels *Grimm: The Chopping Block*, *Supernatural: Night Terror*, *Supernatural: Rite of Passage*, *Buffy the Vampire Slayer: Ghoul Trouble*, *Angel: Avatar*, and *Angel: Monolith*. In January 2012, he released his first fiction collection, *Exit Strategy & Others*. *Supernatural: Cold Fire* is his twelfth novel.

A member of the Horror Writers Association, International Thriller Writers, International Association of Media Tie-In Writers and the Garden State Speculative Writers, John resides in southern New Jersey with his wife, three children, a dog and a cat.

John maintains his official author website at www.passarella.com, where he encourages readers to send him email at author@passarella.com, and to subscribe to his free author newsletter for the latest information on his books and stories. To follow him on Twitter, see @JohnPassarella.